Frank Merriwell's Chums

BURT L. STANDISH

Author of the celebrated "Merriwell"
stories, which are the favorite reading of
over half a million up-to-date (1904)
American boys.

BOOKS FOR ATHLETICS

LONDON
IBOO PRESS HOUSE
86-90 PAUL STREET

Frank Merriwell's Chums

BURT L. STANDISH.

BOOKS FOR ATHLETICS

Layout & Cover © Copyright 2020 iBooPress, London

Published by
iBoo Press House

3rd Floor
86-90 Paul Street
London, EC2A4NE UK

t: +44 20 3695 0809
info@iboo.com II iBoo.com

ISBNs
978-1-64181-941-1 (h)
978-1-64181-942-8 (p)

Frank Merriwell's Chums

BURT L. STANDISH

Author of the celebrated "Merriwell"
stories, which are the favorite reading of
over half a million up-to-date (1904)
American boys.

BOOKS FOR ATHLETICS

CHAPTER I.

FRANK ASKS QUESTIONS.

September was again at hand, and the cadets at Fardale Military Academy had broken camp, and returned to barracks.

For all of past differences, which had been finally settled between them—for all that they had once been bitter enemies, and were by disposition and development as radically opposite as the positive and negative points of a magnetic needle, Frank Merriwell and Bartley Hodge had chosen to room together.

There was to be no more "herding" in fours, and so Barney Mulloy, the Irish lad, and Hans Dunnerwust, the Dutch boy, were assigned to another room.

Like Hodge, Barney and Hans were Frank Merriwell's stanch friends and admirers. They were ready to do anything for the jolly young plebe, who had become popular at the academy, and thus won both friends and foes among the older cadets.

Barney was shrewd and ready-witted, while Hans, for all of his speech and his blundering ways, was much brighter than he appeared.

Still being plebes, Merriwell and Hodge had been assigned to the "cock-loft" of the third division, which meant the top floor on the north side of the barracks—the sunless side.

The other sides, and the lower floors, with the exception of the first, were reserved for the older cadets.

Their room contained two alcoves, or bedrooms, at the end opposite the door. These alcoves were made by a simple partition that separated one side from the other, but left the bedrooms open to the rest of the room.

Against the walls in the alcoves stood two light iron bedsteads, with a single mattress on each, carefully folded back during the day, and made up only after tattoo.

The rest of the bedding was carefully and systematically piled on the mattresses.

In the partitions were rows of iron hooks, on which their clothing must be placed in regular order, overcoats to the front, then rubber coats, uniform coats, jackets, trousers, and underclothing following, with a bag for soiled clothing at the rear.

On the broad wooden bar that ran across the front of these alcoves, near the ceiling, the names of the cadets who occupied the bedrooms were posted, so inspecting officers could tell at a glance who occupied the beds.

At the front of the partition the washstand was placed, with the bucket of water, dipper, and washbowl, which must always be kept in a certain order, with the washbowl inverted, and the soap-dish on top of it.

Rifles were kept in the rack, barrels to the front, with dress hats on the shelf, and a mirror in the middle of the mantelshelf. Accoutrements and forage saps were hung on certain hooks, and clothing and other things allowable and necessary were always to be kept in an unvarying order on a set of open-faced shelves.

The broom and slop-bucket were to be deposited behind the door, the chairs against the table, when not in use, and the table against the wall opposite the fireplace.

At the foot of each bed the shoes were placed in a line, neatly dusted, with toes to the front.

It was required that the room should be constantly kept in perfect order, and Merriwell and Hodge were called on to take turns, week and week about, at being orderly, and the name of the one responsible for the appearance of the room was placed on the orderly board, hung to the front of the alcove partition.

Back of the door was another board, on which each was required to post his hours of recitation, and to account for his absence from the room at any inspection.

In fact, a rigid effort was made at Fardale to imitate in every possible way the regulations and requirements enforced at West Point, and it was the boast that the school was, in almost every particular, identical with our great Military Academy.

Of course, it was impossible to enforce the rules as rigidly as they are at the Point, for the cadets at Fardale were, as a class, far younger, and the disgrace of expulsion or failure in any way was not to be compared with that attending unfortunates at the school where youths are graduated into actual service as officers of the United States army.

Many of the cadets at Fardale had been sent there by parents who could not handle them at home, and who had hoped the discipline they would receive at a military school would serve to tone down their wildness. Thus it will be seen that many harum-scarum fellows got into the school, and that they could not readily be compelled to conform to the rules and requirements.

For all that Frank Merriwell was a jolly, fun-loving fellow, he was naturally orderly and neat, so that it seemed very little effort for him to do his part in keeping the room in order.

On the other hand, Bartley Hodge was naturally careless, and he had a persistent way of displacing things that annoyed Frank, although the latter said little about it at first.

Whenever the inspecting officer found anything wrong about the room, he simply glanced at the orderly board, and down went the demerit against the lad whose name was posted there. It made no difference who had left a chair out of place, hung a coat where it should not be, or failed to invert the washbowl, the room orderly had to assume the responsibility.

Now, it was the last thing in the world that Hodge could wish to injure Merriwell, but three times in Frank's first week as room orderly he was reported for things he could not help, and for which Bart was entirely responsible.

Merriwell had risen to the first section in recitation at the very start, while Hodge, who had been placed in the third, was soon relegated to the second.

Frank was trying to curb his almost unbounded inclination for mischief, and he was studying assiduously.

On the other hand, while Hodge did not seem at all mischievous by nature, he detested study, and he was inclined to spend the time when he should have been "digging," in reading some story, or in idly yawning and wishing the time away.

One day, after having taken his third demerit on his roommate's account, the inspector having detected tobacco smoke in the room, Frank said:

"Why don't you swear off on cigarettes, Bart? They don't do a fellow any good, and they are pretty sure to get him into trouble here at the academy."

Hodge was in anything but a pleasant frame of mind, and he instantly retorted:

"I know what you mean. You are orderly, and I ought to have spoken up and told the inspector I had been smoking. I didn't know what it was he put down, but I'll go and confess my crime now."

He sprang up petulantly, but Frank's hand dropped on his arm, and Merriwell quietly said:

"Don't go off angry, old man. You know I don't want you to do anything of the sort. I will take my medicine when I am orderly, and I know you will do the same when it comes your turn."

"Well, I didn't know——" began Bart, in a somewhat sulky manner.

"You ought to know pretty well by this time. I am not much given to kicking or growling, but I do want to have a sober talk with you, and I hope you will not fire up at anything I say."

"All right; go ahead," said Hodge, throwing himself wearily into a chair, and thrusting his hands deep into his pockets. "I'll listen to your sermon."

"It isn't to be a sermon. You should know I am not the kind of a fellow to preach."

"That's so. Don't mind me. Drive ahead."

"First, I want to ask how it is you happened to let yourself be put back in recitations?"

"Oh, Old Gunn just put me back—that's all."

"But you are fully as good a scholar as I am, and you could have gone ahead into the first section if you had braced up."

"Perhaps so."

"I know it. You do not study."

"What's the use of boning all the time! I wasn't cut out for it."

"That's the only way to get ahead here."

"I don't care much about getting ahead. All I want is to pull through and graduate. Then I can go to college if I wish. These fellows who get the idea that they must dig, dig, dig here, just as they say they do at West Point, give me a pain. What is there to dig for? We're not working for commissions in the army."

"From your point of view, you put up a very good argument," admitted Frank; "but there's another side. It surely must be some satisfaction to graduate well up in your class, if not at the head. And then, the more a fellow learns here, the easier he will find the work after entering college."

"Work? Pshaw! There are not many fellows in colleges who are compelled to bone. I hate work! I thought you were the kind of a fellow who liked a little fun?"

"Well, you know I am. Haven't I always been in for sport?"

"But you're getting to be a regular plodder. You don't do a thing lately to keep your blood circulating."

"I am afraid you do too much that is contrary to rules, old man. For instance, where is it that you go so often nights, and stay till near morning?"

"I go out for a little sport," replied Bart, with a grim smile.

CHAPTER II.

A GHASTLY SUBJECT.

ut you know the consequences if you are caught," said Frank, warningly.

"Of course I do," nodded Bart, "but you must acknowledge there is not much danger that I shall be caught, as long as I make up a good dummy to leave in my place on the bed."

"Still, you may be."

"That's right, and there's where part of the sport comes in, as you ought to know, for you are quite a fellow to take chances yourself, Merriwell."

"That's right," admitted Frank. "It's in my blood, and I can't help it. Anything with a spice of risk or danger attracts and fascinates me."

"You are not in the habit of hesitating or being easily scared when there is some sport in the wind."

Frank smiled.

"I never have been," he admitted. "I have taken altogether too many risks in the past. A fellow has to sober down and straighten up if he means to do anything or be anything."

Bart made an impatient gesture.

"Any one would think you were a reformed toper, to hear you talk," he said, with a trace of a sneer.

"Not if they knew me," said Frank, quietly. "Whatever my faults may be, I never had any inclination to drink. I have had fellows tell me they did so for fun, but I have never been able to see the fun in it, and it surely is injurious and dangerous. I don't believe many young fellows like the taste of liquor. I don't. They drink it 'for fun,' and they keep on drinking it 'for fun' till a habit is formed, and they become drunkards. Now, I can find plenty of fun of a sort that will not harm me, or bring——"

"I thought you weren't going to preach," interrupted the dark-haired boy, impatiently. "Let me give you a text: 'Thou shalt not put an enemy into thy mouth to steal away thy brain,' or something of the sort. Now, go ahead and spout, old man."

Frank's face grew red, and he bit his lip. He saw that Hodge was in a most unpleasant humor, and so he forced a laugh.

"What's the matter with you to-day, Bart?" he asked. "I haven't seen you this way for a long time."

"Oh, there's nothing the matter."

"It must be staying up nights. Where do you go?"

"If you want to come along, and have some fun, I will show you to-night."

Frank hesitated. It was a great temptation, and he felt a longing to go.

"Well," he said, finally, "I have not broken any in quite a while, and I believe I'll take a whirl with you to-night."

"All right," nodded Bart. "I'll show you some fellows with sporting blood in their veins."

"But I want you to understand I do not propose to follow it up night after night," Frank hastened to say. "A fellow can't do it and stand the work that's cut out for him here."

"Bother the work!"

"I'll have to work to keep up with the procession. If you can get along without work, you are dead lucky."

"Oh, I'll scrub along some way, don't you worry; and I will come out as well as you do in the end."

That night, some time after taps, two boys arose and proceeded to carefully prepare dummies in their beds, arranging the figures so they looked very much like sleeping cadets, if they were not examined too closely. Bart was rather skillful at this, and he assisted Frank in perfecting the figure in Merriwell's bed.

"There," he finally whispered, with satisfaction, "that would fool Lieutenant Gordan himself."

They donned trousers and coats, and prepared to leave the room in their stocking feet.

Bart opened the door and peered cautiously out into the hall.

"Coast is clear," he whispered over his shoulder.

In another moment they were outside the room. Along the corridor they skurried like cats, their feet making no noise on the floor.

Frank was still entirely unaware of their destination, but, as they had not taken their shoes, he knew they were not to leave the building.

Frank cared little where they went, but he realized Hodge was leading the way to a remote part of the building, where the rooms were not entirely taken, as the academy was not full of students.

All at once, Bart sent a peculiar hiss down the corridor, and it was answered by a similar sound.

A moment later they scudded past a fellow who was hugging in a shadow where the lights did not reach.

"Who's that?" whispered Frank.

"That's the sentinel," replied Bart.

Then they came to the door of a certain room, on which Hodge knocked in a peculiar manner.

A faint sound of unbarring came from behind the door, which quickly opened, and they dodged into the room.

As yet there was no light in the room, and, still filled with wonder, Frank asked:

"Was that the regular sentinel out there, Bart?"

"That was our sentinel," was the reply.

"But where are the regular sentinels? I did not see one of them."

Faint chuckles came from several parts of the room, and Hodge replied:

"At a certain hour each night the duties of the regular sentinels take them away long enough for me to get out of my room and in here. See?"

"They must be in the trick?"

"The most of them are. When it happens that one is not, we have to look out for him, and dodge him. To-night those on duty on this floor were all fixed."

Then somebody cautiously struck a match, by the flare of which Frank saw several fellows were gathered in the room.

A lamp was lighted, and Merriwell looked around. Besides Bart, he saw Harvey Dare, George Harris, Wat Snell and Sam Winslow.

"Hello, Merriwell, old man," some greeted, cordially, but cautiously. "Glad to see Hodge has brought you along."

Frank was instantly seized by an unpleasant sensation—a foreboding, or a warning. Harris and Snell were not friends of his; in fact, in the past, they had been distinctly unfriendly. Dare he knew little about, as they had never had much to do with each other. Sam Winslow was a plebe, having entered the academy at the same time with Merriwell, but Frank had never been able to determine whether he was "no good" or a pretty decent sort of fellow.

Had Frank been governed by his first impression, he would have found an excuse to bid that company good-night immediately, but he did not like to do anything like that, for he knew it would cause them to designate him as a cad, and he would be despised for doing so.

He had gone too far to back out immediately, so he resolved to stay a while, and then get out as best he could.

At the window of the room blankets had been suspended, so no ray of light could shine out into the night to betray the little party.

At a glance, Frank saw the room was not occupied by students, for it contained nothing but the bare furniture, besides a box on the table, and the assembled lads.

Bart saw Frank looking around, and divined his thoughts.

"I suppose you are wondering where you are? Well, this is the room in which Cadet Bolt committed suicide. It has been closed ever since, as no fellow will occupy it. It is said to be haunted."

This appealed to Frank's love of the sensational. Besides that, he fancied he saw an opportunity for some sport that was not down in the programme, and he smiled a bit.

"Of course it isn't haunted," he said. "I don't believe there is a fellow here who believes in ghosts?"

"I don't."

"Nor I."

"Nor I."

"Such stuff is rot!"

"I don't believe in anything I can't see."

Thus the assembled lads expressed themselves, and Frank smiled again.

"While I do not believe this room is haunted," he said, "I once had a rather blood-curdling experience with something like a disembodied spirit—an adventure that came near turning my hair snowy white from fright and horror. I will tell you about it. The original of my ghost happened to be a fellow who committed suicide, and he——"

"Say, hold on!" gurgled Wat Snell, who had declared that believing in ghosts was "all rot." "What are we here for—to listen to ghost stories or to have a little picnic?"

"Oh, drop your ghost yam," said George Harris, who had asserted that he did not believe in anything he could not see. "You may tell it to us some other time."

"But this is a really interesting story," insisted Frank. "You see, the fellow shot himself three times, and when he did not die quickly enough to be suited, he cut his throat from ear to ear, and his specter was a most ghastly-appearing object, bleeding from the bullet wounds and having a gash across its throat from——"

"Say, will you let up!" gasped Harris. "If you don't, I'll get out!"

"Oh, I don't want to break up this jolly gathering," said Frank,

14

his eyes twinkling, "but I was just going to tell how the ghost——"

"Cheese it!" interrupted Sam Winslow. "Talk about something besides ghosts, will you? You are not given to dwelling on such unpleasant subjects, Merriwell."

"But I thought you fellows didn't take any stock in ghosts?"

"We don't," grinned Harvey Dare; "and that's just why we don't want to hear about 'em."

"We've got something else to do besides listen to yarns," said Harris. "Let's proceed to gorge." And he began opening the box that sat on the table.

CHAPTER III.

AN IRRESISTIBLE TEMPTATION.

"Harris is lucky," said Sam Winslow. "His folks send him a box every now and then, and he gets it through old Carter, at the village."

"I have hard enough time smuggling it in," said Harris, "and I share when I get it here."

"For which we may well call ourselves lucky dogs," smiled Harvey Dare. "A fellow gets awfully weary of the regular rations they have here."

"That's right," agreed Frank. "I often long for the flesh pots of Egypt, or almost anything in the way of a change of fare."

"Well, here's where you get it—if you'll agree not to spring any more ghost yarns on us," said Harris. "Just look over this collection of palate ticklers, fellows."

"Fruit cake!" gasped Sam, delightedly. "Oh, how my stomach yearns for it!"

"Cream pie!" ejaculated Wat Snell. "Yum! yum! Somebody please hold me!"

"Tarts!" panted Harvey Dare. "Oh, I won't do a thing to them!"

"Look at the cookies and assorted good stuff!" murmured Bart, ecstatically. "I shall be ready to perish without a tremor after this!"

"Permit me to do the honors," said Harris, grandly. "Just nominate your poison, and I will deal it out."

So each one called for what he desired, and Harris supplied them, using a pocket-knife with which to cut the cake and pie.

"Aren't you glad you came, Merriwell?" asked Sam, with his mouth full of fruit cake.

"Sure," smiled Frank, as he helped himself. "I shall not regret it, if it gives me indigestion."

Frank believed Wat Snell was a sneak, but he did not fancy it would be at all necessary to accept the fellow as a friend just because they had met under such circumstances. He meant to use

Snell well, and let it go at that.

The boys thoroughly enjoyed their clandestine feast. It was a luxury a hundred times dearer than a feast from similar things could have been had there been no secrecy about it and had it been perfectly allowable.

They gorged themselves till they could eat no more, and the contents of the box proved none too plentiful for their ravenous appetites. When they had finished, nothing but a few crumbs were left.

"There," sighed Harvey Dare, "I haven't felt so full as this before since the last time Harris had a box."

"Nor I," said Wat Snell, lighting a cigarette. "Have one, Merriwell?"

Frank declined to smoke, but his example was not followed by any of the other lads. Each one took a cigarette and "fired up."

"You ought to smoke, Merriwell," said Dare. "There's lots of pleasure in it."

"Perhaps so," admitted Frank; "but I don't care for it, and, as it is against the rules, it keeps me out of trouble by not smoking."

"It's against the rules to indulge in this kind of a feast, old man. You can't be too much of a stickler for rules."

"It doesn't do to be too goody-good," put in Snell, insinuatingly. "Such rubbish doesn't go with the fellows."

"I don't think any one can accuse me of playing the goody-good," said Frank, quietly. "I like fun as well as any one, as you all know, but I do not care for cigarettes, and so I do not smoke them. I don't wish to take any credit to myself, so I make no claim to resisting a temptation, for they are no temptation to me."

"Lots of fellows smoke who do not like cigarettes," assured Sam Winslow.

"Well, I can't understand why they do so," declared Merriwell.

"They do it for fun."

"I fail to see where the fun comes in. There are enough improper things that I would like to do for me not to care about those things that are repugnant to me. Some time ago I made up my mind never to do a thing I did not want to do, or did not give me pleasure, unless it was absolutely necessary, or was required as a courtesy to somebody else. I am trying to stick by that rule."

"Oh, don't talk about rules!" cut in Dare. "It makes me weary! We have enough of rules here at this academy, without making any for ourselves."

"Come, fellows," broke in Hodge; "let's get down to business."

"Business?" said Frank, questioningly. "I thought this was a case of sport?"

"It is. You mustn't be so quick to catch up a word."

The table was cleared, and the boys gathered round it, Hodge producing a pack of cards, the seal of which had not been broken.

"You'll notice that those papers are all right," he said, significantly. "Nobody's had a chance to tamper with them."

"What do you play?" asked Frank, to whose face a strange look had come on sight of the cards.

"Oh, we play most anything—euchre, seven up, poker——"

"Poker?"

"Yes; just a light game—penny ante—to make it interesting. You know there's no interest in poker unless there's some risk."

The strange look grew on Frank Merriwell's face. He seemed in doubt, as if hesitating over something.

"I—I think I will go back to the room," he said.

"What's that?" exclaimed several, in amazement. "Why, you have just got here."

"But I am not feeling—exactly right. What I have eaten may give me a headache, and I have a hard day before me to-morrow."

"Oh, but we can't let you go now, old man," said Harris, decidedly. "You must stop a while. If your head begins to ache and gets real bad, of course you can go, but I don't see how you can get out now."

Frank did not see either. He had accepted Harris' hospitality, had eaten freely of the good things Harris had provided, and the boys would vote him a prig if he left them for his bed as soon as the feast was finished. It would seem that he was afraid of being discovered absent from his room—as if he did not dare to share the danger with them.

Frank was generally very decided in what he did, and it was quite unusual for him to hesitate over anything.

There is an old saying that "He who hesitates is lost."

In this case it proved true.

"Oh, all right, fellows," said Frank, lightly. "I'll stop a while and watch you play."

"But you must take a hand—you really must, you know," urged Harvey Dare. "Our game is small. We'll put on a limit to suit you—anything you say."

"I do not play poker, if that is your game."

"Don't you know how?"

"Well, yes, I know a little something about it, but I swore off more than a year ago."

"Nobody ever swears off on anything for more than a year. Sit in and take a hand."

Still he refused, and they finally found it useless to urge him, so the game was begun without him, and he looked on.

The limit was set at ten cents, and it was to be a regular penny ante game.

There was some hesitation over the limit, which Bart named, winking meaningly at one or two of the fellows who seemingly started to protest.

Surely there could not be much harm in such a light game! No one could lose a great deal.

The first deal fell to Bart, and he shuffled the cards and tossed them round in a way that betokened considerable dexterity and practice.

The boys were inclined to be jolly, but they were forced to restrain their feelings as far as possible, for, although the rooms near them were unoccupied, there was danger that they might be heard by some one who would investigate, and their sentinel might not be able to give the warning in time.

As Frank Merriwell watched the game, a peculiar light stole into his eyes, and he was swayed by ill-repressed excitement. He was tempted to get up and go away for all that anybody might say, but he did not go; he lingered, and he was overcome by an irresistible longing—a desire he could not govern. Finally, he exclaimed:

"What's the use for me to sit humped up here! Give me a hand, and let me in."

CHAPTER IV.

A GAME OF BLUFF.

hat's the talk, old man!" exclaimed Harvey Dare, with satisfaction. "Now you are beginning to appear natural."

The other boys were only too glad to get Frank into the game, and room was quickly made for him, while he was given a hand.

The moment he decided to play, he seemed to throw off the air of restraint that had been about him since he discovered the kind of company Bart Hodge had brought him into. He became his free-and-easy, jolly self, soon cracking a joke or two that set the boys laughing, and beginning by taking the very first pot on the table after entering the game.

"That's bad luck," he said, with a laugh. "The fellow who wins at the start usually loses at the finish, so I may as well consider my fortune yours. Some of you will become enormously wealthy in about fifteen minutes, for I won't last longer than that if my luck turns."

He soon betrayed that he was familiar with the game, and luck ran to him in a way that made the other boys look tired. He seemed able to draw anything he wanted.

"Say!" gasped Sam Winslow, in admiration; "I shouldn't think you'd want to play poker—oh, no! If I had your luck, I'd play poker as a profession. Why, if you drew to a spike, you'd get a railroad! I never saw anything like it."

Wat Snell had been losing right along, and he sneered:

"There's an old saying, 'A fool for luck,' you know."

"It applies in this case," laughed Frank. "If I wasn't a fool, I wouldn't be in this game."

"What's the matter with this game?" asked Harris. "Isn't the limit high enough to suit you?"

"That's the matter," said Dare, swiftly. "Let's raise the limit."

"Let's throw it off," urged Snell. "What's the use of limit, any how?"

Frank shook his head.

"I don't believe in a no-limit game," he said. "There are none of us millionaires."

"And for that very reason, none of us will play a heavy game," said Sam. "We have played a no-limit game before, and nobody ever bets more than a dollar or so. That doesn't happen once a game, either."

"Twenty-five cents is usually the limit of our bets," declared Harris.

"Then raise the limit to a quarter," said Frank. "I am willing to give you fellows a show to get back your money."

But they did not fancy having the limit a quarter, and quite a long argument ensued, which resulted in the game being resumed as a no-limit affair.

"There!" breathed Wat Snell, "this is something like it. Now I can do something. If a fellow wanted to bluff he couldn't do it on a ten-cent limit."

Hodge had said very little, but he seemed willing and ready to throw off the limit.

The change of limit did not seem to affect Merriwell's luck, for he continued to win.

"I believe you are a wizard!" exclaimed Sam Winslow. "You seem to read a fellow's cards."

Wat Snell growled continually, and the more he growled the more he lost.

"Oh, wait till I catch 'em by-and-by," he said, as he saw Frank rake in a good pot. "I won't do a thing to you, if I get a good chance!"

"If you have the cards, you will win," was the reply. "They are coming for me now, and I am simply playing 'em."

Hodge had lost something, but he said little, being more than satisfied as long as Frank was winning.

Thus the hours passed.

By one o'clock Frank was far ahead of the game, but he still played on, for he knew it would not seem right for him to propose stopping.

Dare, Harris and Winslow were nearly broken, but they still hung on, hoping for a turn in their direction. Snell had plenty of money, for all that he had been the heaviest loser.

Finally there came a good-sized jackpot, which Dare opened. Snell was the next man, and he promptly raised it fifty cents. Winslow dropped out, and Hodge raised Snell fifty cents. Then it came Frank's turn, and he simply staid in. Harris was dealing, and he dropped out, while Dare simply "made good."

This gave Snell his turn, and he "boosted" two dollars.

"Whew!" breathed Winslow. "That settles me. I'm out."

Hodge was game, and he "came up" on a pair of nines.

Snell was watching Merriwell, and the latter quietly pushed in two dollars, which finished the betting till cards were drawn, as Dare dropped out, after some deliberation.

"How many?" asked Harris, of Snell.

"Don't want any," was the calm reply.

Hodge took three, as also did Merriwell, which plainly indicated they had a pair each.

"Snell has this pot in a canter," said Harris.

Snell bet five dollars, doing it in a way that seemed to say he was not risking anything.

Hodge dropped his nines, which he had not bettered, and that left Merriwell and Snell to fight it out.

"This is why I object to a limit being taken off a game," said Frank. "It spoils the fun, and makes it a clean case of gambling."

"It's too late to make that kind of talk," sneered Snell. "You are in it now. Do you call?"

"No," replied Frank, "but I will see your five dollars, and put in another."

This created a stir, but Snell seemed delighted.

"I admire your blood," he said, "but the bluff won't go with me. Here's the five, and I will raise ten."

Now there was excitement.

Frank's cards lay face downward on the table, and every one was wondering what he could have found to go up against Snell's pat hand. He was wonderfully calm, as he turned to Bart, and asked:

"Will you loan me something?"

"Every cent I have," was the instant reply, as Hodge took out a roll of bills and threw it on the table. "Use what you want."

There were thirty-five dollars in the roll. Frank counted it over carefully, and then put it all into the pot, raising Snell twenty-five dollars!

When he saw this, Snell's nerve suddenly left him. His face paled and his hands shook.

"Whoever heard of such infernal luck as that fellow has!" he grated. "Held up a pair, and must have fours now!"

Frank said not a word. His face was quiet, and he seemed waiting for Snell to do something.

"If you haven't the money to call him——" began Harris.

"I have," declared Snell; "but what's the use. A man can't beat fool-luck! Here's my hand, and I'll allow I played it for all it is worth."

He threw the cards face upward on the table, and smothered exclamations of astonishment came from the boys.

His hand contained no more than a single pair of four-spots!

"Then you do not mean to call me?" asked Prank.

"Of course not! Think I'm a blooming idiot!"

"The pot is mine?"

"Yes."

"Well, I will allow I played this hand for all it is worth," said the winner, as he turned his cards over so all could see what they were.

Wat Snell nearly fainted.

Merriwell's hand was made up of a king, eight spot, five spot, and one pair of deuces!

It had been a game of bluff, and Frank Merriwell had won.

CHAPTER V.

FRANK'S REVELATION.

reat Caesar!" gasped Harvey Dare. "Will you look at that! That is what I call nerve for you! That is playing, my boys!"

Wat Snell rose slowly to his feet, his face very white.

"It's robbery!" came hoarsely from his lips.

"Steady, Snell!" warned Harvey Dare. "You were beaten at your own game—that's all."

Snell knew this, but it simply served to make his rage and chagrin all the deeper.

"I am not a professional card player," he said, bitterly, "and I am no match for a professional."

He was more deeply cut by the manner in which he had been beaten than by the loss of his money.

"Nor am I a professional," came quietly from Frank Merriwell's lips, as he quickly sorted from the pot the money he had placed therein. "I simply sized you up as on the bluff, and I was right. I don't want your money, Snell; take it. I set into this game for amusement, and not with the idea of beating anybody to any such extent as this."

Snell hesitated, and then the hot blood mounted quickly to his face, which had been so pale a few moments before.

"No, I will not take the money!" he grated. "I take the offer as an insult, Merriwell."

"No insult is intended, I assure you."

Snell was shrewd enough to know he would stand little chance of getting into another game of poker with that company if he accepted the money, and so he made a desperate effort to control his rage and play the hypocrite.

"I don't suppose you did mean the offer as an insult, Merriwell; and I presume I was too hasty. I am rather quick at times, and, as Dare says, I was beaten at my own game, which made me hot.

You had nerve, Merriwell; take the money—keep it."

The words almost choked him, but he pretended to be quite sincere, although his heart was full of bitterness and a longing to "get even."

It was some time before Frank could be persuaded to accept his winnings, and, when he did finally take it, he was resolved to return it quietly and secretly to Snell, at such a time that no one else could know anything of it.

This matter was scarcely settled when there came a peculiar rap on the door.

"Who's that?" asked Frank, in some alarm.

"It's our sentinel," assured Harris. "His time on post is up."

The door opened, and Leslie Gage entered the room. Gage had been Merriwell's bitter enemy at one time during the summer encampment, having made two dastardly attacks on Frank, who had been generous enough to rescue him from death after that, and had saved him from expulsion by refusing to give any testimony against him.

For all of this generosity on Merriwell's part, Gage still bore deep down in his heart a hatred for the plebe who had become so popular at the academy. This he tried to keep concealed, pretending that he had changed into a friend and admirer.

"Hello, Merriwell," he saluted. "Been having a little whirl with the boys?"

"I should say he has!" replied Snell. "He has whirled me wrong end up, and I feel as if I am still twisted."

Then the whole play was explained to Gage, who chuckled over it, and complimented Frank on his nerve.

For all of this apparent restoration of good feeling, Frank was discerning enough to detect the insincerity of both Snell and Gage.

Gage had done his duty as guard, and there was no one on the watch now. None of the boys felt like taking the place, so it was decided to call the "session" over for that night.

"You must come again, Merriwell," said Dare. "You have given us the sensation of the evening, and you must let Snell have a chance to get square."

"Yes," said Snell, "all I ask is a fair chance to get square. If I fail, I won't say a word, and I'll acknowledge you are the best fellow. Let's shake hands, Merriwell, and call it quits for the time being."

"That's the stuff!" came from Sam Winslow. "Now everything is quiet on the Potomac again."

Frank shook hands with Snell, and a few moments later the boys began to slip from the room and skurry along the corridors to their rooms, which all reached without being challenged by the sentries.

Bart was filled with satisfaction and delight, and before getting into bed he whispered to Frank, not daring to speak aloud in that room:

"That was the prettiest trick I ever saw! And I was delighted to see you rub that fellow. He hasn't done a thing to me but win every time I have held up a hand against him of late."

Frank said nothing, and had there been a light in the room, Bart would have seen that his face bore an expression that was anything but one of satisfaction.

Merriwell did not sleep well during the few hours before reveille. His slumber was filled with dreams, and he muttered and moaned very often, awaking Hodge once or twice.

"I guess he is still playing," thought Bart.

At reveille Frank was, as a rule, very prompt about springing out of bed and hurrying into his clothes and through his toilet. On the morning after the game, however, he continued to sleep till Hodge awakened him by a fierce shaking.

"Come, come, man!" said Bart; "turn out. Are you going to let a little thing like last night break you up?"

Frank got up wearily and stiffly.

"I didn't sleep well," he said.

He was quite unlike his usual spirited self.

"Get a brace on," urged Bart. "You want to be on hand at roll-call."

Finding it was necessary to "get a brace on," Frank did so, and was able to leave the room in time to go rushing down the stairway and spring into ranks at the last second.

After breakfast, as Bart was sprucing up the room, and Frank was vainly trying to prepare himself for the first recitation, but simply sat staring in a bewildered way at the book he held, the former said:

"You don't know what a slick trick you did last night, Merriwell! Why, I'd given almost anything if I had been the one to soak Snell in that fashion."

Frank put down the book, and rose to his feet, pacing twice the length of the room. All at once he stopped and faced Bart, and his voice was not steady, as he said:

"You didn't mean any harm, old man, but you did me a bad turn last night."

Bart stared, and asked:

"How?"

"By taking me where I could sit into a game like that. I am going to tell you something. I have one great failing—one terrible fault that quite overshadows all my other failings and faults. That is my passion for cards—or, to put it more strongly and properly, my passion for gambling."

Bart whistled.

"You don't mean to say that you have a failing or a fault that you cannot govern, do you?" he asked.

Frank put out one hand, and partly turned away. Instantly Bart sprang forward and caught the hand, saying swiftly:

"There, there, Merriwell—don't notice it! I didn't mean anything. You are sensitive to-day. Hang it all, man! do you think I want to hurt your feelings without cause! I shouldn't have said it, for I see you are not yourself."

"No, I am not," confessed Frank. "You know every fellow has a secret. I did not intend to tell mine. I believe I was born with an intense passion for gambling."

"And you cannot govern it?"

"Well, I have been able to do so during the past year."

"Oh, you are all right; you have a strong mind and——"

"Every strong mind has a weak spot. I began gaming by playing marbles, and the passion grew on me. When I had money, I gambled for cents and nickels. As I grew older, I learned to play cards, and I gambled for larger sums. If I knew that a game was going on I would leave everything to get into it. Once I 'appropriated' money from my mother's purse to gamble with."

Frank stopped. His face crimsoned as he uttered the words, and he showed his deep shame and humiliation. But he quickly added:

"That was my first and last theft. The shame and disgrace of exposure by my mother was nearly more than I could endure. But she did not know I played cards for money. Thank God! she never knew! She died when I was twelve years old.

"I never knew much about my father's business. He was much away from home, and I saw him but little. After mother's death, I went to live with my uncle. Still I played cards for money, and the passion grew upon me. A little more than a year ago I was rapidly developing into a young gambler. Then came news of my father's sudden death in California, and I swore I would never play cards again. Last night I broke my oath."

"What was the cause of your father's death?" asked Bart, by way of saying something.

"He was shot over a game of cards in a gambling-house," replied Frank, hoarsely.

27

CHAPTER VI.

THE PLOT.

WAT Snell and Leslie Gage were roommates, and they certainly made a delectable pair.

Gage was naturally the leader, being the worse of the two. He was a daring and reckless sort of fellow—one who would not stop at anything, and who would have recourse to almost any measure to gain his ends.

This revengeful fellow had never forgiven Merriwell for what he considered a great injury. Gage had been the pitcher on the regular ball team, but, by superior skill, Merriwell had supplanted him. That was enough to produce in Gage's heart a feeling of undying hatred for the successful plebe.

It made no difference that Frank had, in all probability, saved him from death after he had twice attempted to kill Merriwell. Gage had been shrewd enough to see that he must dissemble if he would remain in the academy, and so he pretended to be repentant and to think Frank one of the finest fellows in the world, while his hatred and longing for "revenge" still lay hidden, black and hideous, in a secret corner of his heart.

Snell was quite a different sort of bad boy. He regarded Gage as his superior, and he was ready to do almost anything for the fellow, but he could not imitate Leslie's daring, and he kept his own vileness so much concealed that many square, honest lads believed he was a really good fellow. Bart Hodge had begun to think Snell was a sneak and bad, but he had no proof of it, and so he kept still.

Wat was in anything but a pleasant mood the day after the game of cards. He flung things round the room in a way that caused Gage to regard him with wonder, as it was so much unlike the usual quiet, crafty roommate he knew.

"What's the matter with you, Wat?" he asked, in surprise. "You must be ill. Go directly and place those things where they belong, for we never know when one of those blooming inspectors will pop in. I am room orderly this week, and am going to have things kept straight, for I can't afford to take any more demerit. My record is bad enough as it stands."

So, with a little grumbling, Wat went about and restored to order the things he had disarranged, but he could not help thinking how often, when he was room orderly, he had been obliged to follow Gage about, and gather up things he had displaced.

"What's the matter?" repeated Leslie, who suspected the truth. "You don't seem to feel well, old boy."

"Oh, it's nothing," replied Wat. "I was thinking of last night."

"And raising all this row because you happened to drop a dollar. Why, that's the run of the cards."

"Oh, it wasn't what I lost that made me mad."

"Then what was it?"

"Why, I was thinking that that fellow Merriwell won."

"And I presume you were thinking how he won the last pot, eh?"

"Yes"—sullenly.

"You don't love Merriwell a great deal?"

"I should say not! I despise the fellow!"

"And you'd like to get square?"

"Wouldn't I!"

"I suppose you mean to do so?"

"If I ever get the chance—yes."

"I fancy you are aware that I am not dead stuck on Merriwell myself?"

"Yes, I know."

"I have an old score to settle with him, and I will settle it some way. I failed in one or two attempts to do him up, for——"

"You were altogether too bold, partner mine; and it's a wonder you were not expelled from the academy. You would have been if Merriwell had blowed on you."

"That's right, and he would have done so if he had known what was good for him. He is soft!"

"In some things he may be soft, but you must acknowledge he is hard enough in others. He has a way of coming on top in almost everything."

Gage could not deny this, and it made him angry to think of it.

"You are right," he said, fiercely. "I suppose I was foolish to fight him in the way I did. That big bully Bascomb got a hold on me, and he has been blackmailing me ever since. Hang that fellow! I'll choke the wind out of him yet!"

A crafty look came to Snell's face, and he said:

"There are ways to down a fellow without showing your hand."

"I suppose so; but it usually takes too long to suit me. I like to jump on an enemy at once, and do him up."

"Well, I hope you are satisfied that Merriwell is the kind of a fellow who will not be jumped on that way?"

"It seems so."

"Then it is possible you are ready to try some other method?"

Their eyes met, and Wat grinned significantly.

"How do you mean?" asked Leslie, eagerly. "You have some kind of a scheme?"

"That fellow won some money off me, and I refused to take it back. He must show up again, and give me a chance to square the score. He is bound in honor not to refuse to do so."

"That's right," nodded Gage.

"Well, you are rather handy with the cards, and I reckon you will not find it hard to fleece him."

"Oh, I can beat him out of his money, but that is poor satisfaction when you want to disgrace a fellow and drive him out of the school."

"We'll find a way for that, if we can get him to following the game."

"I don't know as I see how."

"His parents are dead."

"Well?"

"He is supported by a rich uncle, who sent him here to this school."

"What of that?"

"His uncle gives him a regular allowance. If Merriwell exceeds that allowance, there will be inquiries as to what he has done with his money."

"I begin to see."

"This uncle is a stern, crusty old fellow, and he would be furious if he should accidentally find out that his nephew is gambling. The chances are about ten to one that he would take him out of Fardale and turn him adrift to hustle for himself."

Gage's eyes began to glitter, and the smile about his mouth was most unpleasant to see.

"Snell," he said, "you have a head on your shoulders! You are a dandy schemer! But how will this uncle find out that Merriwell has been gambling?"

"There are several ways for him to find it out. If we can get hold of a few of Merriwell's IOU's, they might be sent to the uncle for collection."

"I see; but first we must run him out of ready cash."

"Of course. By the time he has lost all his money, he will be eager to play to win it back. We must lend him money, and take his IOU's."

"We'll do it!" Gage jumped up, struck Snell a blow on the back, and then grasped his hand, giving it a shake.

"We'll do it!" he repeated. "Merriwell's goose is beautifully cooked!"

Snell smiled in his crafty way.

"I am glad you take to the scheme, for with your aid, there ought not to be any trouble in carrying it out."

"Oh, we'll work it! But how did you find out so much about Merriwell? That's what sticks me. He has been sort of a mystery here, as none of the fellows knew exactly where he came from, or anything about his folks."

"Oh, I took a fancy to get posted concerning him. At first I didn't see how I was going to do so. That was during camp, and Hans Dunnerwust tented with him then. I cultivated the thick-headed Dutchman, and succeeded in getting into his good graces. So I often visited Hans in the tent when Merriwell and Mulloy, that Irish clown, who thinks Merriwell the finest fellow in the world, were away. I kept my eyes open, and one day I spotted a letter to Merriwell. I swiped it instanter, and it helped me out, for it was from his uncle."

"You're an artist in your line, Wat!" exclaimed Leslie, approvingly.

"That letter didn't give me all the information I desired," continued Snell, "but I found I had a friend living in a town adjoining the one Merriwell hails from, so I wrote and asked him to find out a few things for me. He rode over on his wheel, and found out what I have told you."

"Why, you are a regular detective, old man!"

"Merriwell's mother," continued Wat, "has been dead several years. No one seems to know much about his father, except that he was nearly always away from home, and he died suddenly in California a little more than a year ago. I haven't been able to find out that he left any property, so Merriwell is dependent on the generosity of a rather crabbed and crusty old uncle, whose head is filled with freaks and fancies. He seems to be just the kind of a man who would be easily turned against a nephew who had, as he would consider it, gone astray."

"That settles Merriwell! If we cannot get the old uncle down on him, we are pretty poor schemers."

They looked at each other and smiled again. A precious pair of youthful plotters they were!

"We must be slick about this business," warned Snell. "We mustn't let anybody but ourselves get the least wind of it."

"Certainly not."

"And we must do our prettiest to pull the wool over Merriwell's eyes, for you know he is rather discerning in some things, and he may be inclined to be wary. We must seem to think he is the finest fellow in the world."

"That will be pretty hard," said Leslie, with a wry face, "but I have been doing something in that line of late, and I will keep it up. That business doesn't come so easy for me as it does for you."

"You can do it, if you try. And I shall depend on you to skin him with the papers."

"That won't be hard, if he plays square."

"I don't think there is any doubt about that. He is one of the kind of fellows who doesn't know enough to play any other way."

"Then Frank Merriwell's name is mud—with a capital M."

CHAPTER VII.

SPREADING THE SNARE.

he plot was laid, the snare was set, but the game seemed wary. For some time Frank Merriwell remained away from those midnight gatherings in the room of the student who had committed suicide.

"Hang the luck!" exclaimed Gage. "Is he going to keep away right along?"

"He must not be allowed to do so," said Leslie. "He must be shamed into coming."

"That may not be easy."

"It should not be difficult with a fellow like Merriwell. He must give me a chance to get even."

"Hodge doesn't try to get Merriwell out again."

"No. He says he will not influence him to attend the gatherings."

"What's the matter with Hodge?"

"I don't know. He is ready enough to come himself."

It was true that Bart had positively refused to use his influence to induce Merriwell to attend again one of the secret parties. He had been greatly moved by Frank's revelation, and he had resolved not to lead Frank into the path that was so fascinating and so dangerous for him. He did not know that the evil was already done—the fever was burning in Merriwell's veins.

Frank had been waiting an opportunity to speak with Snell in private, and it came one day when he met the fellow on the grounds outside the academy.

"Hello, Snell," he saluted. "I have been looking for you."

"And I have been looking for you," said Wat, meaningly. "Why haven't you ever come round since that night? Aren't you going to give a fellow a show to get square?"

"I am not going to play cards any more!"

"What?" cried Wat, in apparent astonishment. "That beats anything I ever heard! You have beaten me out of a good roll, and now——"

"I have been looking for you that I might return every cent you lost that night, so you cannot consider me mean if I do not give you a chance to get even over the table. If you will tell me just how much you dropped, I'll make it good now."

An eager look came to Wat's face, but it quickly vanished, for he realized that he would defeat himself if he accepted the money.

"What do you take me for!" he cried, with apparent indignation. "I am not that kind of a fellow!"

"You need never fear that I will say anything about it, for I pledge you my word of honor to say nothing. All I want is to make sure you do not feel that I have any money that belongs to you."

"I don't care whether you say anything about it or not, Merriwell. That does not keep me from accepting the money. I tell you I am not that kind of a fellow. You won it, and you will keep it, unless you have nerve enough to give me an opportunity to win it back."

This did not suit Frank at all, for the money had lain like a load on his conscience. He had sworn not to gamble again, and he had broken his oath. But, what was worse, so long as he kept that money, he felt that he really ought to give Snell a chance to get square. There seemed but one way to get out of playing again, and that was to make Snell take back the money.

But it was useless for him to urge Wat; not a dollar would the fellow accept.

"You can't give me back anything," declared Snell. "You won that money by having the most nerve—at that time. But you can't repeat the trick, old man," he added, jovially. "Come around to-night, and see if you can."

Frank shook his head.

"No," he declared, "I shall not come."

"Oh, what's the use, Merriwell! We want you to come, and all the fellows are saying it is not like you to win a few dollars and then stay away. I have told them over and over that I do not believe you are staying away because you are afraid I will win the money back. You're not that kind of a fellow."

At that moment Snell seemed very sincere, and Frank said:

"Thank you. I am glad to know you do not believe such a thing possible of me. Still, I shall not come."

"Oh, yes you will!" laughed Wat. "It can't be that you're afraid of being caught. If anybody says so, I'll swear I know better. You have nerve enough not to care for that. Come around to-night. We'll look for you."

Snell hurried away, knowing full well that he had said things which must worry Merriwell, if they did not drive him into coming to the midnight card parties.

Wat was right. Frank was worried not a little, for he could not bear to fancy that some of the boys thought him mean in staying away. Hodge saw Merriwell was troubled, but the dark-haired boy remained silent.

In the meantime, finding Hodge would do nothing to bring Merriwell round. Gage and Snell tried their best to make friends with Hans Dunnerwust and Barney Mulloy, as these boys were particular friends of Merriwell's, and might be induced to use some influence over him.

Barney, however, was wary. He did not fancy either Gage or Snell, and he repulsed their advances.

To Hans, the temptation of a midnight supper on cakes and pies was too much to resist, and he was added to the circle that gathered in the room of the suicide.

Hans could play poker, and the game being made small enough to suit him, he came in and won about two dollars, which made him swell up like a toad, and declared:

"Uf you poys know some games vot I can play petter as dot boker, shust you name him, und I vill do you at dot. Oh, I vose a dandy on trucks, ain'd it? Shust keep your eye on me, und I vill learn some tricks vot you don'd know alretty yet."

Snell did his best to make Hans believe he was a great favorite, and then he told him how Frank had won the only time he had appeared in the game, and had never come around since.

"Some of the fellows seem to think he is afraid I will win the money back," said Wat; "but I don't take any stock in that, for Merriwell's not that kind of a fellow. Still, I don't like to have such ideas concerning him get into circulation."

"Dot vos vere I vos righdt," nodded Hans. "He don't peen dot kindt uf a feller ad all, you pet me my shirt! Dot Vrankie Merrivell vos a taisy, undt he don'd peen afrait a show to gif anypody. You vait till I tell him vot dose fellers say. I pet me your life he vill gome aroundt bretty kuveek righdt avay."

"Oh, don't say anything about it!" exclaimed Snell, as if he really wished Hans to keep silent. "Merriwell knows his business. His friends will stand up for him, no matter what others may say."

"Vell, I vos going to toldt him dot shust der same. Uf he don'd peen aroundt here der next dime, I don'd know der kindt uv a feller vot he vos peen yet avile."

"Well, don't mention that I said anything. He might fancy I

thought him afraid to come round."

"I don'd call your name at all, don'd you let me vorry apout dot."

Snell knew the Dutch boy would lose little time in communicating with Frank, and he was right. Hans did not see that Frank was little like his usual jovial self, and he did not know in what a turbulent state of mind the unfortunate plebe was left.

Bart was not a little worried over Frank, for he saw how the lad had changed in a short time, but he hoped that Merriwell would come round in time, and be his old jolly self.

That evening, a short while before taps, Frank asked:

"I suppose it is another card party to-night?"

"Yes," replied Bart, "a few of us are going to get together."

"Will Snell be there?"

"I presume so."

No more was said. Bart rose and slipped out of the room at the usual time, thinking Frank was asleep.

But Frank was not asleep, and Hodge was scarcely gone when he, too, arose and began to arrange a dummy in his bed.

CHAPTER VIII.

THE HAUNTED ROOM.

The little party of card players was expectantly awaiting the appearance of Bartley Hodge.

There was to be no feast this night—nothing but cigarettes and draw poker.

Hodge appeared at last, and he brought a disappointment to at
least two of the party, for Frank Merriwell was not with him.

Leslie Gage and Wat Snell exchanged glances that were full of
meaning.

Sam Winslow was on guard outside, it being his turn to fill that
unenviable position.

"Hello, Hodge," saluted Harvey Dare. "Now we are ready to
proceed to business."

"Dot vas righdt," nodded Hans Dunnerwust, who was on hand.
"I vos goin' to smoke cigarreds to-nighd dill I vos sick, und haf a
pully dime."

"Why doesn't Merriwell ever show up again?" asked Leslie
Gage.

"That's it," joined in Wat Snell, "why doesn't he come round and
give a fellow a show to win back some of that money he won off
us? Is he afraid?"

"You know well enough that Frank Merriwell is not afraid," said
Bart, quickly.

"Well, it looks that way," declared Leslie.

"Yes, it looks that way," echoed Wat.

"Possibly he has too much sense to spend his nights here," said
Hodge. "If I had known that much, I wouldn't have gone back
a class. Merriwell is in the first section, and he is making right
along."

"Well, he is a different fellow than I thought he was," asserted
Snell. "Until lately, he has seemed quite a fellow for sport, but he
is degenerating into a drone."

"Such drones are the fellows who get along well in school and in the world."

"Bah! Give me a fellow with blood in him!" came contemptuously from Gage.

Leslie had grown desperate, having come to the conclusion that Frank was not to be cajoled into playing poker any more. He now determined, of a sudden, that he would take another tack, and see if he could not anger Merriwell into coming.

Hodge remembered that Gage had tried to injure Frank in the past, and the dark-eyed plebe was ready to blaze forth in an instant. Although he did not know it, Gage was treading on the very thin crust that covered a smoldering volcano.

Leslie was not warned by the fire that gleamed in Bart's eyes, for he continued:

"If Merriwell persists in staying away—if he does not show up and give Snell a chance to get square, he is——"

A knock at the door!

It was the regular signal for admittance, and so, after the first start of alarm, George Harris said:

"Open up quickly. It must be Sam, and, if so, there's something wrong in the wind."

Wat Snell opened the door, and, to their amazement, into the room stepped Frank Merriwell!

It was with difficulty that the boys suppressed a shout of welcome.

Snell quickly closed the door, and then the boys rushed at Frank and shook his hand delightedly.

"You're a sight for sore eyes!" exclaimed Wat Snell, joyously.

"Dot vos so!" agreed Hans. "You vould peen a sighd for a plind man!"

"I will take back anything I said, and swallow what I was going to say," came from Leslie Gage. "I didn't think it could be possible you wouldn't come round again, old man."

"Now, we will have a jolly little racket," said George Harris. "And you want to look out for Merriwell. He is a great bluffer."

"But he doesn't bluff all the time," supplemented Harvey Dare. "I found out that he held cards occasionally, for I called him a few the last time he was around."

Frank laughed; it was his old, jolly laugh, suppressed somewhat. He seemed like himself once more, as Bart Hodge instantly noted. He had cast off the strain under which he had been for so long, and now Frank Merriwell, mischievous and full of fun, was on deck again.

But this did not quite please Hodge, who watched his roommate closely, his uneasiness growing as he saw how care-free Merriwell seemed. What had brought about such a change? Had Frank thrown his resolutions to the wind?

"I've got a supply of coffin-nails," said Snell, as he produced several packages of cigarettes. "Help yourselves, gentlemen. Pass them round."

Round they went, and when they reached Frank Merriwell he accepted one.

"I am going to be real dissipated to-night," he laughed, as he struck a match and "fired up." "You may have to carry me to my room on a shutter, for I actually am going to smoke!"

Leslie Gage and Wat Snell exchanged glances of satisfaction.

A black look came to Bart Hodge's face, and he half started up as Frank took the cigarette, acting as if he would utter a warning. Then he settled back in his seat, thinking:

"Let him smoke, if he wants to. One cigarette will do nobody harm."

But Hodge knew in his heart that it was not the smoking of one or a dozen cigarettes that was dangerous to Merriwell; it was the breaking of his resolutions—it was the feeling of abandon and recklessness that had seemed to seize upon him.

Not much time was lost in beginning the game, but now Bart insisted on a proper limit.

"What do you say, Merriwell?" asked George Harris. "What kind of a limit suits you?"

"Anything from five cents to the sky," was the laughing reply. "Fix it to suit yourselves."

Once more Gage and Snell exchanged glances.

Bart stuck for a moderate limit, but he finally agreed to make it a dollar, the ante being five cents.

"Vell, uf I had pad luck, I don'd last long at dot," said Hans. "I don'd haf more as four tollars und sefen cends."

"Merriwell won at the start the last time he was here, and he kept the luck straight through to the finish," observed Harvey Dare. "It isn't often such a thing occurs."

A few minutes later, as Harris beat Frank, the latter said:

"This game starts differently from the other, fellows. I have lost at the beginning, and to keep up the precedent I have established, I must lose all through it."

He said this smilingly, as if he really wished to lose.

As the cards were being dealt, Bart, who sat by his roommate's side, leaned toward Frank, and softly asked:

"What made you come, old man?"

"Couldn't keep away," was the reply.

"Well, be careful—keep watch of yourself."

"Not to-night, Bart. I am going to let loose on this occasion."

Frank played recklessly from the start, and fortune fluctuated with him, for he would forge ahead and then drop behind, but he was never much ahead, nor far behind. For all of his careless playing, he seemed to hang about even.

Leslie Gage was too shrewd to try to get at Frank on this occasion, for he wanted Merriwell to win again, so they would get a still firmer hold upon him.

Wat Snell lost steadily, soon beginning to growl, and keeping it up. Once, under cover of conversation the others were making, he leaned toward Gage and muttered:

"Merriwell is my hoodoo. I can't do a thing with him in the game."

"Keep cool," warned Leslie. "Never mind what happens this time. We'll get at him again."

Hans Dunnerwust managed to blunder along and keep in the game by sheer luck, for he did not play the cards for their face value at any time. Still he made enough to keep on his feet and not have to get out of the game.

"Vell!" Hans finally exclaimed, as he tried in vain to win, "uf I don'd do petter as dot, I vill suicide go und gommit bretty soon alretty."

"By the way, Hans," said Frank, "do you know that the fellow who used to have this room committed suicide here?"

"Shimminy Gristmas!" gurgled the Dutch boy. "You don'd say dot!"

"Yes, I do, and the room is said to be haunted by his spook, which cannot rest in its grave."

"Vell, dot vos nice! Oxcuse me while I haf a chill!"

At this moment a hollow groan seemed to come from beneath the chair on which Hans sat, and the Dutch lad gave a jump, getting on his feet quickly, and peering under the chair, his face growing pale, as he chattered:

"Vot vos dot, ain'd id?"

Some of the other boys were not a little alarmed, for all had heard it distinctly.

"It—it actually sounded like a groan!" said Wat Snell.

"That's what it did," agreed George Harris.

"But you know it couldn't have been anything of the sort," laughed Frank, "for you fellows do not believe in ghosts."

40

"Who—who—who said anything about ghosts?" stammered Snell.

At this moment another groan, louder and more dismal than the first, seemed to come from directly beneath the table.

There was a scrambling among the boys, as they hastened to get their legs from beneath that table.

"I don'd feel very vell aroundt der bit uf mein stomach," gasped Hans. "I pelief I vos going to be sick alretty yet."

One of the boys held the light, while they all looked under the table, but they did not find anything there.

"Now, that is singular," commented Harvey Dare. "If that wasn't a groan, I never heard one in my life."

"And a real ghostly groan at that!" said Leslie Gage.

"I never did take any stock in this rot about ghosts, but——"

"Beware, young man, how you mock at the spirits of the departed!"

The voice seemed to come from one of the alcove bedrooms, and it was of the sort to make the hair stand on the head of a superstitious person.

"Oh, dunder und blitzen!" panted Hans. "Dot vos a shook! Uf I don't ged avay oud uf here righd off, I peen gone grazy! I don'd vant any shook in mine!"

"It is some fellow playing a joke on us," said Harvey Dare, angrily. "Some one has concealed himself in there. Bring the light, fellows, and we will soon find out."

He started for the alcove, but no one seemed anxious to take the light and follow him. After a moment, however, Frank did so.

All through both alcoves Harvey searched, and his face was rather pale when he and Frank returned to the table.

"What did you find?" asked Wat Snell, thickly.

"Not a thing but dust," replied Harvey. "There hasn't been a living soul in either of those bedrooms since the room was closed after the suicide."

"Ha! ha! ha!" laughed the hollow voice. "You are right. They dare not come, but I am doomed to stay here till this building shall crumble and decay."

"Vell, you may sday till der cows come home!" gurgled Hans; "but I don'd peen caught in here any more bretty soon righd avay, you pet!" and he made a break for the door.

The others quickly extinguished the light, and followed him.

There would be no more gatherings in that room.

41

CHAPTER IX.

IN THE MESHES.

rank Merriwell fancied he had hit upon a scheme to stop the card games from which he could not remain away. Being a skilled ventriloquist, he was the author of the dismal groans and the mysterious voice that had so alarmed the boys.

Bart was not in the secret, and so he wondered, when he heard Frank chuckling to himself, after they had safely reached their room and were getting into bed.

For several days the "gang" was disconsolate, having no place in which they could play a game of cards without fear of detection at any instant.

Frank Merriwell seemed restored to his usual jolly self. He laughed and joked, and did not seem worried over anything.

But the "gang" would not remain long without a place in which to play cards.

One day Frank received an invitation to "sit into a little game" that evening.

Snell tendered the invitation.

Merriwell's face clouded instantly.

"Why, there is no place to play, is there?"

"Sure!" was the reply. "You didn't suppose we'd be knocked out so easy, did you?

"Where do you play?"

"Come along with Hodge to-night, and he will show you. You have been there before."

But Frank did not come along.

Three nights he knew of Bart rising and stealing out of the room. Then there was an interval of two nights, during which Bart, plainly too much used up to stand the strain, or else out of money, remained in his bed.

When Hodge arose again, and prepared to go out, he heard a stir in Merriwell's alcove.

"Are you awake, Frank?" he asked, softly.

"Yes," was the reply, "and I am going with you."

Bart hesitated. He was tempted to undress and return to bed, but he had received his money from home that day and, having lost heavily the last time he played, he was anxious for "satisfaction."

"I'm not Merriwell's guardian," he thought. "I guess the fellow is able to take care of himself."

So he told Frank to dress fully for going out, and to take his shoes in his hand.

Together they crept from the room, slid along the corridor, watched a favorable moment to get past the sentinel, and finally found their way into a room where the "gang" was waiting.

There was much whispered satisfaction when Merriwell was known to be with Hodge.

Then the window was softly opened, and one by one the boys descended the fire-escape, which ran past that window. The last one out closed the window, having arranged it so it could be readily opened from the outside.

Behind the messhall they sat down on the ground and pulled on their shoes.

It was a cool, starry night,

"I rather fancy I know where we are bound," said Frank.

"Where?" asked Bart.

"To the old boathouse, down the cove."

"Sure. You are a good guesser, old man."

Then the thought came to Frank that it would be a good thing for Fardale Academy if that boathouse should burn to the ground. It was there plebes generally received their first hazing, and there most of the fights between the cadets took place.

To the boathouse they went, and this night luck ran against Frank, for he lost heavily.

"There," he said, as he and Bart were returning together, "I can stay away from the game now, and no one will have a right to accuse me of meanness, for I have dropped more than I made at both of the other games I have been in."

"That's right," assured Bart, "you may do as you like now, and I'll fight the fellow that dares open his trap about it."

But Frank had taken the false step that leads to others, and he was to find it no easy thing to keep away from the game that fascinated him so. For a little time he succeeded, but he was uneasy and in a bad way so long as he knew a game was going on. Night after night he heard Bart dress and slip out, and the longing to accompany him grew and grew till it was unbearable.

"What's the matter with Merriwell?" one of his classmates asked of another. "He was making right along at one time, and we all thought he would head the class, but now he is making an average of less than 2.5."

"Oh, he is flighty," replied the other. "Do you notice that he doesn't seem to be as jolly and full of fun as he was once."

"I believe he is in some kind of trouble," declared the first. "He doesn't ever get a max lately."

By way of explanation, let us state, a "max" was the highest mark obtainable, or 3; 2.9 or 2.8 was considered first class, 2.5 was really good, 2 was fair, and below that it fell off rapidly too, which meant utter failure.

Frank was, indeed, in trouble. He found it impossible to keep away from the poker parties, and so, one night after Bart had departed, being unable to sleep, he got up and followed his roommate again.

Gage and Snell were rejoiced, for they saw they had Merriwell fairly within the meshes. All that was needed now was to close the net carefully and draw it tighter and tighter about him, till there was no possible escape.

This trick was accomplished with consummate skill. Frank's luck seemed to have deserted him, but at first his losings were just heavy enough to provoke without alarming him. Sometimes he would win a little, and then he would fancy his luck had turned, but the tide soon set the other way.

Made angry by his petty losses, he followed the game with dogged persistency. And those petty losses soon began to grow larger and larger. His money melted away rapidly, and still fortune frowned on him.

In vain Hodge counseled his friend to drop the game and stay away. Such advice was now wasted on Frank, and it made him angry.

"It's too late!" he hotly declared. "I am going to see the thing through!"

And so the meshes of the snare closed around him.

CHAPTER X.

DOWNWARD.

In vain Gage and Snell tried to get hold of some IOU's with Frank Merriwell's name on them. Frank's money was exhausted, and he stopped playing suddenly. Gage offered to loan him money, but he had not forgotten the past, and not a cent of Gage's cash would he touch.

Then Snell tried it, but was no more successful.

This made them both angry.

"Confound the fellow!" said Gage, fiercely. "We've got him badly tangled; but he seems to have taken the alarm, and I'm afraid he will break away."

"We must not let him do so," said Snell. "If we lose our fish now, we'll never land him."

"What can be done?"

"That is for us to study out."

And so they set about plotting and trying to devise still other schemes to disgrace Frank, and drive him from the academy.

In the meantime, a feeling of revulsion had seized Frank Merriwell. Of a sudden he had perceived whither he was drifting. He realized what false steps he had already taken, and he was heartily ashamed of himself.

Among his treasures was a medal of honor presented to him by Congress for twice saving the life of Inza Burrage, a pretty girl who lived in Fardale, and whose brother, Walter, was a cadet at the academy. Once he had fought a mad dog with no weapon but a clasp-knife, and kept the creature from biting Inza, and once he had saved her from death beneath the wheels of the afternoon express, which flew through Fardale village without stopping.

Coming across this medal where he kept it choicely deposited, it suddenly brought to him an overwhelming feeling of self-abasement and shame.

What would Inza Burrage think of him if she knew of his weakness—knew that he was playing cards for money, and making associates of such fellows as Gage and Snell?

It was true that she did not know either Gage or Snell for what they really were at heart, but Frank did, and there really seemed no excuse for him.

He tried to excuse himself by saying he had been led into temptation through Hodge, but, in another instant he felt meaner than before.

"You ought to be ashamed, Merriwell!" he told himself. "You have all the influence in the world over Hodge, if you use your power skillfully, and, instead of trying to shoulder the blame on him, you should be disgusted with yourself for making no attempt to save him from such company and such practices!"

Then he thought of the money he had lost. How could he stop without making an effort to win it back? If he could have one good streak of luck and win enough to make himself square, he would stop.

This very desire to "get square with the game" has been the ruin of more than one promising youth.

So he told himself over and over that he would stop as soon as he "got square."

Saturday came round. Inza Burrage had sent him word through her brother that she would visit Belinda Snodd that afternoon, and he might see her there, if he cared to call.

Belinda Snodd was the daughter of John Snodd, a rather queer old fellow, who ran an odd sort of boarding-house for summer people who visited the Cove, on which Fardale Academy was situated. Snodd each year boarded a number of applicants for admission to the academy until they had prepared themselves for examination and been accepted or turned away. Frank had boarded there when he first came to Fardale, and so he knew the family well.

But how could he meet Inza that afternoon? He was in no mood to meet her. She had regarded him as a hero—as being very near perfection. If she knew the truth——

"I can't do it!" Frank muttered. "Not till I face about squarely can I see her again."

But, as the afternoon came round, he was seized by a great longing to catch a glimpse of her, at least. Mechanically he began dressing, as if he were going to call on her.

Hodge was reading a book. He flung it aside, with an impatient exclamation that was followed by a yawn.

"I'm tired of that old thing!" he cried. "I am tired of everything!"

"You need a rest, Bart," said Frank. "You are not getting enough sleep."

"I am getting as much as you. I say, Frank, don't you think living is a bore, anyway?"

"Not when a fellow lives right."

"Right? What do you mean by that? Isn't a chap to have any sport?"

"Yes; but there are two kinds of sport—so called. One is healthy, invigorating, delightful, like baseball and football, for instance. The other is fascinating, injurious, debasing, like poker."

Bart stared at Frank a moment, as if he were somewhat puzzled, and then said:

"I guess you are right, old man. I hadn't ever thought of it just that way before. I'd swear off and try to keep away from the game, if I wasn't in so deep."

"You have lost quite an amount lately."

"Yes, I have been knifed deep. Gage has astounding luck."

"Do you think it is all luck?"

Bart looked surprised.

"Why, to be sure. The fellow plays a square game."

"Why should he? You know, as well as I, that he is not square by nature."

"That's right; but his cards are cut every time, and he doesn't know enough to put 'em up."

"There are other ways of cheating besides putting the cards up."

"That's true, but I do not believe Gage is on that lay. He simply has beastly big luck."

"Perhaps."

"You do not think so?"

"I do not know. You will remember that Gage has no particular love for either of us, and we have both lost heavily."

"Do you mean to quit playing?"

"Possibly."

Hodge looked doubtful, for he now understood how strong must be the temptation for Merriwell to follow the game.

Frank completed dressing, and left the academy. He turned his footsteps in the direction of Snodd's, but still he had no intention of going there. Keeping under the brow of the hill, he passed around to a large grove in the rear of Snodd's buildings.

It was early October now, and the air was bracing and exhilarating, for all the afternoon was mild. The trees were flaming with color, and the leaves had begun to sift down. In the grove squirrels romped and chattered.

It seemed good to Frank to get away alone under the shadow of the trees. New strength and new life came to him, and new resolves and determinations formed themselves unsought and unbidden in his mind. He felt that it was a privilege and a blessing to be alive.

Had he felt free to meet Inza then, he would have been quite happy.

He flung himself down beneath a great tree at the edge of the grove, where he could see Snodd's buildings. For a long time he lay there, thinking and dreaming.

Suddenly he started up. Three figures were leaving the buildings and coming toward the grove. He saw they were three girls, and he instantly recognized one of them as Inza. The others were Belinda Snodd and one of the village girls, with whom Frank was slightly acquainted, Mabel Blossom, generally known as May Blossom.

"They are coming here!" exclaimed Frank. "They must not see me!"

He arose hastily, and scurried away into the grove, and he did not stop till he had reached the shore. There he sat down amid some rocks, and remained a long time, as it seemed to him.

But he could not resist the temptation to steal back and see if the girls were still in the grove. He finally arose and did so.

As he passed through the grove and came out near the old picnic-ground, he suddenly halted and stepped behind a tree, for he had come upon two persons in earnest conversation.

They were Inza Burrage and Leslie Gage!

CHAPTER XI.

TRUSTING AND TRUE.

Instantly a surge of jealousy swept over Frank Merriwell. How did it come about that Gage had met Inza there? Was it by appointment?

Belinda Snodd and May Blossom were in plain view a short distance away, and Wat Snell was trying to make himself agreeable to them.

Without intending to eavesdrop, Frank paused there a moment, unconsciously listening. He heard Inza say:

"The others cannot hear you now, Mr. Gage, so you can tell me the important thing you have to reveal."

"I don't know as you will be pleased to hear it," said Gage, with an attempt at great apparent sincerity, "for it is about your friend, Frank Merriwell, and you will not like to hear anything unpleasant of him."

Inza drew herself up proudly.

"You cannot tell me anything of Mr. Merriwell that will make me think less of him," she declared, her dark eyes flashing.

That was enough to chain Frank to the spot; he could not have slipped away then had he desired to do so.

"Perhaps not," said Gage, with a significant smile, "but I think I can."

"How has Frank Merriwell ever injured you that you should be slandering him behind his back?"

For an instant this staggered Leslie, like a blow in the face, but he swiftly recovered.

"Oh, Merriwell has never injured me, and I haven't the least thing in the world against him," he said, smoothly; "but I do take an interest in you, and it makes me sorry to see you so absorbed in a fellow utterly unworthy of your friendship—utterly unworthy to be spoken to or even noticed by you."

Gage spoke rapidly, for he saw she was eager to interrupt him.

Her face grew pale, and she stamped one small foot angrily on the ground, as she flung back:

"This is not the first time you have tried to injure him, and you should be ashamed! Why, he saved you from the Eagle's Ledge, after you had fallen over Black Bluff."

"Which was exactly what any fellow would have done for another under similar circumstances. That is not to his credit. I beg you to listen. It has taken me some time to make up my mind to tell you the truth—to warn you, and now I must. To begin with, Merriwell comes of an uncertain family, although, I believe, he has an uncle who has some money, and that uncle is paying the fellow's way through Fardale Academy."

"What do I care about his family, so long as I know him to be a noble fellow! You forget, sir, that he has twice saved my life!"

"No, I have not forgotten. I do not blame you for being grateful, but you must know the whole truth about him. Frank Merriwell is a gambler—he plays cards for money."

"I don't believe it!" were the words that came from Inza's lips, and sent a thrill of shame through the lad behind the tree.

"But it is true, and I can prove it. I will prove it, too! If I prove it to your satisfaction, Miss Burrage, will you cut the fellow, and have nothing to do with him in the future?"

Frank leaned forward, holding his breath, eager to hear the answer.

It came promptly and decisively:

"No!"

Gage caught his breath.

"Do you mean to say you will still be friends with a regular gambler like Merriwell?" he asked.

"I do not believe Frank Merriwell is a gambler—you can never make me believe it!"

"But I will bring proof."

"Even then I will believe your proof is hatched up against him."

This made Gage lose his head.

"Why, you are awfully stuck on that cad!" he cried. "You are altogether too fine a girl for him!"

He suddenly caught her in his arms, and tried to embrace her. She struggled, and cried out for help.

Like a panther, Frank Merriwell bounded from behind the tree. He caught Gage by the collar, and tore Inza from his grasp. Then Frank's fist shot out, landing with a sharp spat right between Leslie's eyes. A second later Gage came in violent contact with the ground.

"Frank!" exclaimed Inza, as he supported her.

Wat Snell and the two girls with whom he had been talking had witnessed the entire affair. They now came hurrying toward the spot.

"The miserable cur!" cried Frank. "I will——"

"Don't touch him again!" urged Inza. "Oh, you struck him an awful blow!"

In truth Frank had given Gage a heavy blow, and it was some seconds before the fellow made a move. Snell helped him sit up. Leslie put his hand to his head, and stared in a dazed way at Frank.

"Are you hurt much, old man?" asked Wat, sympathizingly.

"I guess not," mumbled Gage. "What did he strike me with?"

"His fist."

"Why, it seemed like a rock!"

Wat helped him to his feet, and the two stood glaring at Frank, who regarded them with supreme scorn.

"Shall we sail in and do him up?" asked Wat, excitedly.

"Yes," said Leslie; "we will give him a good drubbing."

Instantly Frank placed Inza to one side, and boldly faced the two young rascals.

"I don't believe you both can whip me, the way I feel just now," he cried. "I think I can give you more fight than you want, so just sail right in."

They hesitated. There was something about Merriwell's look and bearing that seemed to warn them against attacking him. To Wat Snell it suddenly seemed quite probable that Frank would prove more than a match for both of them.

"There are ladies present," he said, hastily. "We cannot fight in the presence of ladies."

"Very thoughtful!" came scornfully from Frank's lips. "Possibly the ladies will step aside long enough for us to settle this little matter."

"Oh, don't fight with them, Frank!" pleaded Inza. "There are two of them, and——"

"That is not enough. I am good for two such sneaking scoundrels as they are! Don't worry about me."

"Hear the blowhard!" sneered Snell.

Frank seemed on the point of springing toward him, and Wat hastily dodged behind Leslie, saying:

"Give it to him, Les, if he wants to fight!"

This showed how much Gage could depend on Snell in a scrimmage, and the former instantly decided that it was not best to try to get revenge on Merriwell just then.

"There will be no fighting here," he said, loftily, "but I shall not forget Merriwell's blow, and he shall pay dearly for it. I will make him wish he had not been so free with his fist."

"As for you, Miss Spitfire," turning to Inza, "you must feel proud to have a friend in a fellow of his class! Do not forget what I told you about him and——"

"Silence, sir!" cried Inza, contemptuously. "You had better go away at once. I wouldn't believe such a contemptible creature as you under any circumstances!"

"All right, all right," growled Gage, scowling blackly. "You will find out in time that I told the truth. This is not the end of this matter. Come, Wat, let's go. If I stay any longer, I'll have to whip Merriwell before all of the present company."

So the delectable pair moved away together, and Gage's revengeful heart was made still more bitter by the ringing laugh of scorn Inza Burrage sent after them.

CHAPTER XII.

THE SNARE IS BROKEN.

hen Frank parted from Inza that afternoon, he had made a free and full confession of his fault. She had listened with pained surprise, almost with incredulity, but she had not shown the scorn that Frank felt he fully deserved. However, she had exacted a pledge, which he had freely given, and, returning to the academy, he felt that he was himself once more. His step was elastic, his heart was light, and he whistled a lively strain.

That evening he had a long talk with Bart.

"Come, Bartley," urged Frank, "drop this card-playing, and give attention to your studies."

Bart was in a bad mood, as he had been much of the time lately, and he laughed harshly.

"You're a fine fellow to give that sort of advice when you cannot keep away from the game yourself!" he said.

"But I can keep away," came quietly and decidedly from Frank's lips.

"Prove it."

"I will. I am not going to play any more. I have been a fool, and I am ashamed of it."

"That is easy enough to say, but—— Well, we will see what we will see."

"You doubt my ability to keep away from the game?"

"Haven't I reason to do so?"

"You surely have. But look here, Bart; you know as well as I the kind of fellows we are running with when we play cards with that gang. Neither you nor I care to call Gage and Snell our particular friends."

"That's right."

"And Harris is a kind of uncertain fellow—neither one thing nor another."

"Sure."

"Sam Winslow hasn't enough stamina to resist temptation of any sort."

"Go on."

"Harvey Dare is a pretty decent chap, but he doesn't care a rap what people think or say of him."

"Well?"

"Hans Dunnerwust has been inveigled into the game, and I am going to do my best to make him break away."

Bart drew a deep breath.

"Go ahead, Frank," he said, "and I hope you may succeed in your missionary work. You didn't name my failings, but I have them, or they have me, for I can't break away from them."

"You can if you will try. Make a desperate effort, Bart. Think how differently you are situated than I, who was born with a passion for gambling."

Bart rose impatiently.

"Drop it, old man," he growled. "I've lost too much to knock off now. I am going to play to-night."

"To-night? Why, it is Saturday night!"

"Yes."

"If you begin playing, you will not stop before Sunday comes in."

"Perhaps not."

"You don't mean to say that you are going to play on Sunday?"

"The better the day, the better the deed," mocked Bart.

Frank said no more, but he formed a firm resolution. He would find a way to save his roommate and break up the card game. Gage and Snell were welcome to all they had won off him, but he would bring their career to an end.

How was he to do it?

Surely he could not report them, for that would place him beneath a ban among the cadets.

He studied over the problem.

That night, when Hodge arose to slip away, Frank got up also, and began to dress. Bartley heard him, and was surprised.

"Where are you going, Frank?" he whispered.

"With you," was the quiet reply.

"But I thought——"

Hodge stopped; he would not say what he thought. But he told himself that he had known all along that Frank could not keep away.

They got out of the academy, and made their way to the old

boathouse, where the company was already assembled.

Gage and Snell were there, but neither of them spoke to Frank.

Bart sat into the game immediately, but, to the general surprise, Frank declined.

"I am short, and I don't feel like playing to-night," he said. "I've got a book I want to read, and it wasn't possible for me to have a light in quarters, so I came along."

He declined all offers of money, and sat down to read the book. He turned his back to the table, so the light fell on the pages from over his shoulder, and in a short time he seemed too much absorbed in the book to observe anything that was going on.

The game became very warm. It was without limit, and Hodge lost from the first. Both Gage and Snell were winning steadily.

Still Merriwell seemed to read on calmly. But he was not reading a great deal. In the palm of one hand he had a small mirror concealed. By the aid of this mirror, he was watching the movements of Gage and Snell.

And he was making some very interesting discoveries!

At length there came a large pot. Hodge and Gage stayed in and raised till every one else fell out. Hodge took one card; Gage, who was dealing, took two.

Then there was betting such as had never before been known in that old boathouse.

Hodge's face was pale, and he refused to call, for he believed his time to get square had come. He put in his "paper" for more than fifty dollars, after his money was exhausted.

Finally the game came to an end, and Gage proclaimed himself the winner.

He started to take the money lying on the table. Like a leaping tiger, Frank Merriwell came out of his chair, whirled, thrust Leslie's hands aside, and pushed the money toward Bart.

"Not this evening, Mr. Gage!" he said. "I am onto your little game, and it won't work any more with this crowd!"

The boys sprang to their feet.

"What do you mean?" asked Gage, hoarsely, his face very pale.

"I mean that you are a sneak and a cheat!" said Frank, deliberately. "I mean that you are too mean and contemptible for any honest fellow in this academy to ever have anything to do with! I mean that you have deliberately robbed your companions by means of crooked appliances made for dishonest gamblers! That is exactly what I mean, Mr. Gage."

Leslie gasped, and managed to say:

"Be careful! You will have to prove every word, or——"

"I will prove it! I have been watching you, and I have seen you repeatedly make the pass that restores cut cards to their original position. I have seen you hold back at least three of the top cards in dealing, and give them to Snell or take them yourself. Those cards will be found to be skillfully marked, and that pack is short. Boys, count those cards!"

The cards were counted, and the pack proved to be four cards short.

"Here is one of the gambler's appliances of which I spoke," said Frank, thrusting his hand under Leslie's side of the table and wrenching away something. "It is a table hold-out, and it contains the four missing cards. This is the kind of a fellow you are playing cards with, gentlemen."

The faces of the boys were black with anger, Wat Snell being excepted. Seeing his opportunity, Snell quickly slipped away, and before he could be stopped, had bolted from the boathouse.

Gage took advantage of the excitement to make a break for liberty, and he, too, got away.

"What a howling shame!" said Harvey Dare, in disgust. "We'd tar and feather them both. Anyway, they'll have to get out of the academy."

The boys who had put money into the game were given what they had invested. The rest was turned over to Hodge. It made his losing nearly square.

"This settles me," he said, grimly. "I am done playing. No more of this business for me."

"Stick to that, and you will be all right," said Frank Merriwell, in a low tone.

Leslie Gage knew what must follow. The story was bound to spread among the cadets, and he would find himself scorned and shunned. He immediately ran away, and it was reported that he had gone to sea.

Wat Snell had not the nerve to run away, but he found himself the most unpopular fellow at the academy, shunned by the cadets generally, and regarded with contempt.

The exposure of Gage's crookedness broke up the poker parties for that season, at least; and Frank was happy, for he had saved himself and rescued Hodge and Hans Dunnerwust.

But he was happiest in receiving the approbation of Inza Burrage, who learned, through her brother, what Frank had done.

CHAPTER XIII.

THE "CENTIPEDE" JOKE.

Sh!"

"What's up?"

"There's a carmine haze on the moon."

"That's clear as mud! What's the racket?"

"You room next to Mulloy and Dunnerwust?"

"Yes."

"Well, you will hear the racket just about the time taps sound."

"But I want to know what's up," persisted the second speaker, whose curiosity was aroused. "Has somebody put up a job on those two marks, Mulloy and his Dutch chum?"

"You've guessed it."

"Who?"

"Guess again."

"Merriwell."

"Right. Take your place at the head of the class."

This hasty and guarded conversation was carried on between two plebe cadets who had met in a corridor of the academy "cockloft." The first speaker was a jolly-faced little fellow, whose name was Sammy Smiles, and whose companions had failed to invent a nickname for him that fitted as well as his real name—Smiles.

The other boy's name was also Samuel, or the first part of his name was Samuel; but the cadets declined to have two Sams among the plebes, and so Samuel Winslow had gradually come to be known as "Poke."

"What's Merriwell up to now?" asked Poke, a look of delighted suspense on his face. "He's making things rather lively round here lately."

"You bet!" grinned Sammy Smiles. "There's more fun in him than there is in a barrel of monkeys."

"But what's he up to now?" reiterated Winslow. "Don't keep a fellow in suspense!"

"He smuggled in a basket of crawfish."

"Well?"

"Well, you don't suppose he got 'em to eat, do you?"

"'Course not. Is he going to make the Dutchman eat them?"

"No, but they may take a few bites out of the Dutchman."

"You don't mean——"

"He's put the crawfish into Dunnerwust's and Mulloy's beds."

"Jeewhiz!"

Poke clapped a hand over his mouth, and looked round hastily. Then he asked:

"How could he do it? Beds ain't made up till after tattoo, and he wouldn't have time to——"

"Tattoo sounded fifteen minutes ago. It doesn't take Mulloy more than two minutes to make up his beds. Hans is slower, but I hustled 'em both up to-night. I dodged into their room the instant tattoo sounded, and told 'em Gray wanted 'em both to come to his room, but they mustn't come till after their beds were made, for they might stay till it was too late to make the beds before taps. They both hustled up the beds, and then skipped over to see Gray. Merriwell was watching, and he didn't lose more than an hour getting that basket of crawfish into their room, and stowing the lively little birds in the beds. Oh, my! won't there be a howl when they yank themselves into bed!"

Sammy Smiles doubled up with suppressed laughter. He was convulsed at the thought of what would happen when the Dutch boy and the Irish lad hastily jumped into their beds.

"Merriwell takes the cake," Poke declared, with a chuckle. "He's been on a regular frolic for the last week, and he can invent more kinds of fun than any fellow living—besides himself."

"That's right," agreed Sammy. "Frank is a dandy! Things would be rather dull here this winter if it wasn't for him."

"Well, he'll never let them get dull, and I believe he is the best fellow that ever lived!"

"Right again," nodded the other lad, with a moment of seriousness. "Merriwell is the prince of good fellows, and there's not a white man in the academy who wouldn't fight for him. I know some fellows are down on him, but that's pure jealousy. They're sore because he has become so popular. I don't believe he cares much."

"If he wouldn't stick up for Hodge the way he does——"

"That shows his loyalty. I can't see what he finds to admire in Hodge, though the fellow can fight and play ball. He and Frank do not seem very well matched for roommates. I don't see how

Merriwell can keep from working jokes on Hodge all the time. Jingoes! but wouldn't I laugh if he had put some of those crawfish in Hodge's bed!"

This fancy convulsed Sammy again, and, just then, Poke hissed: "'Sh! Somebody's coming! Skip!"

Both made haste to get into their rooms, and, as Sammy roomed with Ned Gray, he found Barney Mulloy and Hans Dunnerwust being entertained there. Ned was telling them stories, and pretending to be greatly absorbed in their society. As Sammy slipped in, with the inevitable grin on his face, although he was doing his best to suppress it, Ned looked up and asked:

"How's the weather outside?"

"It is settled," replied Sammy, with a meaning wink.

"Do you think it will be a cold night?"

"It will be for some folks."

"When the weather is cold down East, they call it nipping."

"Well, it will be nipping to-night for some people."

"In that case, somebody will have to be stirring."

"That's right."

"Yaw," said Hans, with a lazy yawn, "I pet me your life some folks peen plame fools enough to peen sdirring to-nighd. Dot makes me dired. Vy in dunder don'd dey gid in dere peds und sday dere, ain'd id?"

"Oh, some people don't know enough for that," said Ned Gray. "And then there are people who are afraid to go to bed at this season of the year."

"Vot vos dot? Afrait uf vot?"

"Centipedes."

"Vot vos cendibedes?"

"They are a creature with a poisonous bite, and they are all sizes from the bigness of a pea to one as large as your hand."

"Oh, phwat are yez givin' av us!" cried Barney Mulloy, derisively. "Is it idiots or fools ye take us fer, Oi dunno?"

"Oh, I am telling you the sober truth," declared Ned, with the utmost seriousness, while Sammy Smiles got behind the visitors and stuffed his handkerchief into his mouth to keep from shrieking with laughter. "The centipedes of tropical countries are smaller than our regular winter centipedes, which are sometimes as large as a man's hand. Their bite is deadly poison."

"Dunder und blitzens!" gasped Hans. "I don'd tole you dot!"

"Get away wid yer blarney!" exclaimed Barney, disbelievingly. "Pwhat do yez take us fer, Oi warnt to know? It's nivver a bit do ye shtuff sich a yarrun down aour throats, me b'y."

"You are not compelled to believe it."

"Cintipades in th' winter!" snorted the Irish lad. "Thot bates th' band!"

"Well, you may think what you like, but you may see some of our winter centipedes some time, and then it is possible you will feel that you owe me an apology."

"Vot does cendibedes look like, ain't it?"

"They have long, leg-like claws, and are covered with hard shells."

"Und dey pite?"

"Well, I should say so."

"Put, vy vos some beoples afrait dose cendibedes uf to go to ped? You tole me dot."

"Well, these winter centipedes are great creatures to seek warm corners, and so they get into beds."

Sammy Smiles was ready to roll on the floor. He could not keep his laughter bottled up, and it burst forth in a gurgle, which he quickly changed to a most distressing cough.

"Wan thing is sure," said Barney; "nivver a cintipade is loikely to get inther our beds, fer we make 'em up ache noight, so we'd see th' craythers if they wur there."

"I believe one of them has never been seen in the academy," came seriously from Ned's lips. "The strict discipline of the institution is too much for them, and they keep away."

Barney grinned.

"Thot's all roight, me b'y. Some doay Oi'll tell yez about th' big shnakes we hiv in Oireland. Oi hivn't toime to-night."

"Und I vill dell you apoud der big Injuns vot dere vos der Rhine on, in Shermany," said Hans. "Maype you haf heardt uf dose poem enditled 'Big Injun on der Rhine,' ain'd id?"

"Oh, well, that's all right!" said Ned, with a wave of his hand, as if he was not quite pleased.

Then he looked at his watch, and exclaimed:

"Great Scott! we've got but one minute left in which to undress and get into bed before taps!"

He leaped up and began undressing, and, with exclamations of alarm, the Irish lad and the Dutch boy hustled from the room, losing no time about getting into their own and undressing.

"Did Merriwell fix it?" asked Ned, of Sammy.

"You bet!" was the reply. "Extinguish the flicker, and wait for the general war-dance. It will take place in a very few seconds."

So they extinguished the light, and awaited the outburst that must soon come.

CHAPTER XIV.

LIVELY TIMES.

arney and Hans dashed into their room, and tore themselves out of their clothes, which, however, they took care to hang in order on the pegs placed along the partition that divided one end of the room into two alcoves.

Long practice enabled them to undress with great swiftness.

By the time taps began to sound they were ready to jump into their beds.

Barney quickly extinguished the light, but Hans lost no time in getting under the blankets, while the Irish lad made a leap to do so.

Then came a cry of astonishment and fear from Hans.

"Shimminy Gristmas!" exclaimed the Dutch boy. "Vot dot vos I touch me to, ain'd id?"

"Shut up!" growled Barney. "Bad cess to yez! do yez phwant th' officer av th' guarrud doon on us! Kape shtill, ur——"

"Wa-ow!" howled Hans, uttering a wild shriek of pain and terror. "I vos caught in der ped my leg by! Dunder und blitzens! I vos bit mit der toe on!"

"Begorra! ye hiv gone crazy, ye son av a Dutch chazemaker! Kape shtill thot howlin', ur——"

Then Barney's tone suddenly changed, and he let out a yell that would have awakened Rip Van Winkle from his long nap.

"Saints defind me! I'm bitten in siventane different places intoirely! Wurra! wurra! Musha! musha! Th' bed is full av crawling crathers!"

"Cendibedes!" howled Hans.

"Cintipades!" shrieked Barney.

Out of the beds they scrambled in hot haste, and to each one six or eight of the crawfish were clinging.

"Wao-w!" roared Hans.

"Whoop!" bellowed Barney.

"I peen kilt alretty yet!" shrieked the Dutch boy. "I peen bit all ofer py does cendibedes!"

"Begorra! there's a bushel av th' craythers hangin' to me!" shouted the Irish lad. "Oi'm a dead b'y intoirely!"

"Hel-lup! hel-lup!" howled Hans, dismally.

Out into the center of the room danced the two boys, fighting, clawing, striking at various parts of their bodies, where the crawfish persistently clung. They collided, and both sat down heavily on the floor.

"It's kilt we are!" moaned Barney.

"Dot peen near knockin' mine prains oud alretty yet!" declared Hans.

"Loight th' lamp!!

"Hel-lup! hel-lup! hel-lup!"

In some way they scrambled to their feet, and both lunged for the door, which they beat upon with their fists, as if they would tear it down.

"Docther!" bellowed Barney.

"Toctor!" screamed Hans.

"Will yez get away fram thot dure, so Oi can open it?"

"Ged avay dot toor from mineself!" flung back the Dutch boy. "I ged me to dot toor first, und I peen der first von oud!"

"Oh, ye will, will yez! We'll see about thot!"

Biff! smack! thud! thump! The two frantic boys were hammering each other in the darkness of their room, while the listening jokers were convulsed with merriment.

The uproar had aroused that entire section of the academy. The sentinel came down the corridor at the double quick, just as Frank Merriwell, partly dressed, leaped out of his room and flung himself against the door of the room from which the racket issued.

Other boys came swarming into the corridor, and the excitement was intense.

Merriwell burst into the room, and, a moment later, dragged out Hans and Barney into the lighted corridor.

The crawfish were still clinging comfortably to various portions of the garments in which the two lads had gone to bed. Seeing the creatures, Hans uttered a howl of agony louder than any that had yet issued from his throat.

"Cendibedes!" he wailed. "I vos a tead boy! I vos peen bit in more as nine huntred und sefenteen blaces alretty yet! Vere vos dot toctor?"

"They're centipades sure!" groaned Barney. "An Oi didn't belave there wur such craythers! Ouch! ouch! How they boight! Take 'em off!"

But the two lads danced, kicked and beat about them with their arms so that no one could remove the crawfish.

The boys who were witnesses of this "circus," nearly choked with laughter. Sammy Smiles had a fit, and rolled on the floor, clinging to his sides.

All the while Frank was apparently making desperate efforts to quiet the boys and remove the crawfish, but, at the same time he was saying just loud enough for them to hear:

"The bite is deadly poison! The only antidote is equal parts of new milk and vinegar taken internally. About a gallon should be absorbed, while a chemically prepared poultice of H2O, tempus fugit, and aqua pura should be applied to each and every bite."

"Bring' on yer new milk and vinegar, begorra!" roared the Irish boy, wildly. "It's a barrel ur two Oi'll drink av th' sthuff!"

"Somepody dose boultices make britty queek alretty!" shouted Hans. "I vant dwo huntred und elefen for dose bites vot I haf all ofer mein body on!"

"Keep still!" ordered the sentinel. "Stand still while those crawfish are removed."

"You peen bitten all der dime dose cendibedes py, und I pet me my poots you don'd keep very sdill yet avile! We-e-eow! Dey vos eadin' me ub alretty yet!"

"Get away wid yez, ye spalpane!" shouted Barney, and one of his wildly waving fists struck the sentinel between the eyes and knocked him over instantly.

"Remember it is vinegar and milk that you want, and you must have it," shouted Frank, in the Irish lad's ear. "Every second you delay about procuring it makes your chances all the more desperate."

"Begorra! Oi'll hiv it directly, av there's anything av th' sort in th' ranch!"

Then Barney made a break for the stairs, with Hans a close second, and the boys could not resist the temptation to rush after them.

Never before had there been such an uproar heard in Fardale Academy, and the commotion had brought Professor Gunn and his two principal assistants, Professor Jenks and Professor Scotch, from their rooms on the floor below the "Cockloft."

"What can be the meaning of this outrageous hub-bub?" cried Professor Jenks, who, on account of his exceeding height, was known as "High Jinks."

"Goodness knows!" exclaimed Professor Gunn, peering over his spectacles in a horrified way at his companions. "It must be a mutiny——"

"Or a murder!" chattered Professor Scotch, who was a very small man, and was generally known as "Hot Scotch," because of his fiery red hair and peppery temper.

"Let us proceed together to investigate," came resolutely from Professor Gunn's lips.

"All right," said High Jinks, bravely. "Lead the way, sir."

"Be cautious, gentlemen—be cautious!" urged Hot Scotch, his face pale and his teeth rattling together. "Such dreadful shrieks have never before assailed my ears—never! They are certainly cries of mortal agony!"

"Oh, you can go to your room, and lock yourself in, if you are afraid!" came scornfully from the tall professor's lips.

"Who's afraid!" bristled the little man, instantly. "You will find I am not afraid of you, sir! I am ready to——"

"Gentlemen! gentlemen, silence!" came commandingly from Professor Gunn's lips. "I will not have this unseemly bickering! If you are ready, come on."

So they moved toward the stairs, High Jinks resolutely keeping by Professor Gunn's side, while Hot Scotch lingered a little in the rear, clinging to the tail of the head professor's coat.

Just as they reached the foot of the stairs and were about to ascend, feet were heard rushing along the corridor above, and then Barney Mulloy came plunging down the stairs, with Hans Dunnerwust riding astride his neck, both in their nightclothes, with a few crawfish still clinging to them.

The three professors were unable to get out of the way, so the frantic boys plunged straight into them, and all fell in a struggling, squirming mass on the floor.

CHAPTER XV.

WARNED.

At the head of the stairs swarmed the plebes, who were convulsed with laughter.

"Oh! oh! oh!" gasped Sammy Smiles, clinging to his sides. "Somebody please do something to stop me from laughing! Ha! ha! ha! If I don't stop soon, I'll die! Oh, dear! oh, dear! I am sore all over!"

"Help!" cried Professor Gunn.

The boys on the floor below the Cockloft were out by this time, and they were enjoying the spectacle quite as much as the plebes above.

Frank had rushed into his room, and he came forth with a bag that contained something that moved and snarled. Reaching the head of the stairs, he quickly opened the mouth of the bag and extracted two cats. He had slipped on a pair of heavy gloves, and he succeeded in holding the cats securely, while he said to Ned Gray:

"Quick—take the string that held the mouth of the bag—tie their tails together! Lively!"

Ned caught up the string, and worked swiftly, tying the cats' tails tightly together.

When this was accomplished, Frank gave the felines a fling toward the group at the foot of the stairs.

The cats struck one on either side of Professor Gunn's neck, and, as their tails were tied together, they hung there, but not quietly.

With wild howls of agony, they began clawing each other, incidentally, by way of diversion, socking their claws into the professor's face now and then, and ripping up a few furrows in that gentleman's countenance.

Professor Gunn howled louder than the cats, and tried to fling them off; but they clung to him as if they loved him, and continued to shower marks of affection upon him.

"Great Scott!" gasped Ned Gray. "If it is ever found out that you were at the bottom of this, Merriwell, you will be expelled sure!"

"Then I shall perish in a good cause," laughed Frank. "Fun is better than medicine, and we were beginning to stagnate."

"Help!" cried Professor Gunn, in tones of deep anguish. "Take these beasts away! They are devouring me!"

"Meow! me-e-eow! S'pt! s'pt! Me-e-e-e-ow!" howled the cats, as they continued to scratch the professor's face till it began to look like the colored map of a country that had been disturbed by a violent earthquake.

Somehow Hot Scotch had gotten into a wrangle with High Jinks, whom he was holding down and punching vigorously.

"Hit me in the ribs, will ye! Pound me in the eye, will ye? Tackle me when down, will ye? Well, I've got a score against you, and I'll settle it now!"

"Take him off!" squealed Jenks, thrashing about with his long legs. "Save me! save me!"

Having untangled themselves from the mass and become freed of the crawfish in the struggle, Hans and Barney sat on the floor and stared in astonishment at the spectacle. The sight was too much for the risibilities of the Irish boy, and he forgot that he had been severely bitten by "centipades."

"Begorra! Dutchy, this is a roight loively avening, Oi do belave," he chuckled. "Will yez look at this fer a racket, Oi dunno! Hurro! Sail in, b'ys!"

"Vell, I don't efer seen der peat uf dot!" gasped Hans, his eyes bulging. "Uf dot don't peen a recular fight, I vos an oysder!"

"Now, boys, it's time to take a hand," said Frank Merriwell. "Be lively! Gather up the crawfish, and throw 'em out of the windows. Work quick! Here, Windsor, dispose of this bag!"

His words put the cadets in motion. Down the stairs he ran, and quickly gathered up every crawfish he could find, while others followed his example. Then, leaving the boys to take care of the cats and separate the fighting professors, he bounded up the stairs and hurried to the room occupied by Barney and Hans, where he removed every crawfish he could find in the beds or upon the floor. He worked with great swiftness, and accomplished all this in a very few seconds.

In the meantime, some of the boys who had been in the joke from the start, took hold and aided Frank to clear out all signs of the crawfish, while others hastened to Professor Gunn's assistance, and pulled off the cats, removing the string from their tails.

Barney and Hans were beginning to call for the doctor again, declaring they had been bitten by "centibedes," or "cintipades," and Professor Gunn was glaring over a handkerchief held to his bleeding face, while High Jinks and Hot Scotch stood apart and glowered at each other, ready to resume hostilities at the slightest provocation.

Lieutenant Gordan was on hand, looking very stern, and asking a few very pointed questions. He fully understood a practical joke had been perpetrated, and woe to the perpetrator if the lieutenant found proof against him. Gordan was stern and as unwavering as the hills in the discharge of his duty.

But the lieutenant found five very excited and incoherent persons in the group that had assembled at the foot of the stairs. Professors Jenks and Scotch would not say much of anything, only mutter and glare daggers at each other, while Professor Gunn was too furious and too confused to tell anything straight. Barney and Hans declared over and over that they had been bitten by "centipedes," and showed the wounds. The jumbled story told by them puzzled the lieutenant more than anything else.

Having been released, the cats had taken flight.

Lieutenant Gordan did not say much, but the expression on his face told that he meant to investigate the affair thoroughly. The time, however, was not suitable for an investigation, and so he ordered everybody to their rooms. Barney called for a drink of milk and vinegar, but the lieutenant assured him that he was not in danger of dying immediately if he did not obtain what he desired, so both the Irish lad and the Dutch boy were sent to their rooms, like the others.

In a brief time silence settled over the academy, and no one could have fancied there had been such an uproar there a short while before.

In the morning, Bartley said to Frank.

"What in the world has got into you, old man? You are full of the Old Harry, lately. You will have this academy turned bottom up, if you keep on."

Frank smiled.

"We've got to have something to break the monotony," he said. "A fellow gets tired of plugging away at his studies all the time."

"That's so," admitted Bart, who was a dark-faced, reserved sort of boy; "but such tricks as you perpetrated last night are dangerous."

"How?"

"What if Lieutenant Gordan finds out you were at the bottom of it? You know what will happen."

"Sure!"

"Well, you are taking big chances for a little fun."

"A little fun!" echoed Frank. "Didn't you consider that something more than a little fun last night? It struck me as a roaring farce."

A faint trace of a smile came to Hodge's dark face.

"You enjoy anything of the kind far more than I do, Merriwell," he said. "I like fun of a different sort."

"Well, I fancy you will acknowledge I take some interest in other sports, Bart?"

"That's all right, Frank; you are the leader of our class in everything, because you are a natural leader. But you have a dangerous rival."

"Think so?"

"I know it. There is a fellow in this school who is aiming to stand at the head in athletics. Up to a few weeks ago he remained in the background, so that little or no notice was taken of him; but he is coming to the front now, and I believe he means to give you a hot race for first position. He has even declared openly that he is a pitcher, and means to make a try for a position on the team."

"That's all right, Bart. I am not hoggish enough to want all the honors, and, if we play as much ball as we intend to next spring and summer, we'll need another pitcher. I can't do all the twirling."

"But he says he will not play under you as captain of the team."

"Ha! That is interesting! Now you are waking me up. I suppose the fellow you speak of is Paul Rains?"

"Yes, he is the one."

"Then Rains is something of an enemy, as well as a rival. Well, we'll see who is the better man."

CHAPTER XVI.

PAUL RAINS.

he short, dark days of winter had brought about changes in Fardale Academy. Drills had been discontinued, and, except for weekly inspections and occasional guard duty, there were no formations under arms. The hours for study were longer, as also were the lessons. Some of the plebes were negligent and regardless of the fact that the January examinations were close at hand, while others were "boning" steadily, doing their level best to stand well in their classes.

For all of his mischievous disposition, Frank was studying enough to hold his own in his class, and he was looked on favorably by his instructors. He was magnetic, and had a winning way, so that he made many friends, always among the better class at the school. No one, either man or boy, is ever popular without having enemies, and this was true of Frank; but his enemies were those who were jealous of him, or those with whom he did not care to associate, for the best of reasons.

Hodge was not a fellow to make friends, being haughty and proud, and Merriwell obtained many enemies because he roomed with Bart, and seemed to stand up for the fellow.

The friendship of the two lads was rather remarkable, considering how they had once been enemies, and how Hodge had worked hard to injure Frank.

Among the plebes there were a few who stood head and shoulders above their companions in athletics. Hodge went in for fencing, and Professor Rhynas declared he would make a master of the foil. Hugh Bascomb, with a pugilist's thick neck and round head, was spending all his spare time boxing, and it was said that he could strike a blow that would stagger an ox. His admirers declared it was a beautiful sight to see him hammer the punching-bag, and they assured him over and over that he was certain to make another Sullivan. Naturally, this gave Bascomb the "swelled head," and he got an idea into his brain that he was really cut out for a fighter, and that nobody in Fardale could stand up before him for four rounds.

Day after day Barney Mulloy took a long pull at the rowing machine. Ned Gray spent his spare time on the horizontal bars or the trapeze, and Hans Dunnerwust tried his hand at everything, making sport for the spectators.

Among the plebes there were two lads who seemed all-round athletes. They were Paul Rains and Frank Merriwell.

Paul did not like Frank. In fact, he was envious of Merriwell's popularity, although he did his best to keep the fact concealed. Being a sly, secretive person, it was but natural that Rains should come to be considered as modest and unassuming. In truth, he was not modest at all, for, in his secret heart, there was nothing that any one else could do that he did not believe he could do. And so, while appearing to be very modest, he was really intensely egotistical.

Rains had not been given much attention for a time after he entered the academy, but his athletic abilities, for he was really a capable fellow, although his capabilities were limited, were bringing him into notice.

Jolly, open as the day, Frank did not know what it was to be crafty or secretive. He had a way of saying things he thought, and he did not understand people who kept their fancies and ambitious desires bottled up.

Hodge had not been the first to give Frank a hint that he had a rival in Rains, but he was the first to tell him that Rains had declared he would not play on the ball team if Merriwell was captain.

Frank remembered that, and he wondered what Rains could have against him. Frank was never able to understand one fellow despising another because the other was popular, for it was natural for him to wish everybody good luck and success, and he always rejoiced in the success of any fellow he knew, providing, of course, that the success was of the right sort.

Lieutenant Gordan made a rigid investigation of the racket caused by the "centipedes," but he failed to fasten the blame firmly on any one. Not one of the boys who knew the facts would expose Merriwell, and both Barney and Hans, discovering their wounds were not fatal, grinned and declared they were not sure there had been anything in their beds, but they thought they had felt something.

Professor Gunn was very indignant to think the culprits could not be discovered.

"It is a disgrace to the school!" he told Lieutenant Gordan. "Just look at my face, sir! I am a picture!"

The lieutenant did not crack a smile.

"You have no one but yourself to blame for your condition, sir," he said.

"Eh? eh? How's that? how's that?" sputtered Professor Gunn. "I don't think I understand you, sir."

"Then I will make it clear. If you had remained in your room, as you should when the disturbance occurred, you would not have received those injuries."

"But, sir—but I am the principal of this school. It is my place——"

"It is your place to keep in your room, sir, when there is an outbreak like the one under discussion, and allow me to straighten matters out. If you had done so, I might be able to get at the bottom of this affair and discover the guilty jokers; as it is, you and your associates complicated matters so that I do not seem able to do much of anything."

Having spoken thus plainly, Lieutenant Gordan turned on his heel, and left the professor in anything but a pleasant frame of mind.

It was a day or two after the occurrence of the "great centipede joke," as the crawfish affair came to be termed, that Paul Rains and Hugh Bascomb were having a bout with the gloves in the gymnasium. Quite a number of spectators had gathered, and Frank Merriwell sauntered up and joined the group.

Professor Rhynas was giving his attention to another department of the gymnasium, and he had left Bascomb to meet all comers and "give them points."

Bascomb was not finding it a very easy thing to give Rains many points, although he believed he could knock the fellow down any time he wished to do so by simply letting drive one of his sledge-hammer blows.

But Bascomb had not thought of striking Rains with all his strength. He had discovered that Rains disliked Merriwell, and that was enough to establish a bond of friendship between the big plebe and the lad with whom he was boxing.

Bascomb hated Frank, but he feared him at the same time.

"Nobody seems able to get the best of that fellow," he had thought a hundred times. "It seems to be bad luck to go against him, and so I am going to keep away from him in the future. Poor Gage! Merriwell was bad medicine for him."

Bascomb was a coward, but he could hate intensely in his two-faced, treacherous way.

The moment Merriwell joined the group, Bascomb noted it.

"He's watching Rains," mentally decided the big plebe. "He wants to see what the fellow is made of."

Rains seemed aware that Merriwell was a spectator, for he braced up and gave Bascomb a merry go for a few minutes, forcing the big fellow back, and seeming to tap him with ease and skill whenever and wherever he chose.

When this little flurry was over, Rains threw off his gloves, and declared he had had enough.

"So have I," said Bascomb, with a grin. "You're the best man I've put the mittens on with yet. I believe there is a fellow not more than a hundred miles from here that thinks he is some one with gloves, but you can do him dead easy. More than that, I think he knows it, and I don't believe he has the nerve to stand up and face you for a whirl."

"Oh, I don't want to box with any one," said Rains. "Keep still, Bascomb."

"You may not want to box, but you can down Frank Merriwell just the same," declared the big plebe.

CHAPTER XVII.

THE BULLY'S MATCH.

moment of silence followed Bascomb's distinctly-spoken words, and the eyes of nearly every one were turned on Merriwell, to whose face the hot color slowly mounted.

"What's the matter with you, Bascomb?" he finally asked. "What do you want to draw me into this affair for? I don't know as I have any desire to put on the gloves with Rains."

The big fellow grinned in a way that was distinctly insulting.

"I don't think you have," he said. "You wouldn't cut any ice with him."

"You may be right; but I don't quite understand how you know, as I have never stood up with you."

"Oh, that wasn't necessary; I've seen you spar, and I have your gage. You don't run in the class with Rains."

At this juncture Rains made a move as if he would quiet Bascomb, but the big fellow quickly went on:

"I'm not going to keep still any longer. You're too modest, Rains. You keep in the background, and let fellows like Merriwell take the lead in everything, when you should be a leader. You are a better all-round man than Merriwell any day, and you can knock corners off him any time he has nerve enough to put on the mitts with you. He's a dandy to push himself to the front, but——"

That was a little more than Frank could stand. The jolly look had vanished from his face, and he faced Bascomb, saying sharply:

"Look here, my friend, I reckon you are saying one word for Rains and two for yourself. I haven't mixed up with you for reasons that you very well understand, but I don't propose to take much of your talk. If there is any difference between Mr. Rains and myself, we will settle it at another time; but if you want to get a rap at me, now is the accepted occasion, and I will put on the gloves with you."

Bascomb had not been looking for this, and he was taken aback for a moment. Still, although he knew Merriwell was a far better all-round athlete, he believed he could more than match him in boxing, so he eagerly accepted the opportunity.

"I'm your man," he said. "Peel off and get into gear. It won't take me long to show you there are a few things you do not know."

He laughed in a disagreeable way, and Hodge, who had overheard all, bit his lips to repress an outburst of anger.

"The sneak!" whispered Bart to Frank, as the latter stepped aside to take off his coat and vest. "He means to use his sledgehammer blow on you. He won't box for points, but he will try to soak you. Look out for him."

"I am not afraid of him."

"That's all right; but you know he has been practicing that blow, and they say it is terrible. He is cut out for a prizefighter, and is no fit boxing antagonist for a gentleman."

"I shall look out for his 'wicked left,' as I have heard the boys call it."

"He wants to provoke you into a fight with himself or Rains."

"I thought as much; but he may change his mind after we spar, if he does not catch me foul by an accident."

"He is tricky."

"I will watch out for his tricks."

"Look out for his cross-buttock. He's stout as a moose, and he will give you a nasty fall."

For all of his warning words, Bart had great confidence in Frank. They had fought once, shortly after coming to Fardale, and Hodge had found Merriwell more than his match then. Since that time, Frank had missed no opportunity to pick up points in boxing, and his advancement had been great.

Still there was a chance that, by some accident, Bascomb might land once with that "wicked left," or might seek to injure Merriwell by a fall, if he found that he was matched in every other way, so Bart was on hand with his words of warning.

It did not take Frank long to get ready, and it was not long before the two boys faced each other, adjusting the gloves upon their hands. Then they came up to the scratch, and the word was given that started the contest.

Bascomb started in at once with a series of false motions intended to confuse Merriwell, but they simply brought a faint smile to Frank's face, and he remained as placid as ever until——

Just as Bascomb had decided to rush, Merriwell rushed. There was a flashing of their gloves. The big fellow struck twice, and both blows were met by a ready guard.

Biff! biff! biff! First with the right, and then twice with the left Frank struck the big plebe. None of them were heavy blows, but they all stung, and the angry blood surged to Bascomb's face, as he saw Merriwell leap back beyond his reach, laughing a bit.

"Mosquito bites!" said Bascomb, derisively.

"But they count."

"Who cares. I will more than square that in a minute."

"All right; I am waiting."

Once more they were at it, toe to toe, hands moving slightly, light on their feet, ready to dodge or spring, ready to strike or guard. Blows came, one landing on Merriwell's cheek, and another on his shoulder; but more than twenty were dodged or guarded, and Bascomb was struck twice for every blow he gave.

Frank was watching for that left hand body blow, and it came at last, just when Bascomb thought it must count.

In that case Bascomb deceived himself.

The blow was struck swiftly enough, but Frank stopped it with a right hand guard, and, with his left, countered heavily on Bascomb's mouth, sending the big fellow's head back.

Bascomb was surprised, and he showed it. He was also thoroughly angered, and he proceeded to "wade into" Merriwell like a cyclone.

On the other hand, Merriwell was cool as ice, and he made every blow count something, for even when they failed to land they kept the big fellow busy.

Time after time Bascomb rushed in, but Merriwell was light as a feather on his feet, and he danced nimbly about, tapping the other fellow now here, now there, smiling sweetly all the while, and showing a skill that was very baffling to Bascomb.

"Hang him!" thought the big fellow. "He is a regular jumping jack. If I don't land a blow on him pretty quick, I am going to clinch."

This he soon did, catching Frank for the cross-buttock throw.

For a moment it looked as if Merriwell would be flung heavily, and Hodge drew his breath through his teeth with a hissing sound that turned to a sigh of relief as he saw his friend thrust forward his right foot between Bascomb's, break his wrist clear and catch the big fellow behind the left knee with his left hand, while he brought his right arm up over Bascomb's shoulder, and pressed his hand over Bascomb's face, snapping his head back and hurling him off sideways.

This was done quickly and scientifically, and it convinced Hodge that Bascomb could not work the cross-buttock on Merriwell.

Hugh Bascomb was disgusted and infuriated by his failure. He had counted on having a soft thing, and he was actually getting the worst of the encounter.

Time was called, and a breathing spell taken.

Then they went at it again, and this time both worked savagely, their movements being swift and telling.

Watching this battle, Paul Rains began to believe that he was not yet quite Merriwell's match at boxing.

"But I am a better man than he is at most anything else," thought the fellow.

Smack! smack! smack!

Merriwell was following Bascomb up like a tiger, and the big fellow was forced to give ground. Again and again Frank hammered the desperate plebe, getting few blows in return and seeming to mind none of them no more than drops of rain.

Bascomb's face wore the look of an enraged bull. Suddenly, with a quick side motion, he snapped off the glove on his left hand.

Then, with his bare first, he struck straight and hard at Frank Merriwell's face!

CHAPTER XVIII.

RAINS' CHALLENGE.

Bascomb's movement had been noted by the spectators, and a cry of astonishment and warning broke
from many lips.

"Look out!" shouted Bart Hodge.

Frank had seen the movement, and he needed no warning.

Like a flash, he ducked to the right, and Bascomb's bare fist
missed his face and shot over his shoulder.

At the same instant Frank countered with his left, striking the
big fellow on the chin, and hurling him backward with force
enough to send him reeling.

Leaping forward, Merriwell followed up his advantage, and
Bascomb received two terrible blows, one of which knocked him
down as if he had been struck by a cannon ball.

Then Frank flung off both his gloves, his face flushed, and his
eyes flashing, as he exclaimed:

"Two can play at your game, fellow! If you want to try a round
with uncovered knuckles, pick yourself up and come on!"

Snarling like a wounded dog, Bascomb scrambled to his feet;
but here the spectators surged between the two, Rains catching
hold of the big plebe, while Hodge grasped Merriwell.

"Easy, Frank!" warned Bart. "Are you crazy? You know what it
will mean if you fight in the gym. Rhynas has noticed it now—
he's coming."

"Confound that fellow!" muttered Frank. "I don't often get started this way, but it was such a dirty trick that——"

"Never mind, now. Keep still, or Rhynas will hear."

"Let me get at him!" Bascomb had snarled. "I will beat the life
out of him!"

"Stop! stop!" said Rains, swiftly. "You are making a fool of yourself! You can't fight here!"

"Can't I? Well——"

"No, it is against the rules. If you press this, you will be expelled, for the affair will be investigated, and it will be proved that you bared your hand, and Merriwell was forced to do so to defend himself."

"Oh, I could hammer him!"

"Well, there is plenty of time. Steady, now! Here is the professor. He has scented a row. Can't you play cool, and pretend it was a joke? Quick!"

Then Frank was surprised to see Bascomb come forward, laughing in a sickly way, as he said:

"You're pretty flip with your hands, Merriwell, and that's right. I hope you won't lay up anything against me because I lost my glove. I was so excited that I didn't know it was gone."

It was on Frank's tongue to give Bascomb the lie, but, for once in his life, Hodge was the cooler of the two, and he warned his friend by a soft pressure on the arm.

Then, seeing Professor Rhynas listening, with a dark look on his face, Frank laughed, and retorted:

"I don't mind a little thing like that, Bascomb, as long as you didn't strike me. I rather think I held my own with you, and so we will drop it."

"Yes," said Bascomb, "we will drop it—for the present."

The way he spoke the words seemed to indicate that, though they might let it drop for the present, the affair was not settled between them, by any means.

Rhynas now demanded to know the cause of the excitement, and he was told that Bascomb had knocked his glove off, and then, in his excitement, had struck a blow.

The professor looked blacker than ever.

"Such a thing is not possible," he declared. "This is no resort for fighters. If you fellows have any differences to settle, settle them elsewhere. I propose to run this department so there can be no slurs cast upon it, and I will not have fighting, quarreling or loud talking here."

The professor was very strict, and they knew he meant every word he spoke, so they did their best to pacify him with smooth words and apologies.

The man, however, was too shrewd to be deceived, and he knew very well that the two boxers had come very near fighting in the gymnasium while he was present. However, he could do nothing but warn them, which he did, and then went about his affairs.

The spectators of the little bout had been given something to talk about, for, up to that moment, they had not dreamed there was any one in the academy who could stand up before Bascomb's "wicked left" and not be unmercifully hammered.

Merriwell had been touched very few times with Bascomb's left, for he had constantly been on the guard for any blow that might come from that point, and he had thumped the big plebe most aggravatingly all through the affair.

But, what was most significant, after Bascomb had flung off one glove and struck at Frank with his bare fist, the smaller and more supple lad had sailed in and shown that he could put pounds into his blows, for he had driven Bascomb back and knocked him down.

This feat had caused Paul Rains to gasp with astonishment, and, in his heart, he was forced to acknowledge that he doubted if he were yet a match for Merriwell.

Hodge alone, of them all, had believed all along that Frank was more than a match for Bascomb.

Now the spectators began to realize that Merriwell was not given to boasting or "showing off," for he had made no pretense to be the champion boxer, and he had allowed them to think Bascomb was more than a match for anybody in the academy.

When forced to meet some one in a contest that should be a test of skill, Frank had chosen to meet Bascomb, which showed he had been confident in himself all along, for all that he had not thrust himself forward.

In his heart, Rains was very sore, for he had just met Bascomb, and, while he had made a good display, the big fellow had shown that he was the superior.

"Merriwell is putting me in the shade without running up against me at all," thought Paul. "I have lost ground with the fellows right here. How can I recover?"

It did not take him long to decide that he must go against Merriwell in some kind of a contest—and beat him.

"You are very clever with the gloves, Merriwell," said Rains, stepping forward, and speaking placidly; "but I would like to see what you can do jumping."

"Is that a challenge?" asked Frank, quietly.

"If you wish to regard it as such."

"Oh, I am not anxious; I simply wanted to know just what you meant it for."

"Then let it go as a challenge."

"For what—high jump, or broad jump?"

"Both."

"That's the talk!" laughed one of the spectators. "Now we will have more sport!"

"All right," laughed Frank. "I will go you, though I have not been doing much jumping lately, and I am not in my best form."

"That will sound all right if you beat," said Rains; "but it will not do for an excuse if you lose."

"All right; let it go. I won't try to make any other excuse in case you are the victor."

In a mass the boys surged toward a piece of ground just outside of the gymnasium adapted to jumping.

"What shall it be first?" asked Frank, as he stood at the edge of the long strip of turf.

"Running long jump," decided Rains.

"That's agreeable. You challenged, and I presume we are to take turns for three jumps, the one who makes the best leap out of the number is the winner?"

"That's all right."

Hodge spoke up quickly:

"What do you mean by taking turns? Is one to jump three times, and then the other jump three times?"

"No, I mean for us to alternate," explained Frank. "First one jumps, and then the other."

Hodge nodded his satisfaction.

"That is fair, and it is much better than the other way," he declared.

The rivals made preparations for the contest. By lot it fell to Rains to lead off.

Rains was smiling and confident.

"If there is anything I can do, I can jump," he told Bascomb, in an aside. "I will beat him by a foot, at the very least."

"I hope you will beat him by a yard!" muttered the big fellow, sullenly. "I want to see him taken down. He has been a leader long enough."

"Oh, I will manage to win some of his glory away from him before the spring campaign opens," said Rains, confidently. "Don't you worry about that; but," he added, swiftly, "don't repeat my words to anybody. I am not going to boast, but I am going to do something. That's the proper way."

"Sure," nodded Bascomb. "I guess you can do it, too."

In his heart, however, Bascomb did not feel at all sure that Rains would prove the victor in the jumping contest.

"Merriwell is the hardest fellow to beat that I ever saw," he told himself. "It doesn't seem possible to down him, and keep him down. If one seems to get the best of him for a bit, he bobs up serenely directly, and comes out on top. It is just his luck!"

If Bascomb had said it was just Merriwell's pluck he would have hit the truth, for Frank, besides being physically capable, was endowed with any amount of determination, having a never-say-die spirit that would not give up as long as there was a ghost of a chance left to pull out a winner.

In the words of the boys, "Merriwell was no quitter."

"Ready," called the fellow who had been chosen for referee. "Rains will set the stint."

CHAPTER XIX.

JUMPING.

here was a determined look on Paul's face, as he walked to one end of the long strip of turf that ran down one side of the gymnasium.

"He is built for jumping," said one of the spectators. "There is a fine pair of legs, if I ever saw a fine pair."

"That's right," agreed another; "and he is full of snap and ginger. He will give Merriwell a hard go."

"But Merriwell is no slow coach at anything," broke in a third. "I never saw a fellow who seemed able to make such a record at all sorts of sports. Who would have thought that he could face Bascomb? Look! Rains is going to start! See him crouch for the run! He is like a young panther! Now he's off!"

Down the line of turf darted Paul, reached the white line, rose gracefully into the air with a pretty spring, and sailed forward in a handsome jump that brought a round of applause from the spectators.

The measurers immediately ran the tape.

"Seventeen feet and four inches," was the announcement.

A shade of disappointment came to the faces of the spectators, for that was far below the Fardale record.

Rains, however, winked quietly to Bascomb, as if to say that the first jump was a teaser, just to see what Merriwell would do.

Frank now took his position, ran swiftly and lightly down the turf, and made the jump. He seemed to be doing his best, or nearly that, yet he did not reach but a little beyond Rains' mark.

"Seventeen feet, six inches and a quarter," announced one of the measurers.

"I wonder if that is anywhere near his limit?" thought Paul, as he slowly walked back to the starting point. "I think I will have to give him a stint this time."

As he faced the mark, he gathered his energies in every part of his body, felt his muscles strain, knew his nerves were at their highest tension.

"He's going to lay himself out this time," said one of the spectators to another. "Seventeen feet will not be mentioned again."

Down the strip shot Rains. He reached the mark, and went flying through the air like a bird, bringing a cry to the lips of those watching, for they saw he had gone far ahead of the first jump.

"That was a beauty!" exclaimed Bascomb, speaking to Wat Snell, who stood watching.

"It was a good jump," said Snell; "but Merriwell will beat it."

"What makes you think so?"

"Because that fellow always beats at everything. I had rather have his luck than a license to steal! I've quit trying to down him, for I found I was bound to get the worst of it if I kept it up."

"Oh, his time will come."

"Perhaps so; but it isn't coming in a hurry."

"Nineteen feet, three inches and a third," announced the measurer.

"Hooray!" shouted one of Paul's delighted admirers.

"That's the stuff! Merriwell will have to shake himself, if he means to beat that."

But Frank had friends who were confident that he would still hold the lead.

"Wait till the next measurement is taken," they said.

Frank's manner, as he took his place for the start, seemed to indicate that he believed the task before him a difficult one.

"He's doubtful," muttered one of Paul's friends.

"He's losing courage," said another.

Pressing his lips together, Frank made the run, and the watchers held their breath as he jumped.

"He's tied Rains!"

"Not much! He's behind!"

"Rains holds the lead!"

"Great Scott! is that Merriwell's best!"

Bascomb thumped Wat Snell on the back.

"What'd I tell you!" he laughed in Snell's ear. "This is right where Merriwell loses some of his glory. Rains has beaten him."

"This time, perhaps," admitted Snell; "but there is another jump to follow, and the best score made is the one that decides the contest. You will find Merriwell is not beaten yet."

"Why, you talk as if you wanted him to beat!"

"Not much! I would give almost anything to see him beaten at everything he attempts. Don't think for a minute that I am in love with that fellow!"

The tape had been run, and now the announcement was heard:

"Nineteen feet, one inch and one-third."

Rains had beaten Merriwell by two inches on the second jump.

But the contest was not yet over, and there was a chance that Frank would finally redeem himself.

Frank's friends were disappointed. Hodge showed deep chagrin in his face, as he drew Merriwell aside, saying swiftly and guardedly:

"You're making a mistake, old man, if you are holding off for the last jump. The second jump is the one to lay yourself out on always."

"Perhaps I did," smiled Frank.

"What!" gasped Hodge. "And he has beaten you!"

"It looks that way, doesn't it?"

"But—but—I—I won't believe it! You can do better—you must do better! Why, old man, you will lose your grip if you don't beat him!"

"You do not expect impossibilities, do you?"

"No, but——"

"Would you go back on me if I lost this match?"

"You know better, Frank! I would stick by you under any circumstances!"

"Then I shall not feel so bad about losing it."

Hodge gasped and clutched the arm of his roommate.

"For gracious sake, you don't mean to say he had set you a stint you cannot beat? You mustn't lose—you shan't lose! Do brace up, old man! Why, think how those fellows who are envious of you will rejoice if Rains comes out on top! You must win!"

"Well, I will do my best on the next. There goes Rains for the last jump."

With the ghost of a triumphant mile on his face, Paul again took his place at the starting point. The smile vanished, and a look of resolution took its place.

"He is going to try to beat your other jump!" said Bascomb.

"He can't do it," declared Snell.

"Wait and see."

Paul had really resolved to beat his last jump. As he ran, he gathered momentum, gauging the distance carefully, and reaching the mark exactly. The jump was a splendid one, and it was instantly seen that he had actually beaten his former record.

Quickly and carefully the tape was stretched.

"Nineteen feet, nine inches and three-fourths!"

Then there were exclamations of wonderment from all sides, and more than one declared Merriwell was badly beaten. There were not a few among Frank's friends who confessed that he had very little chance, and the faces of those who said nothing showed that they had lost heart to a great extent.

Hodge continued to talk excitedly to Merriwell, who shook his head, looking very grave.

Paul Rains was quietly triumphant, for he felt that he was safely the winner of this contest.

Merriwell and Hodge went up the strip together, the latter still talking and making an occasional gesture. Reaching the starting point, they paused and stood talking.

"By smoke!" laughed Bascomb; "Merriwell doesn't want to try it at all, and Hodge is having hard work to induce him to do so! Rains has this match in a walkover."

"That remains to be seen," said one of Frank's friends, doggedly. "You may be right, but don't you fancy for a moment that Merriwell is going to give up without jumping. He isn't that kind of a hairpin, my boy."

"Well, he might as well give up without another try, for he doesn't stand any show."

"Oh, wait and see—wait and see," was all that Frank's defender could say.

Hodge was now seen to leave Merriwell and come back down the runway, and it was noted that the look on his face was far from one of confidence and satisfaction.

"When Hodge loses confidence in Merriwell, the case is desperate," declared Bascomb.

"That's so," confessed Wat Snell. "I am beginning to hope."

"Merriwell is making ready—he's preparing for the run!"

All eyes were now fixed on Frank, who had taken his position at the starting point. He was seen to dig his toe into the ground to get a brace, and he leaned far forward, with one hand outstretched, then he darted toward the mark.

With the speed of a fawn, Frank came down the run, reached the mark, shot like a leopard into the air, sailed like a soaring bird, and landed safely far beyond Rains' best mark—so far, indeed, that the crowd was too astonished to make a sound, but stood staring as the tape was laid.

"Twenty-one feet and two inches!" came the electrifying announcement.

Then, for all of rules, for all of Professor Rhynas, Frank's friends made the air ring with their wild shouts of applause.

CHAPTER XX.

BASCOMB'S MISTAKE.

Paul Rains was struck with dismay and confusion, which threatened to turn to anger.

He saw the crowd gathering round Frank, and congratulating him. Paul was left quite alone. Not even Bascomb approached him, for the big plebe was too dismayed to say anything or do anything.

Wat Snell simply muttered:

"I knew it!"

His tone expressed his hopeless disgust.

Frank's hand was wrung till his arm ached, and he was told over and over that he would make a new record for Fardale Academy if he chose to enter the athletic contests in the spring.

"If he chooses!" shouted one enthusiastic fellow. "He'll have to enter, whether he chooses or not! You don't suppose we will let a fellow like him remain out of it, do you!"

"I knew you could do it, old man!" murmured Bart Hodge, his dark face flushed with pleasure. "You were bluffing all the while that you pretended to doubt."

"I wanted to see how much confidence you actually had in me," said Frank, with a smile.

"Well, you found out."

"Yes, and that gave me a great deal more of confidence in myself. I tell you it helps to know one has friends whose faith in him cannot be shaken, even when he seems to lose faith in himself."

"Where is Rains?"

"There he is. I wonder if he is satisfied?"

Paul was still quite alone, pretending to examine the spikes in the bottom of one of his shoes.

Frank moved toward his rival, and the others swarmed along.

Seeing them coming, Rains straightened up, and through his mind flashed the thought that he must not show his chagrin, no matter how deeply he felt it, and he must receive Merriwell in a manner that would not make him seem like a cad in the eyes of the fellows.

And so, when Frank came up, Paul said:

"That was a beautiful jump, Merriwell. You beat me fairly and squarely. I can't deny that."

"You are satisfied, then."

"Perfectly."

"Then we will try the high jump next."

"Not much!"

"What do you mean?"

"I mean that I am satisfied for the present. If you can beat me nearly a foot and a half at the running broad jump, you ought to be able to beat me at the high jump. But I am going to try you another whirl by and by."

"You do not hold a grudge?"

"What do you take me for?"

"Shake hands?"

"Of course."

Their hands met, but Frank did not fail to note that Rains shook in a manner that was very cold and insincere.

"I reckon Merriwell has come pretty near showing what he is made of," said Hodge; "and those fellows who have been claiming that he has won his popularity by luck had better keep still in the future."

"That's so!" shouted the crowd, and several who did so had been saying the most disagreeable things about Frank a short time before.

There is nothing in the world so ephemeral as popularity. The individual who is to-day a hero may be an outcast to-morrow. There is nothing harder to hold than the esteem of a set of school-boys. He who is regarded as an idol in the fall may be supplanted by a rival in the spring, and may find himself unnoticed and neglected. Having once become a leader in a school, the fellow who has obtained the position must prove his superiority to all comers in order to hold it. Even then his success will produce jealous enemies, who will seek his overthrow by some means, no matter how unfair.

Frank had not sought popularity; it had come unbidden. Having found himself a leader, however, he had pride enough to hold the position just as long as he was capable of doing so fairly and honestly. But he had already discovered that he would be assailed openly and secretly, and his foes would try to drag him down by any means, fair or foul.

Had Rains been a little more cordial, had he shaken hands with Frank as if he really held no grudge, Merriwell would have been more than glad to hail him as a good fellow and a friend. But the touch of his fingers was enough to reveal the bitterness in his heart. Having disliked and envied Merriwell before, Rains would now dislike and envy him still more.

As soon as he could do so without attracting too much attention, Rains left the excited throng of boys, and hurried away to one of the dressing-rooms.

Hugh Bascomb quickly followed, being the only one among Rains' late friends to note his departure.

Bascomb found Rains rubbing down. Paul did not say a word as the big plebe entered.

"Well," said Bascomb, as he sat down on a stool, "what do you think of Merriwell?"

"I think he is a mighty hard fellow to beat at anything," growled Paul.

"But he can be beaten—eh?"

"How?"

"There are ways."

"What do you mean? Speak plainly."

"You ought to know what I mean," said Bascomb, doggedly, keeping his eyes on the floor. "It isn't always the best trotter that wins a race."

"It will not be easy to beat Merriwell fairly."

"That's right; but you are a fellow of nerve and brains, and you ought to be able to devise some scheme to get the best of him unfairly."

Rains stopped and stared at Bascomb, his face showing that he was angrier than ever.

"Now your meaning is pretty plain," he said, slowly. "I will confess that I dislike Merriwell—that I would give almost anything to get the best of him; but I want you to understand, Hugh Bascomb, that I am no sneak!"

Bascomb still kept his eyes on the floor.

"Oh, what's the use to get on your high horse, Rains!" he said, in his sullen way. "If you dislike Merriwell, as you pretend, and if you hope to down him at anything, you cannot be too much of a stickler for little things. Once get him to going down hill, and we can keep him going. I can help you start him."

Had Bascomb taken more than a fleeting glance at Rains' face, he must have seen that the latter was regarding him with contempt.

"I suppose you have a scheme of your own?" Paul finally observed, in a questioning way.

"Sure."

"What is it?"

"Well, to begin with, I have pretty good proof that Merriwell was the originator and perpetrator of that crawfish joke on Mulloy and Dunnerwust."

"What of that?"

"I think that Lieutenant Gordan would be able to fasten it on Merriwell, if he knew what I know."

"That would mean certain expulsion for Merriwell."

"Of course. All three of the professors were so tangled up in that affair that the fellow would surely be fired, if the blame could be fastened upon him."

"What do you want of me?"

Bascomb cleared his throat, twisted on, the stool, and hesitated. Finally, he said:

"You may be able to devise some other means to get the best of the fellow; but, if you can't, and you are ready to take hold of this, you may see him fired out of the academy, so he will no longer be in your way."

"What do you want of me?" repeated Rains, coldly and quietly.

"Well, you see—you understand—you know I came near getting into trouble once by trying to help Gage do Merriwell up. After that Gage was caught cheating at cards, and had to run away. Everybody knows I hate Merriwell, and they'd all think I blowed if anything came to Lieutenant Gordan's ears. That's why I don't dare make a move. With you it is different."

"What do you want of me?" demanded Rains, the third time.

"I will give you the proofs, and you can carry them to Lieutenant Gordan, who will follow it up, and see that Merriwell is expelled. In that way, I will not get entangled, and no one will suspect you."

With one wide stride, Rains reached Bascomb, caught him by the shoulders, and thrust him backward, thus forcing him to look up.

"You have insulted me!" came fiercely from Paul's lips. "I am no sneak and informer! Did you think I would do the dirty trick you are too much of a coward to try? Well, you made a big mistake! I dislike Merriwell, but I am not ready to make myself contemptible in my own eyes by blowing on him."

Bascomb put up his big hands and thrust Rains off.

"Whom are you calling a coward!" he snarled, as he got upon his feet.

"You!" shot back Paul. "You are a coward and a sneak!"

"Why, I'll thrash you well!"

"No, you won't!" cried Rains, flinging up one hand to stop the advance of the big plebe. "If you lay a hand on me, I will make known to the entire school the scheme you just proposed to me. The boys would tar and feather you."

Bascomb stopped and showed his yellow teeth, while he trembled slightly with anger.

"So that's your trick!" he said, growlingly.

"Yes, that's my trick; and if you blow on Merriwell, I will play the card. You made a big mistake in taking me for a sneak just because I didn't happen to like a fellow who is popular. Get out now, and don't come round me again! I don't belong to your class, and I don't want to have anything to do with you. Get!"

Bascomb hesitated, longing to strike Rains, but not daring to do so. Slowly he moved toward the door, where he paused to growl:

"This is all right! I will get square with you some time. If you blow on me, I will pound the life out of you!"

Then he went out

Rains had shown his manhood.

CHAPTER XXI.

THE RIVAL PROFESSORS.

rofessor Jenks and Professor Scotch were rivals. Each admired and sought to win the affections of a widow of uncertain years, who lived in Fardale village.

For some years Professor Gunn's two assistants had been very friendly, but Nancy Cobb, the widow spoken of, was the rock on which they split.

Their jealousy often caused them to completely forget their dignity, and they did things that made them utterly ridiculous in the eyes of all beholders.

As yet, neither had possessed nerve enough to propose to the widow, and so, wishing to make a sure catch, the elderly lady had clung to both, ready to jump at the first one who should offer himself.

The cause of the ill-will existing between the under professors was well known to the cadets at Fardale Academy, and had provided them with no small amount of sport.

Now it happened that Tad Jones, a village lad who was very well known to Frank Merriwell, was the nephew of the coquettish widow, and the widow made her home with Tad's father and mother.

Tad was a lively youngster, who liked fun, and, in more ways than one, he was "a thorn in the flesh" unto his aunt.

One day he succeeded in seeing Frank, whom he informed that he had put up another joke on his Aunt Nancy.

"I've been imertatin' her handwritin' lately," said Tad, "and I've got so I can scrawl jest like her. Old Scotch and Jenks ain't never run onto each other at our house, but I've fixed it."

Tad grinned gleefully, as he made this declaration.

"Fixed it, how?" asked Frank.

"Why, I writ 'em both a letter, askin' 'em to call to-night at eight o'clock, and I signed Nancy's name. I made the letters jest a little spooney, but not too much so. I'll bet they'll be tickled to death, and they'll come sure."

"And meet there?"

"Yep."

"There's liable to be trouble."

"That's what we're lookin' for," chuckled the fun-loving youngster. "Oh, if they'd jest fight!"

"I'd like to see the circus."

"Come on over."

"I don't know as I can get away. I will come if I can."

"All right. Bring along any of the fellers."

That night Frank found a way to get leave to go to the village, and Hans, whom he had told of the coming "racket," escaped from the building and joined him outside the grounds. Together they went over to the village, and called on Tad Jones.

Tad was waiting for them, and he straightway smuggled them into the house.

"Aunt Nancy's expectin' Professor Jenks to call," he gleefully whispered. "I told her that I saw him, and he said he'd be here to-night, so she's frizzled and primped to receive him."

"You'll get into a scrape," said Frank.

"I don't care for that, if I can see some fun. Come right into the parlor, and we'll all hide. Aunt's up in her room, layin' on the finishin' touches."

Into the parlor they slipped. A fire was burning in the old-fashioned open fireplace, and it was plain that Mrs. Cobb had "spruced things up" to receive company.

"Two of us can git behind the organ in the corner here," said Tad. "The other feller can hide under the sofa."

As the sofa was a long, old-fashioned affair, and any one hidden beneath it could command a view of the entire room, Frank decided to conceal himself there.

This was barely settled when there came a sharp rap on the door.

"Git under cover quick!" hissed Tad. "That must be one of 'em!"

Tad and Hans made haste to squeeze in behind the organ, and Frank crept under the sofa.

"Shimminy Gristmas!" muttered the Dutch lad, "uf id don'd peen britty tight blace here den I ton't know somedings."

"It is all right," returned Tad, who had obtained a position where he could peer out. "Keep cool, and let your hair curl."

Pretty soon Nancy fluttered downstairs, and then Frank heard the high-pitched voice of Professor Jenks in the hall. A moment later, the widow entered the parlor.

"Oh, dear!" she simpered. "What a surprise this is, dear Mr. Jenks! Set right down on this chair close to the fire. You must be cold. Let me take your hat and coat."

"I am rather cold," squeaked the professor, as he peeled off his coat, and allowed her to take it away with his hat. "It is a chilly night. You are cozy in here."

The widow was wonderfully and artistically gotten up in a back-number silk dress, beneath which was an expansive hoopskirt, while all around her face were cork-screw curls, meant to be very fetching. As she was somewhat deaf, although she never acknowledged it, she misunderstood the professor's last remark.

"Oh, yes," she smiled, coming back and sitting quite close to Jenks, "no one can hear. We are quite alone."

"Is that so?" gasped the professor, nervously, looking as if he contemplated flight. "I received your letter."

"You believe I'm better! Why, my dear professor, I haven't bin sick. You must have been misinformed."

"I didn't say that, Mrs. Cobb. I said that I received——"

At this moment there came another sharp rap on the door, and Professor Jenks started as if he had been struck.

"Somebody is knocking," he said.

"Rocking?" smiled Nancy. "Then take the rocking-chair. I like to rock myself pritty well."

"Somebody is knocking—knocking at the door!" cried the professor, in his high falsetto.

"Oh, somebody knocking. I will see who it is. Mrs. Jones doesn't always hear 'em. I sometimes think she is ruther hard of hearing."

As she fluttered out of the room, the professor gasped:

"I'm in a perfect sweat already! I'd rather face a battery! I wonder if she will propose? It's leap year, and she may."

Then he suddenly started to his feet, with an exclamation of surprise and anger, for he heard Professor Scotch's hoarse voice in the hall.

"Confound it!" exclaimed Jenks. "What's brought him here tonight? I don't understand this."

In came Nancy, and Professor Scotch was close behind her.

"It's so good of you both to call!" gushed the widow, girlishly. "We'll have a real lovely little chat."

Professor Scotch started back as he caught sight of his rival, and the two glared at each other. Then Scotch growled:

"You here?"

"Yes, sir," squeaked Jenks, defiantly. "Who's got a better right, I'd like to know?"

"But I'd have you to understand I was invited."

"So was I."

"But I received an invitation from this particular lady."

"So did I."

"Set right down on the sofy, Professor Scotch," urged Nancy. "We'll pop some corn, and eat some apples, and be real sociabul."

"Madame," said the little man, with great dignity, "I think there is some mistake."

"You'd like some steak?" exclaimed Mrs. Cobb, in surprise. "I never heerd of people havin' steak to treat callers on. I don't b'lieve there's a bit in the house. I s'pose you do git awful sick of the food they have over to the 'cademy. Now, if you was a married man, and hed a wife to cook for ye——"

"I say I think there is a mistake in this matter."

"Beefsteak in a platter? Yes, that's a good way to serve it."

The little professor gave a gasp, and collapsed onto the sofa. And Frank promptly jabbed a hatpin up through the sofa, so that it penetrated the professor to a distance of about a quarter of an inch.

CHAPTER XXII.

A LIVELY CALL.

Whoop!" roared the big voice of the little man, and Professor Scotch shot into the air like a jumping-jack out of a box. "Wow!" he howled, clutching convulsively at that part of his person which had felt the hatpin. "What did I sit down on?"

The widow looked frightened, and Professor Jenks looked astonished.

"What did I sit down on?" repeated Professor Scotch, his red hair bristling with anger.

"Why, you sat on the sofa, sir," squeaked Jenks.

"Then there must be a whole nest of wasps concealed in that sofa!" shouted Scotch. "I was stung, or I was stabbed—I don't know which."

"Why, I'm sure I cannot imagine what the matter with you can be," fluttered the widow, in distress.

"Well, I don't know what is the matter with your old sofa."

He spoke so loudly that she understood him, and she immediately turned up her nose.

"Old sofa, sir—old sofa! There is nothing the matter with that sofa. Your language is surprisingly offensive, sir."

"Te-he, he, he!" giggled Jenks. "Now you're getting it, Scotch! You've put your foot in it."

"Beg your pardon—beg your pardon," roared the little man. "I did not mean any offense, Mrs. Cobb, but I assure you there must be a dagger concealed in that sofa, for some pointed weapon entered my person in a most painful manner. If you will excuse me, I'll take this chair, for I really do not dare sit down there again."

The widow gave a sniff.

"Your courage is very limited," she said. "Now, I do love to admire a man with courage enough to——"

"Ex-cuse me," squealed Jenks, elevating his voice. "The sofa is good enough for me."

Down he sat upon it, smiling triumphantly.

Frank still had the hatpin—which he had found on the floor beneath the sofa—ready for use, but he held his hand a bit, knowing he could give Jenks a greater shock if he should be pricked after, he had sat there a while in apparent security.

"Oh, you're a daring blade—you are!" sneered Scotch, fiercely, as he glared at Jenks. "You'd walk right up to the mouth of a cannon—if you knew it wasn't loaded!"

"Well, I never yet got frightened by a hair-cloth sofa," squeaked Jenks.

The widow smiled seductively on the long and lanky professor.

"You don't find nothing the matter with the sofy, do you, professor?" she asked.

"Not a thing," piped Jenks. "It is ever the wicked man who feels the pricks of conscience. Now, my conscience is easy, and so I do not feel——We-e-e-ow! Murder! I'm stabbed! I'm killed! We-e-ow!"

Professor Jenks shot into the air with such suddenness and vigor that he thumped his head against the low ceiling, which seemed to fling him back upon the sofa, and Frank promptly gave him a second dose of hatpin.

"Wo-o-ouch!" squealed the tall professor, bounding up again, and dancing wildly round the room, with his hands concealed beneath the tails of his coat. "That sofa is filled with broadswords and bayonets! It is stuffed with deadly weapons!"

Professor Scotch literally roared with laughter.

"Oh, there's nothing the matter with the sofa!" he laughed. "Just go right back and sit down there. Ha! ha! ha! It is ever the wicked man who feels the pricks of conscience. Ha! ha! ha! Ho! ho! ho!"

"Shut up!" piped Jenks, coming close to Scotch, at whom he shook his fist threateningly. "Shut up, or I will thump you!"

"Don't you dare do it here. If you do, I'll——"

"What?"

"I'll see you later."

"Landy massy!" spluttered Nancy. "I do believe you've both been tooken crazy!"

Behind the organ were two boys who were holding their hands over their mouths to keep from roaring with laughter, while Frank, under the sofa, was finding it no easy task to be silent.

The widow was frightened, and both of the professors immediately sought to reassure her. They pranced up on either side, and Scotch began:

"Don't be alarmed, Mrs. Cobb; we'll not fight——"

"You're not tight? Well, you act as if you were, and that's a fact."

"Oh, go fall on yourself, Scotch!" advised Jenks, dropping into the slang he had overheard some boy use. "This is an unfortunate affair."

"What's the matter with my hair?" indignantly asked the widow, as she caressed her corkscrew curls. "You are getting very personal, sir."

"Ho! ho!" laughed Scotch, guardedly. "Now you are getting it, Jenks!"

"You make me tired!"

"Go have your voice filed, so you won't be an old woman."

"Who be you callin' an old woman?" cried Nancy, catching the words with wonderful quickness. "I must say your language is most surprisin' and offensive, sir."

"Excuse me," roared Scotch. "I was speaking to Mr. Jenks."

"But he isn't a woman," said Nancy, suspiciously. "I don't know why you should use such language to him."

"You've put your foot in it now," snickered the little man.

"And I don't know what he's grinnin' and laughin' about. You both act as if too much studyin' and tooterin' was beginnin' to affect your brains. Now, why, don't you both git married, and give up this awful wearin' life you are leadin'?"

"That's just what I called to see about," declared Professor Scotch, bracing up. "I called to pro——"

"Hold on!" squealed Jenks, excitedly. "I was here first, and I will have my first say. Mrs. Cobb, my heart has long yearned for domestic joys and comforts."

"Oh, I don't keer how much you've earned; it's what you've saved that counts."

"Oh, if I had that voice, I'd go break it!" sneered Scotch. "Try again, Hyson, and you'll get her so twisted that I'll stand a good show of winning her."

So Jenks braced up and tried again.

"I say my heart has yearned——"

"Sody-water or magneeshy is good for heartburn," smiled the widow.

"Ye gods!" gasped Jenks. "I didn't know she was so hard of hearing."

"Oh, sail in and win her!" chuckled the little professor. "You're doing first rate."

"Mrs. Cobb," continued Jenks, "I am not much given to the follies of life. I am a very grave man——"

"And I do so admire a brave man!" gushed Nancy.

While passing through the village on the way to Tad Jones' home, Frank had purchased an automatic mouse. Being wound up, the mouse would run swiftly across the room.

At this juncture, Frank pointed the mouse toward Nancy, and let it go, at the same time giving a squeak, which both professors distinctly heard.

Nancy saw the mouse coming, and she uttered a wild shriek of terror, clutching Professor Jenks around his slender neck.

"Save me! Save me from that terrible beast!" she squawked.

It happened that the professor was quite as scared of a mouse as Nancy could be, and he broke away and jumped up on a chair, squealing:

"Murder! We'll all be bitten!"

In a most remarkably skillful manner the widow sprang up to the top of the center-table, where she stood, in a stooping position, her head against the ceiling.

"Who's scared of a mouse!" sneered Professor Scotch, as he gave chase to the toy, which bumped against various pieces of furniture, and so kept dodging about.

Under the chair on which Jenks stood ran the mouse. Scotch knocked the chair over, and Jenks uttered a wild shriek as he came down astride the little professor's neck. Then both rolled against the center-table, which was upset.

Down came Nancy, like a balloon, nearly smothering the two professors, upon whom she alighted.

This was too much for Tad Jones, who burst into a shriek of laughter, jumped out, and extinguished the light, and shouted:

"Skip, fellows—skip!"

Frank and Hans lost no time in leaving their places of concealment and hustling out of the room, abandoning the two professors to their fate.

CHAPTER XXIII.

SKATING FOR HONORS.

"nefer seen der peat uf dot alretty yet," declared Hans, as he and Frank were hurrying back to the academy. "Uf dot don'd peen der piggest racket vot nefer vos, you dunno vot I vos talkin' apout."

"If it is found that we know anything about it, we will be sure to get into trouble," said Frank. "Should anybody question you, why you must be ignorant as a mule."

"You pet me your life I vos. I vill peen ignorand as a clam."

But it seemed that the professors did not suspect that any of the academy boys had been present, and so no inquiries were made in the school.

Tad Jones, however, was accused of having some of his village chums in the scrape, and, when he refused to tell their names, he was soundly strapped by his father, who had sincerely hoped one of the professors would propose to Nancy and take her away without delay.

Just how the rival professors had escaped was not known, but, if possible, the coldness between them was more pronounced than ever. The feud seemed of a deadly nature, and some of the boys declared that Jenks and Scotch were certain to fight a duel over Nancy sooner or later.

The following Saturday was fine, and that afternoon large numbers of the boys from the academy sought the village pond, where the skating was excellent.

By mid-afternoon there were between two and three hundred skaters on the long pond, while half as many spectators were gathered on the shore.

It was a lively and pleasant scene. Inza Burrage was there, with her chosen companion, May Blossom. Inza was a beautiful skater, and so was much sought as a companion by the boys. Three times did Frank approach her to ask her to skate with him, and each time he saw her carried off by some one else.

She was in a coquettish mood that day, and her merry laughter as she skated away each time proved rather tantalizing to Frank, who finally muttered:

"All right; two can play at that game."

It was almost, if not quite, May Blossom's first attempt at skating, and, although she was doing very well, her company was not in such demand as that of Inza.

Seeing May alone, Frank immediately skated to her side, and he was soon doing his best to instruct her in the correct handling of her feet. They seemed quite absorbed in each other's company, and not even Inza's ringing laugh, as she sped past with Paul Rains, caused either of them to glance up.

At first Inza had not minded Frank's attentions to May, but, as time slipped away, and they still clung together, laughing, chatting, and minding no one else, she began to grow uneasy.

"Oh, she can have him, if she wants him!" muttered Inza, her cheeks beginning to burn. "There are any amount of other fellows."

That was quite true, but, in her heart, she knew full well that there was no other fellow she cared so much for as she did for Frank Merriwell.

From this moment she ceased to enjoy herself, and she could not keep from watching Frank and May, although she tried to do so. She grew petulant, and those who were in her company found her surprisingly crisp and disagreeable.

Whenever she could, she skated past Frank and May, and she always laughed as she did so, but there was a false note in her laughter—it did not seem very sincere.

Paul Rains was a beautiful skater. He could cut fancy figures that took away the breath of the village boys, and all his movements were graceful and rhythmical. He could write his name with his skates, and every letter was perfect and clean cut as if done with a pen. It was not long before all eyes were centered on him, and Inza did not fail to note that he seemed to be the principal attraction on the pond.

So Inza skated a great deal with Paul, hoping to arouse Frank's jealousy; but, to her overwhelming dismay, after he began to skate with May, Frank seemed to forget there was any one else on the pond.

"I believe he really likes her better than he does me!" thought Inza. "And she, knowing all my secrets, knowing how much I think of Frank, is doing her best to cut me out! Oh, that is true friendship!"

She felt like crying with vexation, and, once or twice, tears did come to her eyes; but she forced them back, continuing to skate and laugh.

Arrangements were made for a skating contest to take place very soon. One of the gentlemen of the village offered a "badge of honor" to the swiftest skater on the pond—the one who could win the race.

Paul Rains entered, as also did Bartley Hodge and Sammy Smiles from the academy. Three village boys entered.

Then Hodge sought Frank, saying:

"Come, old man, we want you in this race."

"Oh, I am busy," laughed Frank, noticing that Inza was near, although he did not glance in her direction. "I am teaching Miss Blossom to skate, and she is getting on famously."

"Well, I think she will excuse you a few minutes. You may go on with your lessons after the race."

"Oh, say, can't you get along without me?"

"Can't anyway; you must come along."

"Well, if I must, I must," murmured Frank, with mock distress. "I will see you later, Miss Blossom, and we will do our best to induce that left foot to make the stroke properly."

So, bowing and smiling, he left her, and, in her heart, Inza cried:

"If he skates with her again this afternoon, I'll be outwitted— that's all!"

As Bart drew Frank aside, he hastily and guardedly said:

"You must go into this race to win, old man. Rains' friends have been saying you would not dare skate against him, and that he would have a walk-over if you did."

Frank's teeth came together with a click.

"Is that so!" he exclaimed. "Well, they may be right; but we'll see."

That was quite enough to put him on his mettle, and he lost no time in entering for the race.

A short time later the seven contestants were drawn up in line, waiting the signal.

One mile up the pond a rock reared its head from the ice, where, at low water, there was a tiny rocky island. Every contestant was to "turn the rock" and skate back to the starting point, making a race of two miles in two long, straight stretches.

The gentleman who had offered the badge of honor stood, pistol in hand, ready to give the signal. The contestants leaned forward for the start.

"Ready!"

Muscles were drawn taut, nerves were tingling.

"One! two! three!"—Bang!

Away darted the skaters, and the race had begun.

A cheer went up from the spectators.

Paul Rains took the lead at the very start, for he seemed to jump away at astonishing speed, while the others were gathering headway.

"Rains has a snap this time," declared one. "Merriwell may be able to take the honors at jumping, but he won't be in this kind of a contest."

"Jist wait a whoile an' see about thot, me b'y," said Barney Mulloy, who had overheard the remark. "Frankie is as full av surproises as a horrunet's nest is full av stings."

CHAPTER XXIV.

SKATING FOR LIFE.

During the entire first half of the course there were four of the seven contestants who made a good showing. These were Rains, Merriwell, Hodge and one of the village boys.

Through it all Rains kept the lead, but the village lad was second until the turning point was nearly reached. Then Merriwell settled down to business and took second place, while Hodge pushed the village boy hard.

Rains' heart was full of triumph. Over and over he told himself:

"At last I have found something at which I can defeat Merriwell fairly!"

Rains believed he was safely in advance, and this delusion was not broken till the last half mile of the course was struck. Then he heard somebody's skates ringing close behind, and, looking over his shoulder, he saw Frank bearing down on him like the wind.

Paul's heart gave a great leap.

"By Jove!" he breathed. "That fellow means to press me! But he shall not come in first—he shall not!"

Then he strained every muscle, and, for a few seconds, the distance between them did not seem to diminish.

Frank, however, held steadily to that terrible speed, and Paul began to fear he could not stand it to the finish, for his head was beginning to grow unsteady, and there was a wild roaring in his ears. Through a bluish mist he saw the great crowd on the shore near the starting point, and he knew the eyes of hundreds were upon the contestants.

"I'll die before he shall pass me!" thought Rains.

And then, once more, he heard the skates of his rival ringing clear close at his elbow. One wild look he cast over his shoulder, and there was Merriwell, fearfully near—and gaining!

Paul's heart rose with a bursting sensation into his throat. He had seen that Merriwell's face bore a look of determination—nay, more, a look of confidence.

Oh, for the power to hold out to the end! Again he forced himself to spurt; but, as that mad burst of energy slackened, he felt, rather than saw, his rival reach his side.

Now a great cheer broke from the crowd of excited and delighted spectators, for the two boys were fairly abreast, and neither seemed able to gain another inch on the other.

Rains had shut his teeth, his nostrils were dilated, and his eyes wild in their sockets. The finish line was near, and he must cross it in advance—a yard, a foot, an inch!

But he little knew that Frank Merriwell had reserved for the last supreme moment enough strength to make a final spurt.

Now—now is the time for one or the other to forge ahead!

Another shout goes up:

"Merriwell! Merriwell! He's the winner! Hurrah!"

Frank had forged to the front; but, even as the cheer came from the crowd, he was seen to be flipped into the air, as if he had struck a spring-board, and he came down heavily on the ice. There was no time to recover.

Frank slid over the starting line, prostrate on the ice; but Paul Rains crossed it upright, and at least three yards in advance.

Rains had won!

An accident had prevented Frank from winning, for his skate had struck a flaw in the ice, and he had been thrown with stunning force.

Great was the excitement. Merriwell was picked up and carried to the shore, where a dash of cold water brought him round.

Rains was quite used up for a while, but he soon recovered. His friends crowded round him to offer congratulations.

"You beat Merriwell this time, Paul," they said.

"But he fell," said Paul, bitterly. "That makes the victory anything but satisfactory. However, I will race him again at any time and any place."

Little did he think how soon they would race again.

Within a short time after the finish of the race, a sudden cry of alarm and terror went up from the throng.

"Look—look there! Two girls have broken through the ice! They will be drowned!"

At a certain point in the pond there was a dangerous bit of ice, where some springs deep down at the bottom continually bubbled up and kept the water alive, so the ice did not form solidly. It was supposed that every one knew where this dangerous spot was, so no sign had been placed there.

Now, however, two girls had ventured upon it, and broken through.

"Who are they?"

"Inza Burrage and May Blossom!"

"Save them! save them!"

Several started toward the imperiled girls, but two forms darted out ahead of the rest, and another race between Paul Rains and Frank Merriwell had begun.

This time it was a race for life.

Shoulder to shoulder they started, and, for some seconds, they kept thus.

Then Frank began to forge ahead, for all that Paul was straining every muscle—was doing the very best that he could to save life.

The girls were seen clinging to the broken edge of the ice, which broke beneath them once or twice, but they managed to keep up in some way.

Wider and wider grew the distance between Merriwell and Rains, showing that the former was by far the faster skater in such a case as this.

As Frank drew near the girls, the ice broke again, and both went under.

He did not slacken speed, but, taking care to avoid them, skated straight into the water.

Clinging to each other, the girls came up; but they would have sunk again immediately if he had not been there to clutch them.

Treading water, he held them up, getting close to the ragged edge of the ice.

The water was fearfully cold, but he managed to keep his head out, knowing aid must come quickly.

Paul Rains slackened his speed as he came near the opening in the ice.

"Form a line—get hold of my feet!" he shouted.

Down upon his stomach he went, and he slid forward till he could reach out and grasp one of the girls.

There he lay till another lad clutched his feet, and still others grasped the feet of the one who had hold of Paul.

"Now, Merriwell," said Paul, "if you can break their clutch on each other, we can take 'em out one at a time."

With some difficulty the grasp of the half-drowned girls was broken. Paul held fast to one, and shouted:

"Pull away!"

He was drawn backward, and the girl was dragged from the

water upon the ice.

Quickly she was passed to some one who carried her away to a place of warmth and safety, while Paul Rains crept back to the opening, and the other girl was rescued in a similar manner. Then Frank, nearly exhausted, was drawn out.

With Rains on one side, and Hodge on the other, Frank skated back to the shore, where the great crowd of spectators had witnessed the gallant rescue. How the crowd cheered and flung up their hats!

"Hurrah for Frank Merriwell!" was the roar that went up. "Hurrah!"

"Hurrah for Paul Rains! Hurrah!"

The man who had offered the badge of honor grasped the two lads by the hands, crying:

"You shall both have a badge of honor! This is true heroism, and you are both heroic lads!"

"Hurrah! hurrah! hurrah!" thundered the crowd.

Let us add here that neither Inza nor May suffered any particularly ill results from their plunge through the ice.

Between Inza and Frank the slight misunderstanding was easily adjusted, and May, in her innocent little heart, had never dreamed of "cutting out" her friend. She and Paul Rains afterward became very friendly.

Between Frank and Paul a rivalry continued to exist; but, for the most part, it was of a healthy, generous sort, and Merriwell retained his position as leader, having become more popular than before among the better class of boys at the academy.

CHAPTER XXV.

THE SINISTER STRANGER.

oy, where did you get that ring?"

Frank Merriwell started and looked quickly at the man who had hoarsely hissed the question in his ear. At a glance he saw that the man was a stranger in Fardale village.

The stranger was dressed in black clothes, wore a cloak, with a cape, and had the brim of his hat slouched over his eyes, which were coal-black and piercing. He had a heavy black mustache and imperial, which gave him a rather savage expression, and, withal, he made a somewhat sinister figure.

The night mail at Fardale was not delivered at the academy till the following morning, and Frank had come to the village post office late that afternoon to obtain an expected letter from home, if it had arrived.

He had also hoped that, on his way to the post office, or in returning to the academy, he might catch a glimpse of Inza. Frank was now a welcome visitor at Inza's home, but, being governed by natural tact and delicacy, he did not wish to call too frequently, fearing Inza's parents might regard him as something of a bore.

Shortly after entering the village he had noticed the stranger in black, who seemed to be staring wonderingly at the boy. To Frank's surprise, this man followed him about.

Finally the stranger slipped softly to Frank's side, and hoarsely whispered the question with which this chapter opens. At the same time, he pointed to a peculiar ring which Merriwell wore on the third finger of his left hand.

Frank drew back, looking the man over from head to feet.

"I beg your pardon, sir," he said, in a manner that was intended to repulse further advances.

But the man was not to be choked off thus easily.

"The ring," he repeated. "I asked you where you obtained it."

"I know you did," said the boy, coolly.

"Answer me!" sibilated the stranger, his brows darkening beneath the wide brim of the hat, and a gleam of fire showing in his eyes. "Tell me the truth, boy!"

"I don't know why I should answer you," said Frank. "I do not know you, and I do not understand what right you have to ask me such a question."

The man in black bit his lip, and hesitated. After a moment, he forced a smile that was far from agreeable to see, although he plainly meant that it should reassure the boy, and, in a low tone, he rapidly said:

"That ring is very odd, and it attracted my attention for that reason. I am a great collector of curios, and especially of quaint and curious rings. I have traveled the world over in search of the quaint and curious, and I have a collection of nearly five hundred rings of all patterns, makes and values. This collecting of rings has become a fad, or mania, with me. Whenever I see an odd or peculiar ring, I am immediately seized by a great desire to possess it; but I always want to know its history. It enhances the value of a ring to know its history. I assure you that some rings have very queer histories, indeed."

Frank watched the man closely as he was speaking, and, although it was plain that the stranger was trying to secure the boy's confidence, Merriwell continued to regard him with suspicion and aversion. There was something about this person's dark face and sinister aspect that was extremely repulsive to the lad.

Once more the man smiled, as if making a desperate attempt to thaw the cool reserve of the boy; but he had begun in a very poor way, for Frank remained cold and distant.

"Some of my rings," went on the man in black, "have tales of bloodshed and murder connected with them, and these are interesting in their way. Some recall romances of blighted love or sundered hearts, and these tales are always interesting to the ladies who look over the collection. Some have been worn by great men or great ladies, and some have encircled the fingers of great villains or great criminals. You should understand why I desire to know the history of every ring that comes into my possession."

"Well," said Frank, quietly, "as there is not the slightest possibility that you will ever possess this ring, you can have very little interest in its history."

The stranger fell back a step, and then, with one hand eagerly outstretched, he exclaimed:

"You will sell it for a good price—of course you will?"

"No."

"Why, its real value is insignificant!"

"It is valuable to me."

"No jeweler will give you more than three or four dollars for it—possibly five."

"Well?"

"I will give you ten dollars for that ring."

"It is useless for you to offer me money for it, as I do not intend to sell it."

Frank turned as if he would move away, but he felt a hand clutch his shoulder with a grasp of iron, while the voice of the stranger almost snarled:

"Don't be a fool, boy! I want that ring, and I mean to have it at some price. I will give you twenty-five dollars for it."

"Take your hand off my shoulder, sir!"

"I'll give you thirty dollars."

"Take your hand off my shoulder, sir!"

"Forty dollars!"

"I have warned you twice to take your hand off my shoulder," came coldly from the lips of the boy, on whose face there was now a dangerous look. "I am going to warn you again, and if you do not obey, it will be the worse for you. Take your hand off my shoulder!"

There was a single moment of hesitation, and then the stranger obeyed; but the look on his face was not pleasant to see, and he hoarsely said:

"You are showing a great deal of authority for a stripling. These military schools spoil boys like you by making them think they are men before the fuzz grows on their faces."

There was no doubt in the lad's mind but he was dealing with a desperate man, and Frank fully realized that he had thoroughly aroused the stranger's anger. But Frank could not be bullied, and the man in black was very repulsive to him, for some reason.

Once more the boy started to walk away; but the man was quickly at his side, where he kept, again attempting to be persuasive, although it was plain that he longed to throttle the lad.

"What is the use of being unreasonable! I am willing to do the square thing. I have made you a magnificent offer for that ring, which I am anxious to possess."

"Far too anxious," muttered Frank.

"That is natural," declared the man, swiftly. "Did you ever collect stamps? If you have, you should know something of the mania that seizes upon a collector. It is thus with me. If I see an odd ring I cannot obtain, I feel as if I had been robbed of something that rightfully belongs to me."

He paused a moment in his talk, but Frank walked straight onward, saying nothing.

"I have offered you a ridiculous price for that ring," continued the man. "I cannot afford it, but my mind is set on having the ring. Already I have spent a fortune in my collections, and the time has come when I cannot fling money freely to the winds. Come now, young man, have a little sympathy with me, and sell me that ring."

Under certain circumstances these words might have melted Frank, who was not a cold-blooded lad, by any means; but there was something in the stranger's villainous aspect and repulsive manner that had turned the boy against the man in black and caused him to remain obdurate.

"I told you at first that it was useless to offer me money for this ring," said the boy. "I think you will begin to understand that I meant it."

"At least, you will tell me how it came in your possession?"

Frank hesitated. Surely there could be no harm in telling this, and it might enable him to get rid of the stranger, so he said:

"It was given to me by my mother."

"And your mother—how did she obtain it?" swiftly asked the stranger.

"My father gave it to her. I do not know how it came into his possession."

"Your father and mother——"

"Are dead."

"Ha! And you prize the ring because it was a present from your mother?"

"That is one reason."

"And there is another?"

"Yes."

"What?"

It suddenly struck Frank that he was talking altogether too much, and so he answered:

"I decline to say. I have already told you enough, and I beg you to excuse me. We will part here."

"First answer one more question. What was your father's name?"

"Charles Conrad Merriwell."

The man in black put a hand to his eyes, and seemed to be thinking for a moment. Beneath his breath he muttered:

"Merriwell, Merriwell—I do not know the name."

Then, dropping his hand, he said:

"I will make you one more offer for the ring. I will give you fifty dollars for it. See—here is the money. Don't be foolish—take it! You will never receive another such offer."

He had pulled out some bills, from which he quickly selected a fifty-dollar bank-note, which he tendered to Frank.

The boy drew away.

"You are wasting your time in offering me money for the ring. I am in earnest in declining to sell it. Good-day, sir."

He turned and walked swiftly away.

The baffled man in black stood staring after the lad, his forehead lowering and his white teeth showing a bit through his dark mustache.

"Refuse to sell the ring!" he grated, madly. "All right! I am not defeated. I will have it within a week!"

CHAPTER XXVI.

THE MYSTERY OF THE RING

Frank did not glance back till he turned onto another street, and then he saw the man in black standing quite still where they had parted. The reddish glow of the sunset was behind the man, on which his black figure stood out like a silhouette, the cloak and cape making him slightly resemble a gigantic bat.

The boy shivered a little as he passed beyond the view of the mysterious stranger.

"That man makes my blood cold," he murmured. "There is something decidedly awe-inspiring about him. Somehow, I do not believe I have seen the last of him."

Frank was right; he had not seen the last of the man in black.

Thinking of what had happened, Frank soon came to the conclusion that the man was mad, or else there was some mystery about the ring that was not known to the possessor.

Why had the stranger been so desirous of knowing how the ring came into Frank's possession?

True he had said that he always wished to know the history of such rings as he collected; but Frank had refused distinctly to sell the ring, and still the man had seemed very desirous of obtaining information concerning it.

Why had he asked the name of Frank's father?

These questions presented themselves to the boy for consideration, and he remembered how, on hearing the name, the stranger had confessed that it was unfamiliar to him.

Frank was thinking deeply of these things, when a familiar voice called:

"Hello, Frank! Are you going past without speaking?"

He started and looked up, finding himself in front of Inza's home. It was a fine, old-fashioned house, built years and years ago, and an iron fence surrounded the front lawn. Inza was at the gate, a pretty pout on her face.

The young cadet instantly lifted his cap, as he smilingly retorted:
"I did not see you there, Miss Burrage."

"Oh, bother your 'Miss Burrage!'" she exclaimed. "You know it
was Inza with you long ago—you promised to call me that. No
wonder you didn't see me; you were going past with your head
down, your eyes on the ground, and an expression of profound
abstraction on your face. What in the world were you thinking
of?"

"That's a mystery," said Frank, approaching the gate.

"Indeed!" and she lifted her eyebrows with a pretty Assumption
of offended dignity. "A secret from me?"

"I did not say it was a secret; I said it was a mystery. I was thinking of the man in black."

"Mercy!" She gave a little shiver. "What is the man in black—
some horrible ogre?"

"Well, I fancy he is ogre enough to give you the chills."

"What story did you find him in?"

"Oh, I didn't find him in a story; I met him in real life. I left him
a few minutes ago."

"This is interesting!" she laughed. "Who is he? What's his name?"

"I don't know. Didn't I say he is a mystery?"

"Come, Frank, are you trying to tease me?"

"Not at all. I will tell you all I know about this singular man in
black."

Then, leaning gracefully against one of the iron gateposts, he
related his recent adventure with the unpleasant stranger. She listened with breathless interest, her eyes growing wider and wider,
and an expression of alarm coming to her pretty face.

"Oh, Frank!" she exclaimed, when he had finished; "I know this
terrible man is dangerous! He will do you harm!"

"Oh, I'm not afraid of that," declared the boy, lightly; "but I
would give something to know what there is about this ring that
makes him so desirous of possessing it."

He held up the ring for her to examine. It was an oddly twisted
band of gold, looking like a writhing serpent. It was set with a
peculiar black stone that seemed quite as hard as a diamond, for
all that there were numerous marks and scratches on its smooth
surface.

"It is a horrid ugly old ring," declared Inza. "Anybody must be
crazy to offer fifty dollars for it."

"Unless it bears some value that is not apparent to one who does
not know its secret."

"What value can it bear?"

"That is the mystery. Still, from my mother's words, I am sure my father prized this ring highly. When it came into his possession he was in Southern California or Mexico, and he sent it home to my mother at the earliest opportunity, writing her to be very choice of it, and not to lose it on her life, as it was very valuable. Now, my father never revealed the secret of this ring to my mother, if the ring has a secret; but I am sure that mother believed there was something mysterious about it, for, when she was dying, she gave it to me, telling me never to part with it. Of course I will not sell it."

"Of course not," nodded Inza; "but the horrid old thing may bring you trouble, instead of good."

"Oh, I don't think there is much danger of that."

"The man in black——"

"Will give over his attempt to obtain it when he really knows I will not part with it on any condition."

"He may; but his words, which you have repeated for me, make me believe he will do something desperate in order to get possession of it. You must look out for him—you must be on your guard constantly."

"Why, Inza!" laughed Frank, in astonishment; "I never heard you speak like this before. You really appear as if you felt a foreboding of some terrible thing."

"Perhaps I do," she said, very gravely, for a light-hearted girl.

Frank looked down at the ring on his hand. Surely it was an ugly trifle to make so much trouble.

"Do you see those fine lines on the surface of the stone?" he asked.

They were faintly visible to the naked eye.

"There is something peculiar about those lines," he said. "This stone is so hard that nothing seems to scratch it, and I am sure those lines were not made by the ring accidentally striking against hard objects. They were there when it came into my possession. I do not think another line or mark has been made upon it since I have owned it."

"That is odd."

"Odd! It is remarkable. It makes it appear that these lines were traced there with some instrument that could mark the stone, and that they have a secret meaning."

"Who knows? Possibly that is true."

"And it may be that the man in black can read their meaning."

The red light was dying out of the western sky, and the dusky shadows of advancing night were gathering in the village street, which was overhung by large dark elm trees. Standing by the gate, the boy and girl minded not the approach of darkness as they talked on.

Suddenly Inza uttered a cry and caught Frank's arm, pointing to the opposite side of the street, and excitedly whispering:

"Look—look there! Who is that man skulking along the walk over there?"

"By Jove! it is the man in black!" declared Frank.

CHAPTER XXVII.

ATTACKED ON THE ROAD.

It was in truth the mysterious man who was lingering on the opposite side of the street under the deeper shadows of the elms. That he was watching Frank quickly became evident, but he slowly walked away when he saw he was observed.

"What a villainous-looking creature he is!" said Inza, in a flutter of alarm.

"How could you tell at that distance when it is so dark?" half laughed Frank.

"Oh, it was his general appearance—his black clothes, and that strange cloak and cape."

To himself Frank confessed that the man had seemed rather more awe-inspiring when seen through the gathering darkness than he had appeared near at hand in the stronger light of sunset.

The stranger had moved along the street till swallowed by the darkness beneath the great trees, but something told the boy he was lingering at a distance—watching and waiting.

Despite his strong nerves, the boy felt a cold chill creep along his back. What desperate deed might not the mysterious man in black be contemplating?

The girl was no less impressed.

"Oh, Frank!" she exclaimed, looking up into his handsome face; "I know you are in danger—I am sure of it! That dreadful creature means to do you some injury!"

Seeing how distressed she was, Frank began to feel sorry that he had told her so much.

"You are nervous," he said. "I shouldn't have told you all this stuff about the ring and that man."

Her hand fell on his, which rested on the top of the iron gate.

"You did right in telling me," came softly from her lips. "Who should you have told if not me? We ought not to have secrets from each other."

"I do not fancy we have many secrets that we keep from each other, Inza," he murmured, leaning toward her over the gate. "You know how I have trusted you."

"And have I not trusted you, Frank? I have told you all my delightful little secrets, and I have not told yours to another soul. They say girls cannot keep secrets, but I think you will find out they can."

"Ah, Inza! you are not like other girls."

"Oh, yes, I am!" she laughed. "You think I am not, but I am. Perhaps I am a trifle too old for my years, as papa often says; but the terrible dangers you have rescued me from have been quite enough to add something to my age."

"In the face of every danger you have been brave as few girls could have been."

"That's flattery."

"It is the sincere, honest truth. Do you think I would attempt to flatter you?"

"Frank!"

Their hands met, and he suddenly leaned over the gate and kissed her, in the dusky twilight. She gave a little cry, as of surprise or dismay, retreating swiftly; but Frank clung to her hands, and she did not make a severe struggle to break away, although for a moment there was a playful mockery of a struggle.

Slowly he drew her back to the gate, but she timidly held away, as if she were really alarmed.

"How dare you, sir!" she exclaimed, with a toss of her head. "You are very bold!"

"I beg your pardon," he beseeched, with mock humbleness. "I will agree not to do it again—till I get another good chance."

"Really! How sacrificing you are! You are extremely free."

"Stolen sweets, you know, are the best. But truly, Inza, hadn't I a right to that?"

"A right, indeed! Why, to use a slang expression, that is cheek!"

"Never mind the cheek," he said, laughingly. "I prefer the lips."

And then, before she could divine his intention, he kissed her again.

This time she broke away in earnest.

"Good-night, sir," she called, from up the walk.

"Oh, wait a moment!" he implored. "You aren't going to leave me like this?"

"Oh, but I am."

"How can you!"

"You are getting altogether too free."

She seemed really angry, and a feeling of dismay came over the lad at the gate.

"Inza!"

She had paused

"Well, sir?"

"Don't go away angry, please! I know I had no right to steal those kisses, but I am willing to make amends."

"Oh, you are!" she said, wonderingly, and it seemed to Frank that she was struggling to keep back a burst of laughter. "How will you do it?"

"If you'll come here, I will give them back to you."

That was a master-stroke. A soft laugh came from her lips, and she returned:

"You are a saucy, cheeky fellow, and I am not coming back. Good-night."

"You are not angry?"

"What's the use to be angry with you!"

"Good-night, Inza."

"Good-night, Frank."

As he turned away down the walk, he saw her pause at the door and heard her softly call:

"Frank."

"Yes?"

"I don't like to think of you as a thief. I will take those kisses back some other time."

Then, with another ripple of laughter, she disappeared into the house.

Frank's heart was very light as he walked airily down the street. He had forgotten the man in black for the time, and he whistled a lively air, thinking of the charming girl he had left a few moments before.

It had now grown quite dark, for the moon had not yet risen; but there was a spring-time sweetness in the air, which was not yet enervated by the languorous heat of summer.

Frank passed beyond the limits of the village, where lights were twinkling from the windows of the houses, and he swung down the road toward the cove at a lively gait, still whistling.

At a certain point the road was lined with bushes, and not far away was the village cemetery.

Frank had reached this lonely locality, when, of a sudden, a feeling of uneasiness came over him. Somehow it seemed that he was in danger.

Then came a rustle in the bushes, and, the following moment, a dark form confronted the lad, blocking his path.

Frank recoiled, and through his mind flashed the thought:

"It is the man in black!"

At the same moment, the unknown sprang forward and clutched the lad, snarling:

"Give me that ring! I will have it! Give it up peaceably, or I will choke the breath out of your body! Don't shout! It will be the worse for you if you do!"

Right there and then the man in black met with a great surprise.

Frank grappled with the stranger, and, for some moments, they engaged in a fierce struggle. At length the boy got the best of it, and, as he threw the man, he gave his assailant a terrible up-per-cut blow.

Having freed himself Frank took to his heels and ran down the road toward the academy.

CHAPTER XXVIII.

THE MARKS ON THE BLACK STONE.

Frank fancied he heard pursuing footsteps behind him, but the mysterious man might have spared himself the effort if he tried to overtake the lad, for Merriwell almost flew over the ground.

The lights from the windows of the barracks soon appeared through the trees, and Frank felt relieved when he was safely within the grounds with the academy buildings looming before him.

A short time later he entered his own room in the "Cock-loft," to find Bartley Hodge sitting with his feet on the table, smoking a cigarette and perusing an exciting detective story; but the feet went down to the floor like a flash, and the cigarette and book disappeared with magical swiftness as Frank came in.

"Oh!" said Hodge, with a sigh of relief; "it's you, is it, Merriwell? I thought it might be an inspector."

Frank laughed.

"It would have been rather bad for you if I had been an inspector, for you did not get that book and cigarette out of sight quick enough to fool anybody, and the air is full of smoke. You would have stood a good chance for chevrons next month if you had let cigarettes and novels alone and taken a little more care to avoid demerit."

"Never mind, old man," said Hodge, as he resumed the cigarette and brought forth the detective story again.

"You'll be a corporal sure, and that is glory enough for us. Don't preach. If you should start in on this yarn, you wouldn't give it up till you finished it."

"And that is exactly why I am not going to start in. I enjoy a good story as well as you do, but I cannot afford to read novels, now, and so I refuse to be tempted into looking into any of them."

"This is a hummer," declared Bart, enthusiastically. "It is full of mystery and murder and all that. Beagle Ben, the detective, is a corker! That fellow can look a man over and tell what he had for dinner by the expression around the corners of his mouth. He sees through a crook as easily as you can look through a plate-glass window. And the mysteries in this story are enough to give a fellow the nightmare. I wonder why such mysterious things never happen in real life?"

"Perhaps they do occasionally."

The way Frank spoke the words caused Bart to turn and look him over wonderingly.

"Hello!" he said. "What's struck you? You are breathing as if you had been running, but you're rather pale round the gills."

"I have had an adventure."

"You are always having adventures. You're the luckiest fellow alive."

"This adventure is somewhat out of the usual order," declared Frank. "It might furnish material for a detective story."

"Whew!" whistled the dark-haired lad. "Now you are making me curious. Reel it off for us."

Then Frank sat down and told Hodge the full particulars of his adventure with the mysterious man in black.

A look of wonder and delight grew on Bart's face as he listened, and, when the account was finished, he slapped his thigh, crying:

"By Jove, Merriwell, this is great! Why, such things do actually happen, don't they! Why do you suppose that man is so determined to obtain possession of that ugly old ring? Do you actually believe he is a collector of rings, with a mania for the quaint and curious?"

"It is possible, but, for some reason, I doubt it."

"So do I."

"He did not seem quite sincere in his manner of telling that story, and he was altogether too desperate in his determination to obtain the ring."

"That's right."

"Besides that, he wished to know how it came into my possession, and, when he learned my father's name, he declared he had never heard it before."

"What do you make out of that?"

"Well, it strikes me that this man recognized the ring as one he had seen before."

Bart nodded with satisfaction.

"Just the way I figured it out, old man!"

"He did not seem so anxious to learn the history of the ring, although he pretended that it was his wish to know the history of every ring that came into his possession. In this case he seemed far more anxious to discover how I came to have it."

"And so he must already know its history?"

"Yes."

"What do you know about it yourself, Frank?"

"Not much," was the serious reply. "You know I once told you that my father was much away from home, traveling in the West, where he claimed to have business interests, and it was not till after his death that we knew what his business actually was—that of a note broker—with a passion for gambling?"

"Yes, I remember all this."

"In his wanderings, father somehow got hold of that ring, and it is pretty certain that he considered it very valuable, for he sent it to mother, and wrote her to guard it faithfully, and not to let it part from her on any consideration. He said that he would come for it some day; but he never did. When mother died, she gave me the ring, telling me to keep it always. That is as much of the ring's history as is known to me."

"And that is just enough to make the thing a decided mystery. I have heard of magic rings used by East Indian fakirs and magicians. Perhaps this is one of those rings."

Frank smiled a bit, and shook his head.

"Hardly that, I think," he said. "From its appearance, I should say this ring was made by some crude workman in the West."

"In, that case, what can there be about it that is mysterious or valuable?"

"You have asked me something I cannot answer."

"Let's look at the thing."

Bart held out his hand, and Frank removed the ring from his finger, handing it over.

"It slips off altogether too easily," said Hodge. "I should think you would fear losing it."

"It does come off easy, and, for that reason, I have not worn it much till of late."

"Yes; I never noticed it on your hand till a short time ago."

"I have kept it among my valuables."

Hodge looked the ring all over, examining it slowly and carefully.

"There doesn't seem to be anything about it to make a fellow think it so very mysterious," he said, with a shade of disappointment in his voice.

"No."

"It is just a homely, twisted ring, with an old scratched black stone set in it."

"That's right."

"Perhaps the man in black is crazy."

"It is possible."

"In which case the mystery amounts to nothing."

For a few seconds the two lads sat staring at each other. Then Frank removed a pin from some hidden place, and held it toward Bart.

"Here," he said, "take this and see how easily you can scratch that stone."

Hodge took it, and attempted to scratch the black stone that was set in the ring.

"Why, the thing is hard as flint—yes, harder!" he exclaimed. "The pin will not leave a mark upon it, and it has already turned the point of the pin over."

"Still, as you said, the stone is scratched."

"What do you make of that?"

"It strikes me it was not scratched by accident."

Hodge started and whistled.

"Do you imagine these marks were made here intentionally and deliberately?"

"Doesn't it seem that way?"

"Well, it is not impossible."

"If they were made there deliberately and intentionally, cut by some instrument that could mark that hard stone, doesn't it stand to reason that the one who made them did not do all that work for nothing?"

"Of course."

"Then those marks may mean something."

"By jingoes! you are right!"

"This may be known to the man in black, which makes him so fierce to obtain the ring."

"Sure!"

Again the boys stared silently at each other, but there were traces of eager excitement on the faces of both.

"How are you going to find out what those marks mean, Frank?"

"That is a question easier asked than answered."

"Did you ever examine this stone under a microscope?"

"No."

"Then I advise you to do so without delay. These scratches are not very plain to the naked eye, but a microscope may reveal a great secret to you."

As Bart passed the ring back, Frank said:

"You are right. My curiosity is thoroughly aroused, and I will examine it under a magnifying glass at the earliest opportunity."

"Get leave to look at it under the big glass in the experimenting room."

"I will try it to-morrow."

Until very near taps the boys talked of the mystery of the ring, and that night both of them dreamed over and over of the ring and the sinister man in black.

CHAPTER XXIX.

BART MAKES A PLEDGE.

he following day Frank obtained permission to look at the ring through the powerful microscope belonging to the academy. Bart accompanied him to the experimenting room, and they were soon taking turns in looking at the marked stone.

"What do you make of it, old man?" asked Bart.

"It looks like a map," said Frank.

"Right!" exclaimed the other lad. "It looks like a map, and I believe that is what it is."

There is a river, or road, and mountains, something that looks like a lake, and then a tiny cross. The cross must be a landmark.

"Yes; and you will note that it is at the end of what looks like a river."

"But that must be a road."

"It is, if this is a map, for it runs over that range of hills, or mountains."

"That is plain enough."

"And you will see there is a tiny, snake-like thread that winds away from that spot, which looks as if it was intended for a lake."

"I see it."

"That must be a river, or stream."

The boys were now very excited. All doubts were fading from their minds; the lines on the black stone had surely been intended to represent a map.

But what portion of the face of the earth did it portray? That was a question the ring did not answer.

"Supposing it is a map," said Frank, helplessly; "what good will it do me? I do not know what it is a map of."

"But you may bet your last dollar the man in black knows."

"I don't see how that is going to do me any good.

"It will do him some good, if he gets hold of this ring."

"Well, I shall take care that he does not get hold of it."

The map—if it were a map—on the stone served to more fully arouse the curiosity of the boys, without in any way satisfying them concerning the mystery of the ring.

Frank became so absorbed in trying to discover the true meaning of the map and in getting some light on the mystery that he began to neglect his studies. This, however, was quickly noted by Hodge, who said:

"Be careful, old man; don't let that ring get into your head so that you will lose your chance of standing well up in your class. You are all right in drill work, and you should be appointed a corporal next month."

"Hang the old ring!" exclaimed Frank, petulantly. "I never had anything cause me so much bother before. Whenever I try to study I fall to thinking of it, and I dream of it every night."

Two days passed, and nothing more was seen of the man in black during that time, which led Bart to believe that the mysterious individual had left the vicinity.

"He must have fancied that you would have him arrested for attacking you on the road," said Hodge. "You are not likely to see him again very soon."

"Don't get that impression into your head," returned Frank. "He is not far away. I seem to feel that he is lurking near, awaiting his next opportunity."

"That's tommy-rot! You have let this old ring mix you all up. Don't slip any cogs now, Frank, or you may have the pleasure of seeing your new rival, Paul Rains, appointed a corporal, while you still remain an ordinary cadet."

Frank flushed.

"Rains is not a bad fellow," he said. "He is square."

"He may seem so to you," said Hodge; "but I am suspicious of any fellow who has much to do with Wat Snell and that gang. Frank, it is a wonder to me that you ever came to have anything to do with me afterward—well, you know."

"I shouldn't if I hadn't believed there was some good in you for all of appearances."

"Thank you, old man!" exclaimed Hodge, with genuine feeling. "You are white all the way through, and I believe it is to you I owe credit for still remaining a cadet in this school."

"Nonsense!"

"There is no nonsense about it. You know I tried two military schools before I came here, and I did not remain in either. I could not get along. You have helped me over the hard places, and you have stood by me, through thick and thin, although most of the fellows, disliked me at first, and thought you were foolish in doing what you did. I have been no particular aid to you, but I have led you into temptations and dangers you would have avoided but for the fact that we were roommates and friends. In return, you have saved me many bad breaks, and I am not liable to forget. I did hate you most intensely, but you shall find that I can be as strong in my friendships as I am in my hatreds."

This was saying a great deal for Hodge, who was usually silent and reserved concerning himself. But Bart knew he was speaking no more than the truth, and he felt that the time had come when such an acknowledgment would do him good.

Frank's generous heart was touched by this new revelation of his friend's nature, and he grasped Bart's hand warmly.

"If I have helped you in any way, I am glad to know it," he said, earnestly.

"Well, you have; and you have taken demerit on my account without a murmur. It is selfish of me to cling to cigarettes when 'tobacco smoke in quarters' has been reported against us so many times. By jingoes! I'm going to swear off! They don't do a fellow any good, and they get an awful hold on one. It won't be easy for me to give them up; but I am going to do it. If you catch me smoking another of the things, you may kick me till there isn't a breath left in my body! That's business, and I will stick to it!"

"Good!" laughed Frank. "You have been smoking a good many of them lately, and I have noticed that you complained of your lungs. How can your lungs be in any condition when you are constantly inhaling so much of that smoke! I know of a young fellow with weak lungs who went into quick consumption, and the doctors said cigarettes were entirely responsible. He smoked a number of packages a day. When he started he simply smoked now and then, but the habit grew on him, and at last he was unable to break it."

"I believe any fellow can break off smoking them if he has any will-power of his own."

"I think a fellow should, but you may not find it as easy as you fancy."

"Oh, it will be easy enough for me. When I make up my mind to a thing, I never give up."

"Well, I sincerely trust it will prove so. Every one knows cigarettes are harmful. Yesterday I read in a paper about a boy in a New York hospital who was said to have a 'tobacco heart' from smoking cigarettes. By a tobacco heart it was meant that his heart was so badly affected that it did not perform its action regularly and properly. Sometimes he is convulsed with terrible pains, and gasps for breath. Nearly all the time he moans and begs for cigarettes; but the doctors say he must never smoke another one if he cares to live. As it is, if he should get up, his heart is so weakened that it may go on a strike any time and cause his death."

"Oh, say!" laughed Bart; "that settles it. Now, I never will smoke again. I mean it—you see if I don't."

"I sincerely hope you do. You may become one of the best athletes in this school. Your only trouble has been shortness of breath when you exercise heavily, and that came entirely from smoking. If you give it up, you will soon cease to be troubled that way."

"Well, here's my hand on it, and it is as good as settled. No matter how much I may desire a smoke now, I'll not monkey with the deadly cigarette."

Their hands met again.

CHAPTER XXX.

FRANK AND THE PROFESSOR.

Frank Merriwell was right in thinking he had not seen the last of the man in black. On the third day after his first meeting with the mysterious stranger he was astonished, while ascending the stairs, to see that individual come out of Professor Gunn's room. Frank paused on the flight that led to the "Cock-loft," and watched the man hurriedly descend the stairs.

"Great Scott!" muttered the young cadet. "That is remarkable. I wonder what he was up to in the professor's room? He saw me, but he hustled away in a hurry."

For a moment Frank hesitated, and then he resolved to find out, if possible, what could be the meaning of the stranger's visit. With this object in view, he descended the stairs and approached the professor's door, on which he rapped.

Of late Professor Gunn had been severely troubled with headaches, and, this happening to be one of his bad days, he was stopping in his room, with his head bound up in a cloth saturated with camphor. Frank was obliged to rap a second time, and then the professor's shuffling step was heard, and his cloth-bound head appeared as the door opened.

"What's wanted?" he asked, sharply. "Can't I have any peace and rest? Speak up—what's wanted?"

"I have something to ask you, professor?" said Frank, quietly.

"Ah, is it you, Merriwell? I was going to see you later. Come in."

Not a little surprised, Frank entered the professor's room, standing cap in hand, while the crusty old fellow seated himself in an easy chair, and asked:

"What is it you want to see me about, young man?"

"You were lately visited by a stranger, whom I saw leaving this room a few moments ago."

"Yes, sir—yes."

"That man assaulted me on the highway a few nights ago."

"What's that—what? Assaulted you? This is interesting—decidedly!"

"Yes, he assaulted me; but I managed to give him the worst of it, and got away without being harmed."

"You should have reported the occurrence—you certainly should. That was the proper thing to do—the correct thing, young man. Then I would have known how to receive him."

"I thought he had gone away from this vicinity, but it seems that he has not. Now, I would like to know his name. What is his name, professor, please?"

"Eh? Ah? His name? Let me see. Now that is surprising—really surprising. I do not think he gave me his name."

"Did not give his name? How did he obtain admission to the building?"

"That's so—how did he? I hadn't thought of that. He was the smoothest talker I ever heard; he didn't give me a chance to ask many questions."

"He must have had some sort of business with you."

"He did—that is, he pretended to have. He said he was here to recover some property that belonged to him—property he lost several years ago."

The eyes of the old professor searched Frank's hands and rested on the peculiar ring.

"So that was his trick—the scoundrel!" cried Frank, repressing his anger with difficulty. "I presume he claimed this ring belonged to him?"

"Well—ahem!—he described such a ring, which he said he had seen on the hand of a student here."

"Exactly. And he named me as the possessor of the ring?"

"He said the name of the student's father was Charles Conrad Merriwell. I believe, sir—I am quite sure, in fact—that that was the name of your father."

Frank was fully aroused, and his brown eyes gleamed in a way that showed how indignant he was, although it was necessary to keep his feelings suppressed as far as possible.

"Professor Gunn," he said, swiftly, "that man is a scoundrel!"

"Eh? Ha! Hum! Severe language. Be careful, young man—be cautious. Do not make a statement you cannot stand behind. It is dangerous—very dangerous."

"I can stand behind every word I have said. Why, when he found I would not sell him the ring, professor, he tried to rob me of it! That is not only the act of a scoundrel, but that of a desperado."

"It looks bad—bad," confessed the old professor, who seemed in a somewhat nervous and flustered state. "Tell me all about it— give the full particulars of the occurrence."

Frank did so, telling a straightforward story, to which the professor listened with interest that was apparent, although he now and then pressed his hand to his head, as if the pain were troubling him.

When the story was finished, and Frank had explained what he and Bart had discovered on the black stone set in the ring, the old professor showed that he was quite wrought up.

"Remarkable!" he exclaimed—"re-e-markable! I am surprised—I am puzzled. This man told a very straight story—said the ring was stolen from him in Arizona. He said it was very valuable to him, as it was an heirloom. He could not tell how it came into your possession—he did not try. All he wanted was to recover his property—that was all."

"That was his scheme when he found he could not buy it from me. He did not attempt to make you believe he was a collector of odd rings, professor, for he knew that would do no good, and so he laid claim to the ring. What proof did he give you that it was his property?"

"Eh? Proof? It seems as if he did give proof of some sort, but really I don't know as he did. He was such a plausible person—so very smooth and convincing. Why, I did not think of doubting him. But I know your record very well since entering the academy, Merriwell. It is satisfactory—quite satisfactory. I do not think you are the sort of a lad to tell a deliberate falsehood—no, sir, no."

"Thank you, sir."

"That being the case, I shall have to accept your statement—yes, I will accept it. He said he would call again to-morrow. Let him come! I think I will have an officer on hand—he shall be arrested the moment he shows himself. That's right—that's proper. Hum! ha! Assaulted a cadet of Fardale Academy, did he? Attempted to rob a student at this school, did he? Well, he shall be duly and properly punished—yes, sir."

The professor had worked himself up into a state of considerable excitement, seeming to have forgotten his headache for the time. He got upon his feet and went tramping about the room in his slippers, the heels of which had been trodden down. He perched his nose-glasses far down on his pointed proboscis, and glared over them in a way he had when he was endeavoring to appear very impressive before a class.

Under other circumstances Frank might have smiled at the figure cut by the excited old man, but he was now far too angry himself to note what was ludicrous.

"Take care of that ring, young man," advised the professor—"take the best of care of it. It may be more valuable than it appears. There is certainly something connected with this ring that makes it valuable to this stranger—or else the man is a lunatic—yes, sir, a lunatic. I do not think that—no, I do not. He appeared rational—he was quite sane when he was here—quite so."

"I have ever regarded this ring as simply an ugly ornament that my father ran across and took a fancy to; but now I believe it must be something more."

"It is likely—quite likely. It seems that there is a mystery connected with the ring. It may be solved soon—very soon. This stranger must know a great deal concerning it. Perhaps he will tell what he knows—perhaps he may be induced to tell."

The professor said this in a peculiar way, that seemed to say "strong inducements" would be held out to the strange man in black.

Frank had seen Professor Gunn, and asked his question, but the mystery was deep as ever when the boy left the professor's room.

CHAPTER XXXI.

SNELL TALKS.

Frank was not the only one who had observed the man in black as that mysterious individual was departing. Bart Hodge saw the sinister stranger, and instantly recognized him from Frank's description.

"Great Scott!" thought Bart. "What can that imp of Satan be up to here?"

The man was hurrying from the grounds, and Hodge followed. The man passed the sentry, but Bart was challenged.

"See that man?" said the lad, hurriedly. "I am satisfied that he has been up to some mischief. I want to follow him, and see where he goes."

"You cannot leave the grounds without a pass," said the sentinel, firmly.

"Oh, hang your pass!" cried Bart, warmly, as he saw there was danger that the man in black would escape. "This is an exceptional case."

"A sentry knows no exceptions. If you leave the grounds, you will have to obtain a pass from the office."

"But that man is a robber—a highwayman! If you stand on the rules of the academy now, he will escape, and you may be reprimanded."

"I shall do my duty as sentinel, sir, reprimand or no reprimand."

The man in black was walking swiftly up the road toward the village, his cape flapping behind him in the wind like the wings of a bat. In a few moments he would disappear from view.

"Hang the luck!" grated Hodge, as he turned away in disappointment. "I'd given something to follow him up."

He was inclined to be angry at the sentinel at first, but his friendship with Merriwell had taught him that he should have forbearance when in the right, and should never hold a grudge when in the wrong. Sober reason told him the sentinel had done no more than his plain duty, so the feeling of anger was swiftly banished from Bart's breast.

"I will find Frank and tell him what is up," he thought.

As he walked swiftly toward the barracks, he was met by Wat Snell, who said:

"Hello, Hodge. I want to have a talk with you."

"With me?" asked Bart, in surprise.

Snell had not been friendly for some time, and, of late, he had ceased to speak to Hodge. This had not troubled Bart at all, but he was greatly surprised by this advance on the part of his enemy.

"Yes, with you," assured Snell. "There was a time when you were ready enough to talk with me. I have even known you to follow me up to get a chance to have a word in private with me."

The face of the dark-haired boy flushed.

"That time is past," he said. "What do you want of me?"

"It is my turn now. I want to have a word in private with you."

Bart did not fancy this much. He knew Snell for exactly what the fellow was—a sneaking, revengeful rascal. The thought that he had ever had dealings with such a scamp made Bart's cheeks burn and caused him to regard himself with no little contempt.

He did not care to be seen talking privately with Snell, and he glanced hastily around, to see if any one was watching them.

Snell noted the look, and an angry light came into his eyes, which were somewhat too small and set so near together that they seemed crowding his nose between them.

"Oh, you hesitate over it, do you!" he sneered. "That's like some fellows to go back on their old friends! You won't make anything by it in the end."

"If you have anything to say to me, say it," commanded Hodge, sharply.

"Come over here where the fellows can't see us from the windows," invited Snell, beckoning Bart to follow.

But Hodge did not stir.

"No, sir," he said, firmly. "If you have anything you want to say to me, say it right here."

Snell did not like this. He came back slowly, casting a hasty, doubtful look up to the dormitory windows. After some hesitation, during which he kicked the gravel of the walk with his toe, he began:

"There was a time when you didn't like Merriwell any better than the rest of us, and you have done things that would put you in a pretty bad corner, if they were known."

Hodge's brows lowered in a scowl, and his nostrils dilated, like those of a wild creature that scents danger. He said nothing, but his steady, piercing gaze made Snell keep his eyes on the ground.

"Of course I am not the kind of a fellow to blow anything of the sort," Wat went on, hurriedly. "I simply mentioned it by chance. You seem friendly with Merriwell now, and I thought you might have forgotten."

"I wonder what the rascal is coming at?" thought Bart; but not a word did he speak aloud.

"For the sake of old times, I thought—perhaps—you might do something for some of your old friends—I didn't know but you might. It can't harm Merriwell any in particular—he'll never miss it. It will be a lift for me, and I can make it an object for you."

Snell was floundering, and the look on his face seemed to indicate that he was growing frightened and felt like taking to his heels.

Of a sudden, Hodge became curious to know what the fellow had to say, and so he decided to try diplomacy.

"I do not forget my friends," he said. "What is it you want of me, Snell?"

That gave Wat a little courage.

"Before I tell you, Hodge, I want to say that you will be well paid if you help out a little in this matter, and Merriwell can never know that you were in it. He'll never suspect you. You didn't have any scruples about doing something of the sort once on a time."

"Well, what is it?" demanded Bart, impatiently. "Don't beat round the bush so much."

"Oh, don't be in such a hurry!" fluttered Snell, nervously, far from feeling fully confident of Hodge. "There's money in this. It will be twenty-five dollars in your pocket if you do what I want you to. Are you with me?"

"That depends on what you want me to do. Name it."

"Well, Merriwell has something that doesn't rightfully belong to him. Understand that—it is not his by right. It belongs to a friend of mine, who wants me to recover his property."

"Well?"

"You can aid me, as you room with Merriwell."

"Jupiter!" thought Bart. "I wonder if the mysterious ring is the piece of property Snell means?"

It was with no little difficulty that Hodge held himself in check; but he did not wish Snell to become alarmed, and so he quietly asked:

"What is this piece of property?"

"It is something Merriwell wears every day. I suppose he takes it off occasionally. That would give you your chance. Mind you, it is not rightfully his, but it belongs to my friend, so there is no harm in taking it to restore it to its proper owner. In fact, that is a simple act of justice."

"Why doesn't the rightful owner recover his property in the regular manner?"

"That might prove difficult, or even impossible, as he would have trouble in establishing his claim, and Merriwell might conceal the property. It is not the value of this property that the owner cares so much for; he wants the property itself."

There was no longer any doubt in Bart's mind; Snell was speaking of the ring. The man in black had resorted to another scheme to obtain possession of that ugly ornament.

With the greatest difficulty, Hodge kept cool and placid, as he asked:

"And you want me to steal this property?"

"No, no, no! It would not be stealing it; it would be returning it to its proper owner. Can't you see?"

"Well, if I am going to do this job, I must know what the property is."

"It is the ring Merriwell wears when he is not in ranks—the twisted band, with a black stone set in it."

"And you want me to obtain that ring and give it to you?"

"Yes."

"For which I am to receive twenty-five dollars?"

"Yes. What is your answer?"

"This is my answer!"

Like a flash, Hodge struck out straight from the shoulder, and his fist caught Snell between the eyes.

CHAPTER XXXII.

SNELL'S HATRED.

Smack!

The blow sounded sharp and clear, and Snell quickly found himself stretched on the gravel walk. He looked up in a dazed way, to see Hodge standing near at hand, regarding him with withering scorn.

"You'll pay dearly for this!" gasped Snell, lifting himself to his elbow and glaring at Bart.

"All right," was the hot retort. "I am willing to pay for it. You may have taken me for a thief, but I rather think you have discovered your mistake."

"You weren't so honest once on a time, not so very long——"

"What's that?" cried Bart, taking a threatening step toward the fellow. "I was never a thief, no matter what my other failings may have been; and if you dare insinuate such a thing, I will ram the words down your throat!"

"That's all right—that's all right!" muttered Wat, scrambling up and getting out of reach. "I will report this assault."

"Report it, and be hanged! The fellows in this academy admire a tattler! You will have a very pleasant time if you report it!"

"It was seen. Somebody will tell Professor Gunn."

"Perhaps so; but it isn't best that you are the one."

"I'll—I'll get even!"

"Go ahead. I'd like the satisfaction of fighting you to a finish."

"I will not fight with my fists," blustered Wat, trying to appear very fierce. "There are more deadly weapons."

"Name any weapon you choose. I will be only too glad to meet you. I am a good pistol shot, and Professor Rhynas says I handle the foils fairly well."

"Oh, you're a regular ruffian!" cried Snell, his chin beginning to quiver and his voice choking with anger that brought tears to his eyes. "I will not fight you in any way! I do not pretend to be a match for a ruffian of your sort. But I will get square just the same."

"I presume you will try to square the account in some sneaking manner. Well, I warn you now and here that it will not be healthy if you try any dirty tricks on me. If anything underhand happens to me, I'll know who was the originator of it, and I'll settle with you. That is business!"

With this, Bart turned to walk away, noting that a great many of the cadets were peering from the windows, some of them grinning with delight.

Snell shook his fist at Hodge's back, blustering:

"This is all right—all right, sir! It is not necessary for me to fight you; you are not on the same level with me."

"No," muttered the dark-haired boy, grimly, "I have never sunk as low as that."

The room occupied by Merriwell and Hodge was not on that side of the building, so Frank, who was studying, had not witnessed the encounter between his roommate and Snell.

Fortunately, also, the blow had not been seen by any one but cadets, so it was not liable to come to Professor Gunn's knowledge, unless Wat told of it himself.

Bart found Frank in their room, and Merriwell looked up as the dark-haired boy entered with a quick, nervous step.

"Hello!" he cried, in surprise. "What's happened? Your face is dark as a thunder-cloud, and you look as if you could eat iron."

"Well, I feel as if I wouldn't have any trouble in chewing up a few pounds of iron," replied Bart. "By Jove! old man, I never realized till a few minutes ago how narrow was my escape from being a most contemptible scoundrel!"

"How is that?"

"I was taken for a thief!" grated Bart, his white teeth clicking. "Yes, sir, taken for a thief!"

"It must have been by somebody who does not know you very well."

"That's where you are wrong. It was by somebody who knows me far too well. That is why I feel that my escape from being a scoundrel was a narrow one."

Had he not seen that Bart was so serious and thoroughly in earnest, Frank must have smiled.

"Give us the particulars," he urged. "What did you do when you were taken for a thief?"

"Knocked the cad down!" snarled Bart, smashing his clinched right hand into the open palm of his left.

"That was very proper," assured Merriwell. "You did nicely, my son."

"But I do not feel any the less humiliated. If I had not given him reason to approach me in such a manner, he would not have ventured."

Then Bart related the particulars of his adventure with Snell.

"So, so!" muttered Frank. "That rascal is in this affair. The man in black has chosen a good tool."

"That man is determined to have your ring."

"I should say so. He has been to Professor Gunn and represented that the ring belonged to him." And then Frank took his turn to tell what he had learned from the head professor.

"Well, I never!" cried Bart, as Frank finished. "Why, the scoundrel has the cheek of a brass monkey! He is dangerous, Frank."

"I believe you."

"If I were in your place, I would swear out a warrant for his arrest, and send an officer after him."

"I may be forced to do so."

"And I advise you to keep your eye on Wat Snell."

"I will do that."

"In the meantime, let me take the ring long enough to make an enlarged drawing of those lines, so that you will have the map, if it is a map, even if you lose the ring. You know my ability to copy with pen and ink anything I see. My father wants me to become a civil engineer, and so I am taking a course to suit him; but, when I leave Fardale, I mean to go to an art school, and find out if I am not cut out for an artist."

"How can you make a drawing of the lines?"

"Why, I will place the ring under a microscope, and then it will not be difficult. You know I can be very accurate when I try."

"Yes, I know it, and I will think of your plan. I am inclined to believe it is a good one. Whether I should lose the ring or not, I'd like to have a copy of that map to study."

"I'll find time to do the job to-morrow, if Old Gunn will permit us to use the microscope again."

On the following day, however, Bart found no opportunity to make the drawing.

Frank watched for the man in black, who had said he would call on Professor Gunn again; but the mysterious man did not put in an appearance, and Merriwell waited his time.

Wat Snell was forced to endure no end of ridicule from his companions, as it was the rule at Fardale that a student who had received a blow or an insult must challenge the one who gave it.

If he did not do so, he was regarded as a coward, and his life in school from that time was certain to be far from pleasant.

In his heart Snell was an arrant coward, and he knew that Hodge was really longing for a challenge. Wat felt sure that he would receive a severe drubbing at the hands of the dark-haired boy whom he had angered, and the thoughts of such punishment filled his soul with horror.

"I can't fight him—it's no use, I can't!" he told himself over and over. "He is a turn-coat, anyway! He did not pretend to be so conscientious till after he got thick with Merriwell. Oh, Merriwell is really the one who is at the bottom of all the trouble I have had in this school, and I hate him worse than I do Hodge.

"I'd like to get hold of that ring. Jupiter! seventy-five dollars is a price to pay for an old ring like that, but it's what that strange man in black offered me to secure it for him. There's something mighty mysterious about that ring. I wish I knew what the mystery is. I am going to ask the man when I see him this evening."

That night Snell escaped from the building and the grounds without obtaining leave. He was going to keep an appointment with the man in black.

CHAPTER XXXIII.

PLAYING THE SHADOW.

Snell was followed.

Frank had taken Bart's advice to keep an eye on the fellow, and something in Wat's actions had given him the impression that Snell was up to something that he did not care to have generally known.

With a great deal of skill, Frank kept watch of Snell till the latter slipped from the grounds under cover of darkness.

It was a cloudy night, with the wind moaning far out at sea, and the waves roaring sullenly along the base of Black Bluff, down the shore.

As may be imagined, it was no easy task to follow Wat without losing the fellow in the darkness or getting so close that the "shadowed" lad would discover that somebody was watching him.

Although he was not aware of it, Frank possessed a remarkable faculty for performing such a task. He moved with the silence of a creeping cat, and yet covered ground with sufficient swiftness to keep near Wat.

Something must have made Snell suspicious, for three times he stopped and peered back through the darkness, and three times Frank sunk like a ghost to the ground, escaping discovery by his swiftness in making the move.

Indeed, had it been possible for a third party to watch them, it must have seemed that Merriwell felt an intuition which told him exactly when Snell was going to look back.

Once or twice before they came to the road that led up from the cove, Frank lost sight of the boy he was following, but his keen ears served him quite as well as his eyes.

When the road up the hill was reached Frank was able to follow Wat with greater ease.

Suddenly Snell paused and whistled three times. In a moment a single sharp whistle sounded near at hand, and then Frank, crouching close to the ground, saw a black figure come toward Wat Snell.

The wind that was moaning over the sea swept up the road and caused something to flap around the shoulders of this figure like a great pair of wings.

For all of the darkness, Frank recognized this figure, and he was seized with an indefinable feeling of fear such as he had never felt before.

With an effort, Frank steadied his quivering nerves, remaining quiet to watch and listen.

The person who had appeared in answer to Snell's signal was the man in black, and he quickly pounced upon the boy, like a huge hawk upon its prey.

"The ring!" he cried, hoarsely. "Where is it?"

Wat gave a low cry of fear.

"Don't!" he gasped. "You're hurting me! Your fingers are hard as iron, and they crush right into a fellow!"

"The ring!" repeated the man, fiercely. "Produce it!"

"I haven't got it."

"What?" snarled the mysterious stranger. "You have not kept your word! What do you mean?"

"Don't shake a fellow like that!" quavered Snell. "You act like a madman."

"Answer my questions! Why haven't you kept your word?"

"Couldn't."

"Why not?"

"Didn't get the chance."

"But you said you could get a boy to assist you—the fellow who rooms with this Merriwell."

"I thought I could, but the cad went back on me."

"He refused to aid you?"

"Yes, sir."

"And you have found no opportunity to get hold of the ring yourself?"

"Not yet—but I will, sir," Snell hastily answered. "All I want is to know that you will pay me as you agreed. Don't hold onto my arm so tight; I won't run away."

"Bah!" cried the man in black, as he half-flung Wat from him. "What beastly luck!"

"It is bad luck," confessed Snell, falteringly. "But it isn't my fault. I have done my best."

The man in black said nothing, but stood with his head bowed, the elbow of his right arm resting in the hollow of his left hand, while his right hand, fiercely clinched, supported his chin. The wind continued to flap the cape about his shoulders.

The man's attitude and his silence gave Snell a feeling of fear, and he drew away, acting as if he contemplated taking to his heels, for all that he had said he would not run.

"I do not propose to endure much more of this," muttered the man, at length. "I'll have that ring soon, by some means!"

"You must consider it very valuable," said Wat, curiously.

"Valuable!" came hoarsely from the lips of the man in black. "I should say so! If it were not, I shouldn't be making such a desperate struggle to get possession of it."

The lad who was listening a short distance away, strained his ears to catch every word.

"There must be some secret about the ring?" insinuated Snell. "The gold in it amounts to little, and the old black stone——"

A strange sound came from the throat of the man in black, and then, seeming to fancy that he had admitted altogether too much, he hastened to say:

"The ring is valuable to me; but it is worth little to anybody else."

"I suppose that is because nobody else knows its secret?" came from Snell.

"Secret! Bah! It has no secret!"

But it was not easy to convince Snell that this was the truth.

"Then why should you go to such extremes to get possession of a wretched old thing of that sort?" demanded Wat.

"I have told you. The ring belonged to me—was stolen from me. It has been in our family a great length of time, and was given me by my father. I prize it highly for that reason. I do not know how it came into the possession of this Merriwell family, and I cannot prove my claim to my own property, so I must recover it in such a manner as is possible. That is the truth."

Wat said nothing. Somehow he was doubtful, for it did not seem that anybody who was sane could resort to such desperate expedients to recover an ugly old ring that had no particular value save as an heirloom.

As for Frank, he might have believed the strange man's story, but for the fact that the man had told him something entirely different. One story or the other might be true, but in any case the man in black was a liar.

There was a brief silence, and then Snell asked:

"How am I to know that you will surely pay me seventy-five dollars for the ring? You pounced upon me a few minutes ago as if you would rob me of it if it had been in my possession."

"That was all through my eagerness and excitement," declared the man, soothingly. "I meant you no harm, but I was very anxious."

"Well, I don't know; I am afraid I will be left when I get the ring and hand it over, so I guess I'll——"

"What?"

Wat edged a little farther away.

"I guess I'll throw up the job," he hesitated.

"Do you still think you can find a way to get the ring?"

"Think so! I know I can get it, sooner or later, if I want to."

"Then look here, to prove that I am sincere I will pay you this much in advance. It is a twenty-dollar gold piece. Now you cannot doubt my earnestness and fairness in this matter. If you bring me the ring within forty-eight hours, I'll pay you, besides this twenty, the seventy-five dollars I offered in the first place."

Snell eagerly clutched the piece of money.

"You're a brick!" he cried. "And I'll lay myself out to get that ring. I haven't begun to try the schemes I have in my head. I will meet you here to-morrow night at about this time, and I'll do my best to have the ring. Only, if I haven't got it, I want you to promise not to jump on me and grab me the way you did to-night."

"Don't be afraid. I won't harm you."

"Well, you can scare a fellow out of his boots, and I don't like to be scared."

"I am afraid you are something of a coward," said the man, a trace of contempt in his tone.

But little more passed between them before the man in black turned away toward Fardale village, and Wat descended the road in the direction of the academy.

Frank hugged the ground at one side of the road, and he was not seen by Snell.

But, by the time Wat had gone so far that there was little danger of discovery if Frank moved from the locality, the man in black had vanished in the night.

Still, Frank sprang up and went scurrying lightly up the hill, keeping to the grass at the side of the road, so his feet made scarcely a sound.

He hurried along the road till Fardale village was almost reached, but he saw nothing more of the man in black. The mysterious stranger had vanished as completely as if swallowed up by the earth.

Frank had hoped to trace the man to the place where he was stopping, but he was forced to give this up and hurry back to the academy.

Still he had not wasted his time.

"They will meet there to-morrow night, eh?" he muttered. "Well, it would not be a very difficult thing to have an officer on hand with a warrant for this stranger."

He went straight to his room, hoping to find Hodge there.

He did. Bart was seated in his favorite attitude, with his feet on the table, and a cigarette in his mouth!

CHAPTER XXXIV.

THE RING DISAPPEARS.

art!"

The exclamation of mingled surprise and reproach came from Frank's lips.

Hodge had made a move to conceal the cigarette, but discovered he was too late.

His face turned crimson, and he hung his head with shame.

Frank closed the door, and came to the side of his roommate, on whose shoulder he gently placed a hand, as he asked:

"How does it happen, Bart?"

Bart started to say something, choked a little, and then forced an unpleasant laugh.

"Oh, I'm a liar!" he burst out, hotly. "I have broken my pledge at the first temptation!"

"Why did you do it? You know you said you could leave off smoking cigarettes easily."

"I thought I could."

"And you found out the habit was fastened more firmly on you than you thought?"

"That's about the size of it. I have been longing for a cigarette all day, and, when I came by accident upon this one, finding myself all alone, I could not resist the desire to have a whiff."

"That shows the habit had a firmer hold on you than you thought."

"Yes. I fancied I could leave it off readily enough; but I was mistaken. It seems a fellow never knows what a hold the nasty little things have on him till he tries to stop smoking them."

"And were you going to give up the struggle without another effort?"

"Oh, no! I didn't mean to smoke only this once. That is, I didn't mean to at first, but after I got to smoking I thought it would be a good plan to taper off."

"Which meant that you were going to tamper with the stuff again, and, finally, you would smoke as much as ever, and would not leave off at all."

"Perhaps you're right," confessed Hodge, who showed his shame.

"I am sure I am right; but you will give over the plan of tapering off—you will stop at once. You are not weak-minded enough to let cigarettes get a hold on you that you cannot break."

"Well, I thought I wasn't; but I don't know about it now."

"Oh, this is bad, but it doesn't mean failure. I don't believe you are the kind of a fellow to give in thus easily to an enemy. You have more fight in you than that."

Frank spoke in a confident tone, as if he did not doubt Hodge's ability to conquer the habit, and Bart gave him a grateful look.

All at once, Bart jumped up and opened the window, out of which he fiercely flung the half-smoked cigarette.

"If I hadn't been a fool by nature, I'd never lighted the thing!" he cried, in supreme self-contempt. "Your confidence in me, old man, has given me confidence in myself. This settles it! I am done with cigarettes forever. You'll never again discover me with one in my lips!"

Bart had meant to keep his pledge in the first place, but Frank's failure to reproach him for falling, and Frank's confidence in his ability to stop smoking gave him the needed confidence in himself—filled him with a determination not to be defeated. And from that hour he never again smoked a cigarette.

"Now we're all right again," said Merriwell, heartily, as Bart came back from the window. "Sit down while I relate a very interesting tale to you."

Bart sat down, and Frank told what he had seen and heard through following Snell.

"That sneak makes me sick!" cried Hodge, fiercely. "I'd like to get another chance at him! Why, he's the biggest sneak in this school!"

"That's right."

"Gage couldn't hold a candle to Snell."

"Gage was bolder; Snell is a bigger sneak."

"That's about the size of it. What are you going to do with the fellow?"

"I think it would be well to catch him in company with the man in black when they meet to-morrow night."

Bart slapped his thigh.

"Just the scheme! But who's going to do the catching?"

"It would be a good plan to have an officer from the village on hand for that job."

"Good! You can swear out a warrant for the man for felonious assault, attempted highway robbery, or something of the sort, and have him sent where he won't trouble you again for some little time."

"That's what I thought."

"It seems the only way to get rid of him, and he is mighty dangerous."

"He is desperate."

"Yes; he means to have that ring anyway. I'll find a way to-morrow to draw those lines on paper. I don't care if that man does say the ring is of no particular value, I know better. If the lines are taken off, you will stand a show of finding out what they mean."

Frank was eager to have an enlarged copy of the lines made, for he felt that he could never be sure that he would not lose the ring, even though the mysterious man in black should be disposed of effectually.

"Snell is determined to get himself into serious trouble," said Frank.

"Oh, money will hire him to do any mean, sneaking thing!" came scornfully from Bart's lips.

"If he is caught with this scoundrel in black to-morrow night, he will be under a cloud here."

"He is under a cloud now. Twenty fellows saw me knock him down, and they'll never give him any rest till he sends me a challenge."

"Well, I don't fancy he will send you a challenge."

"Then his life will be made wretched while he remains at Fardale Academy."

"He has brought it on himself."

"Of course. A fellow can't be a sneak and have the respect of anybody who is decent. I found that out long ago."

The following forenoon Bart obtained permission to use the microscope long enough to make a drawing of the lines on the stone set in the mysterious ring.

Before going to recitation, Frank surrendered the ring to Bart, who hesitated about taking it.

"What if I should lose it?" he said.

"You can't," smiled Frank. "There is no danger of that."

"Still, I rather wish you were coming along."

"I can't do that without getting dismissed from recitation, and that isn't possible."

"Well, I will do the job quickly, and I'll have it finished by the time your class is through reciting."

So they parted, and, with the precious ring in his possession, Hodge hurried to the room where the microscope was kept, having provided himself with the necessary materials for making the drawing.

He lost no time in getting to work, and he made rapid progress. As the drawing developed, he grew excited and enthusiastic, for he plainly saw it must be a map of some wild bit of country.

"I'll bet the man who can read this correctly and knows where this country is located, can go straight to a fortune!" muttered the lad. "But I do not see how it is going to benefit anybody who does not know what section of the country this map represents."

It was a warm spring day, and Bart had opened a window near the table at which he was working. A pleasant breeze was stirring.

Although he took care to be quite accurate, it did not take the lad long to complete the drawing.

He was examining it carefully to make sure he had omitted nothing and had made no errors, when a strong wind sucked through the building, swinging open the door of the room.

He rose hastily to close the door, when another breath of wind set the paper on which he had been drawing fluttering across the table. He sprang to catch it, but it avoided his fingers and fluttered out of the window. Thrusting his head forth, he saw it sail away and settle slowly at the foot of one of the great trees amid which the academy buildings stood.

Out of the room darted Bart, and down the stairs he bounded. He was soon outside, and, recovering the paper, which he readily found, he hastened back.

"Great Scott!" he muttered. "I left that ring under the microscope!"

The thought that he had allowed the ring to escape his sight for a moment filled him with anxiety.

What if he should not find it where he had left it a few moments before?

A cold sweat started out on his face, and he literally tore up the stairs and rushed headlong into the experimenting room, the door of which he had left open.

And then, when he looked for the mysterious ring, he found it had vanished!

CHAPTER XXXV.

MORE DANGER.

one!"

Bart staggered as if he had been struck a heavy blow, and his face grew ghastly pale, while his eyes stared at the spot where he had last seen the ring.

It was truly gone. In some surprising manner it had disappeared from the room while he was in pursuit of the paper, astonishing though such a thing seemed.

For a few moments Hodge was quite overcome by this discovery. He sank weakly into a chair, wringing his hands and breathing hoarsely.

How had it happened?

It did not take Bart long to decide that some one must have slipped into the room and stolen the ring while he was after the drawing.

In that case, whoever committed the theft must have been watching for an opportunity, knowing that he had the ring.

Hodge quickly recovered from his stupefied condition, and dashed out into the corridor to look for the miscreant.

"It must have been Snell," was his decision. "I will look for the sneak."

Straight to Snell's room he rushed, but Snell's roommate, who was studying, declared Wat had not been there in the past hour.

This put Bart at sea for a moment. Where could he find Snell?

Looking at the recitation board, he saw that Snell should appear in the recitation room in a very few minutes.

He could not be confronted there. What plan of action could be devised?

He did not wish to give Snell time enough to conceal the ring. If the fellow could be caught with it still in his possession, it might be possible to make him disgorge.

It was time for Frank to return from recitation. The thought of facing Merriwell with the confession that the ring was gone made Bart's knees weak; but he decided that that was the proper course to pursue, and so he hurried to their room.

Frank had just got in, and, by the look on Hodge's face, he instantly saw that something of an alarming nature had happened.

"The ring!" he cried. "Where is it?"

"I think Wat Snell has it," came huskily from Bart's lips.

With one bound, Merriwell caught his companion by both shoulders, staring straight into his face.

"Have you, also, turned? No! no!" he quickly went on. "I do not think that of you, Bart! You are still true!"

"No, I didn't go back on you," said Hodge, thickly; "but I was guilty of criminal carelessness."

"How did it happen? Tell me quick!"

Bart did so, speaking swiftly, so that no more moments were wasted.

"It is probable that Snell has it," said Frank. "He must be apprehended without delay. Come."

He took the lead, and Bart followed at his heels.

But they were not to confront Wat Snell at the door of the recitation room, as Merriwell hoped, for they were not long in learning that the fellow had lately obtained a pass and left the grounds. According to Snell, his uncle was to pass through Fardale village on the noon train, and Wat's presence was desired at the station.

Of course both Frank and Bart immediately decided that this excuse had been used to enable him to reach the village and deliver the stolen ring to the man in black.

For all of their desire to pursue Snell hotly, they were unable to leave without permission, and so valuable time was lost. At length, however, they were on the highway, running side by side toward the village.

Frank had seemed cool and clear-headed, but, not knowing that Bart had fully completed the drawing of the lines on the black stone, in his heart he was feeling very desperate indeed.

Hodge had grown thoroughly angry, and Snell was likely to get hurt when Bart placed hands upon him.

The boys were good runners, and they covered the distance between the academy and Fardale village in a very short time.

Once within the village, they began inquiring for Snell, and it was not long before they discovered people who had seen him. To the post office they went, and then they were told that a boy answering Snell's description had been seen going toward the railway station.

"It would be a corker if the fellow had really come to see his uncle!" said Bart.

"I do not take any stock in that now," declared Frank.

"Nor I; but I don't understand why he is making so many twists and turns since reaching the village. If he has the ring, why didn't he take it straight to the man in black?"

"Perhaps he knows as little about where to find that individual as we do."

"Possibly."

They came in sight of the station, about which were several carriages, while a few people were seen on the platform, waiting for the midday train.

Reaching the station, they came sharply round the first corner, and found themselves face to face with Wat Snell and the man in black.

At that very instant Snell accepted some money and surrendered something to the stranger.

Frank's keen eyes saw that the something was the stolen ring.

With a cry, he leaped forward, flinging Snell aside, and grasping the man.

"Give me that ring!"

A fierce exclamation of fury broke from the stranger's lips, and he swiftly thrust the ring into his pocket.

"Hands off, boy!" he hoarsely commanded. "Hands off, or you will get hurt!"

"I'll never take my hands off you till you give up that ring, you scoundrel!"

The man having encountered Frank before, well knew that the boy possessed remarkable strength, which would not make it an easy thing to shake him off.

"Let go!" he hissed.

"I will not!"

"Then take that!"

Something bright and gleaming, like the blade of a knife, flashed in the man's hand. He struck, and with a cry, Frank, fell heavily to the platform!

CHAPTER XXXVI.

THE SECRET OF THE RING.

Astonished and horrified though he was, Bart Hodge realized that Frank had been stabbed. At that moment, with the lack of resolution that was characteristic of him on occasions of peril, and not through fear, he stood quite still and did nothing.

Without a shout or a sound, the man in black leaped toward the end of the station, where a saddled and bridled horse was hitched to a post.

One slash of the knife set the horse free, and the desperate man leaped to the creature's back, riding rapidly away.

Frank had swiftly risen to his feet, and several persons, who had witnessed the blow, crowded anxiously around him, asking how badly he was hurt.

"It's nothing but a scratch in the shoulder, for I saw it coming, and dodged. Don't mind me. Don't let that man get away!"

"He won't get very fur on that hoss," said the owner of the animal. "She's lame in her off hind foot, an' she'll tarnal soon give out if he pushes her like that."

"Still he will get away if he is not immediately pursued. Come—who'll follow?"

"Into this carriage, boy!" cried a man. "I have a little horse here that will give him a hot chase. Come on!"

"I am the constable," said another man, with great dignity. "I'll foller as soon as I can get a boss saddled."

Realizing that the boy was not seriously hurt, half of those who had been lingering about the station made a rush to join in the pursuit of the murderous stranger. All kinds of teams were pressed into use, and the road was soon filled with a string of pursuers.

Looking back anxiously, the man in black saw them coming, and he grated his teeth fiercely, for he had already discovered that the horse he had appropriated was seriously lamed.

"Let 'em come!" he cried. "I'll not be taken easily! I have the key to a fortune in my pocket, and I will escape with it, if it is in me to do so!"

Ruthlessly and cruelly he pricked the lame mare with the keen point of the knife, which he still held in his hand, and a trail of dust rose behind him.

Out of the village and into the country the lame horse bore the fugitive. Not far from Fardale was a big stone quarry, and, by chance, the man had selected the road which skirted the jagged hole in the ground.

His pursuers were gaining on him, and he continued to use the knife mercilessly as the horse bore him along the road past the quarry.

Of a sudden a large dog bounded into the road in front of the man in black, and the horse which the man bestrode gave a snort and whirled sideways, coming with a crash against the rail which ran along by the roadside.

At that point the rail was somewhat rotten, and a shriek of horror broke from the man's lips as he saw it break. He made one desperate effort to spring from the saddle and escape going down into the quarry with the horse, but the pursuers were dismayed to see man and beast disappear into the yawning hole.

"He won't get away to-day, my boy," said the man in the foremost carriage, at whose side was Frank. "We'll find him down at the bottom of the quarry, dead as a flounder."

Finding a place to hitch the horse at the side of the road, the man did so, and they went forward together, while the other pursuers kept coming up.

Reaching the point where the man and horse had fallen into the quarry, they looked down.

Amid the jagged rocks far below were two motionless forms.

"Come," said the man; "we'll go down there by the regular road."

They passed round the quarry till they found a road that wound downward till it reached the bottom. By this road they descended, with scores of others at their heels.

When they came to the man and the horse, great was their astonishment to hear the man moaning and to see him open his eyes and look at them.

"Why, the critter an't dead yet!" exclaimed the constable. "I think it's my sollum duty to arrest him on the spot."

Frank quickly knelt by the side of the mysterious man, who faintly whispered:

"So I didn't kill you, boy. Well, I have crimes enough to answer for. The ring is here in my vest pocket. Take it. It will never do me any good now."

Frank quickly extracted the ring from the man's pocket, and

slipped it upon his finger.

"I am dying," murmured the man.

"Perhaps not. We'll have you taken back to town, and see what a doctor can do for you."

"No use; I wouldn't live to get there. My time has come. The hidden mine will never reveal its riches to me."

"He is really dying," whispered some one in Frank's ear. "He will not live ten minutes. The wonder is that he is alive at all."

"Who are you? and what is the mystery connected with this ring?" hurriedly asked the boy.

"Never mind my name," came faintly from the lips of the dying man. "It would do you no good to know it. I have lived a wild life—a wicked life. This is the end! Fate brought me to Fardale—fate showed me the ring that bore the chart to the lost mine."

The man stopped and closed his eyes, while the ghastly pallor spread over his face.

A hand held a bottle of liquor to his lips, and he swallowed a few drops, which gave him a few more moments of life. Again his eyes unclosed.

"Once I committed murder for that ring," he whispered. "I killed the Mexican who possessed it. It was a crazy hermit who cut that map on the stone. He discovered one of the richest mines in Arizona, and a fantasy of his deranged brain led him to cut the chart upon the stone, for he cared nothing for the gold himself. When he died, he gave the ring to a Mexican who attended him in his last moments, telling him its secret. In Tombstone the Mexican got drunk and boasted of his riches, showing the ring. That night I killed the greaser, and obtained the ring. I had a partner, and he stole the ring from me. How he came to part with it, and how it fell into the hands of your father, boy, is something I do not know."

He was exhausted, and his voice sunk till Frank could not catch the words. Then he lay still, short breaths fluttering his lips.

Frank feared the man would not rally again, but he did, and the boy panted:

"Tell me where this mine is located. What part of Arizona does the chart represent?"

With a last great effort, the dying man whispered:

"Northwest from Tombstone—lies the—Santa—Catarina—mountains. There—there—is——"

His eyes grew glassy—the last faint breath fluttered over his lips—the man of mystery was dead.

The man in black was buried in the cemetery just outside Fardale village, and the small stone which Frank Merriwell caused to be placed at the head of his grave bears the word "Unknown."

The man had died just as his lips were about to reveal the location of the country depicted by the chart cut on the black stone of the ring that had caused so much trouble. He had mentioned the Santa Catarina mountains, but he had not told what part of the large range the chart depicted.

"If he had lived thirty seconds longer, I should have learned his secret—should have known how to reach the lost mine by aid of the chart. Now——"

"You may be able to reach the mine after all," said Bart, encouragingly. "You have the ring, and you know its value. When you leave school, you may go West and search for your mine, for it certainly belongs to you now. You may find somebody in the Santa Catarina region that will recognize this portion of the country depicted here."

"Long before that the mine may be found by some one else."

"It is possible, but hardly probable. If it were so easy to find, that man would not have made such desperate attempts to obtain possession of the ring."

"Well, I am not going to kick. I have the ring, and his knife did not end my life, as it would if I had not dodged. He slit open my sleeve from the shoulder to the elbow, and brought the blood."

"Oh, you're a lucky dog," laughed Bart. "You are sure to come out on top every time."

Wat Snell found it convenient to take a vacation, but he returned to the academy later, although he found himself regarded with scorn by all save a certain few of his own sort.

Had Frank seen fit, he could have had Wat expelled; but it seemed that, if the fellow had any sense of shame, the way he was treated by the other cadets was quite punishment enough.

Sometimes Frank and Bart would get out the drawing the latter boy had made from the lines on the ring, and they would study over it a long time, but they always found it baffling, and they finally gave up in despair.

Still Frank clung to both ring and chart, hoping they would some day prove valuable to him.

CHAPTER XXXVII.

"BABY."

A year had passed since Frank entered Fardale Military Academy—a year crowded with events and adventures such as made its memory both pleasant and painful.

The time of the June encampment had again arrived.

Frank was no longer a plebe, and the glistening chevrons on his sleeves told that the first year in the academy had not been wasted. He was now Cadet Corporal Merriwell.

The graduates had departed, and the furlough men were away at their homes.

A new squad of plebes had been admitted to the school, and the yearlings, mad with joy at being released from plebedom themselves, were trying every scheme their fertile brains could devise for making miserable the lives of their successors.

During the first two weeks that the plebes had been in the academy the opportunities for hazing them had been few; but immediately on getting into camp the mischievous lads who had suffered the year before, not a few of whom had sworn that nothing in the wide world—nothing, nothing, nothing!—could tempt them to molest a fourth-class man, lost no time in "getting after" the "new stiffs," as the plebes were sometimes called at Fardale.

The yearlings were eager to find fags among the plebes, and they generally succeeded in inducing the new boys to bring buckets of water, sweep the tent floors, make beds, clean up, and do all sorts of work which the older cadets should have done themselves and were supposed to do.

While the penalty for exacting the performance of any menial or degrading task, as well as for hazing, was court-martial and possible dismissal, the yearling generally succeeded in getting the work done without giving orders or making demands, so the plebes could not say they had been coerced into doing those things against their will.

Each yearling sought to have a particular fag to attend to him and his wishes, and no cadet could demand service of another fellow's fag without danger of bringing about trouble.

At first, Frank had resolved to astonish his companions by attending to his own duties entirely by himself, and having no fag; but it was shortly after the new boys came to Fardale that he saw something that made him change his mind.

Among the plebes was a rather timid-looking, red-cheeked lad, who seemed even further out of his element than did his awkward companions. He was shy and retiring, blushed easily, and, at times, had trouble in finding his voice.

Such a fellow was certain to attract attention at any school, and he was soon singled out as a particular object for chaffing by the yearlings.

He blushed to the roots of his hair on being called "Baby," "Mamma's Boy," "Little Tootsy-Wootsy," and other names of the sort applied to him by the cadets.

His real name was Fred Davis, and of the nicknames given him Baby seemed to stick the best, so it was not long before he came to be known by that almost altogether, the officers and instructors being the only ones who did not use it in addressing him.

At the outset Fred was unfortunate in being singled out for guying by Hugh Bascomb, who was a bully by nature, and whose ideas of fun were likely to be of a vicious order.

Bascomb saw he could plague Davis, and he kept at the little fellow, piling it on unmercifully. In fact, he seemed to take a strong dislike to the boy with the pink cheeks, whom he derisively designated as "the dolly boy," and he lost no opportunity to humiliate Davis.

It happened that, on a certain occasion, Bascomb desired that Fred should lie for him, but, to his surprise, the timid plebe absolutely and firmly declined to lie.

"I—I can't do it, sir," stammered the little fellow. "I'd do it if I could, but I can't."

"Why not, pray?" fiercely demanded Bascomb, towering above the shrinking lad and scowling blackly. "That's what I want to know—why not?"

"Because I promised mother I would not lie, and she—she has confidence in me."

"Oh, she—she has!" mocked Bascomb. "You make me sick—you do! I never took any stock in mamma boys. Now you're going to do as I want you to, or I'll make it hot for you."

"I shall not lie, sir."

"All right; wait till you get into camp. Oh, we won't do a thing to you!"

From that time Bascomb did his best to set his companions against Davis, a fact which Frank soon noted.

Knowing that Bascomb was at heart a bully, Frank immediately saw that Davis would have a hard life during his first months in the academy.

Frank's sympathy went out to the little fellow, who had been so tenderly reared that he knew very little of the harsh ways of the world outside his own home. He resolved that the little plebe should be given a fair show.

Somehow Frank divined that Bascomb intended to secure Davis for his fag, and he resolved to balk the bully in this. So it came about that, on the day that the plebes marched into camp, with their bundles under their arms, Merriwell found an opportunity to take Davis into his tent and instruct him in cleaning shoes and setting things to order.

Fred attended to these things cheerfully, never dreaming that they were not a part of his regular duties. When he had finished, Merriwell said:

"That is very satisfactory, Mr. Davis. Immediately after tattoo you may come round and be shown how to make up beds. In the meantime, if any one else should require you to perform service of a similar nature in any tent other than your own, you may inform them that you have already received instructions from me, and that the state of your health will prevent you from doing too much labor of the kind. Do you understand?"

"I think so, sir."

"Very good. You may go."

Frank's duties kept him very busy during the most of the day. He had little time to look after Davis, and he scarcely gave his fag a thought till after supper, when the dusk of evening was settling over the cove, and the "plebe hotels" had been surrounded at various points by mischievous yearlings. Then he took a fancy to stroll around and see how Baby was getting along.

On his way down the street he passed the tent occupied by Bascomb. He might have walked on, but the low, fierce voice of the big cadet caught his ear, and he distinctly heard these words:

"What's that? You refuse to bring water for me? Have done this kind of work already for Merriwell? So Corporal Merriwell has been compelling a plebe to perform menial services? Well, that might cost him those pretty stripes on his sleeves! What do I care for him! I want you to bring that water, and you will bring it."

"But he told me not to do work of this kind for anybody else but myself," came the faltering voice of Fred Davis.

"Oh, he did? Well, that's interesting! I suppose by that he means to lay claim to you. I wonder what Lieutenant Gordan would say if he knew what one of his particular pets has been up to! We'll see who is best man in this affair. Bring that water!"

"I—I don't want to, sir."

"Well, it doesn't make any difference about that; you'll bring it, whether you want to or not. If you don't, I will——"

"What will you do in that case, Bascomb?" quietly asked Frank, as he stepped lightly and quickly into the tent, and confronted the big cadet, who was towering over Fred Davis in a threatening attitude.

Bascomb recoiled, with a muttered exclamation of dismay.

CHAPTER XXXVIII.

SPORT WITH A PLEBE.

erriwell——!"

Bascomb's face showed he was little pleased by the appearance of Frank.

"I believe you were about to tell Mr. Davis what you would do in case he declined to bring a bucket of water for you, sir," said the yearling with chevrons. "Pray, proceed!"

"This—this is an intrusion!" grated Bascomb.

"Really so?" And Frank's eyebrows were uplifted in mock surprise. "I presumed I would be welcome to the tent of a classmate."

"Well, you are not welcome here," growled the big fellow.

"What are you going to do about it?"

"Nothing. If you haven't the instincts of a gentleman——"

Frank interrupted with a laugh.

"Really that sounds fine from your lips, Mr. Bascomb!" he exclaimed. "You were trying to intimidate one smaller and weaker than yourself a moment ago, and yet you have the nerve to talk of gentlemanly instincts. You seem to be venturing on unfamiliar grounds, sir."

Bascomb glared. He longed to punch Merriwell's head, but he felt that Frank was anxious for him to attempt a move of the sort.

"You're a nice chap to talk of intimidation when you have already forced Baby to fag for you!" he cried, hotly.

"I think Mr. Davis will attest that I neither forced him nor asked him to perform any task for me. I simply gave him a few instructions that were sure to be of material benefit to him. But I heard you demanding service, and seeking to compel it with threats. You know what the penalty is for such conduct."

"And I suppose you are just the kind of a fellow to blow. All right; go ahead."

"I scarcely like your tone or your language, Mr. Bascomb; but I am not going to pick it up here and now. However, you have accused me of making Mr. Davis a fag. I presume you know there is a rule in this school that no man has a right to demand service of another man's fag? Knowing this, you tried to make Mr. Davis perform your duties about the tent. Weren't you treading on rather dangerous ground, sir?"

Bascomb looked at the floor, and muttered something.

"You may not have realized what you were doing," Merriwell went on. "In which case, you are pardonable to a certain degree. But I warn you to let nothing of this kind occur again, or you will have the entire camp down on you."

"I know what you mean," grated Bascomb.

"I am very glad you do," came coolly from Frank's lips. "I hoped to make my meaning plain. And I have something more to say. Since the arrival of the new boys, you have seemed to single Mr. Davis out as an especial object for ridicule and torment. I don't know that you have done so because Mr. Davis is small and scarcely a match for you, but it looks that way. Now, Bascomb, if I were in your place, I would let up. If you persist, you are bound to get yourself into serious trouble. I am going to see that Davis has a fair show, and the fellow who crowds him too hard will have some difficulty with me."

Bascomb forced a mocking laugh.

"You seem to fancy you can set yourself up against the whole battalion," he sneered. "I don't believe any plebe ever got through this school without taking his medicine, and I scarcely think you will be able to pull this one through that way. The fellows are not very fond of pets."

"That's all right. The only thing I ask of you is that you let Davis alone."

"Perhaps I will, and perhaps I won't."

"You will if you know what is good for you."

Again the big fellow glared through the gathering darkness, but Frank met the gaze squarely, and Bascomb's eyes dropped.

"That's all I have to say," came quietly from Frank. "You may go now, Mr. Davis. Don't forget you are to receive instructions in making beds after you answer to your name at tattoo."

"No, sir, I will not forget," said the little plebe, and, making a salute, he hurried away, glad to escape from Bascomb's clutches.

Frank stood looking straight at his big classmate, who made a pretense of disregarding him.

"You should take warning by what has happened to several of your particular friends, Bascomb," he finally said. "Harkins resigned to escape court-martial and dismissal; Gage deserted and ran away, and Snell has become the most unpopular fellow in the academy, and all because———"

"All because they ran against you!" snarled Bascomb, madly. "You have had the greatest luck of any fellow I ever saw; but there is a turning point somewhere. You never miss an opportunity to jump on a fellow, and———"

"Now, you are making a statement that you know is absolutely false, sir!" exclaimed Merriwell. "I have never crowded any fellow, and I have never lost an opportunity to cover as far as possible and honorable any wrongdoing a fellow cadet may have been led into. You may not know that I could have caused Snell's expulsion in disgrace if I had wished, but it is true."

"Oh, you are very generous—exceedingly magnanimous! All the matter is, people don't know it."

"You are at liberty to think what you like about it. I have warned you, and you will do well to heed my warning. That is all I have to say."

Frank left the tent, and continued on his way.

Crowds of cadets gathered here and there near certain "plebe hotels" told where the yearlings were enjoying sport at the expense of the new boys.

As Frank came near to the first collection, the familiar voice of his former tentmate, Hans Dunnerwust, attracted his attention.

Forcing his way toward the center of the laughing throng, he found Hans catechising a tall, lank country boy named Ephraim Gallup, who was repeatedly forced to explain that he was "from Varmont, by gum," which expression seemed to delight the listening lads more and more with each repetition.

"Vere vos dot Varmont, sir?" demanded Hans, with a great show of dignity. "Vos it a cidy alretty yet, or vos it a village?"

"Oh, yer gol dern ignerent critter—— Er—er—excuse me, sir! I fergot whut I wuz sayin', dam my skin ef I didn't! Varmont is a State, an' one of ther smartest gol derned States in ther Union, by gum!"

"Vos dot so? I subbose you exbect dot Varmont vos peen large enough to be a cidy britty soon, ain'd id?"

"Wal, gol blame my eyes! Don't you know ther difference betwixt a State an' a city? Ef ye don't, I think you'd best go studdy yer jografry some more."

"Don'd ged so oxcited, sir," cautioned the Dutch boy, with a wave of one pudgy hand. "Id don'd peen goot your health for. Vos dot Varmont a broductive Sdate?"

"Productive! Wal, you bet yer last dollar! We kin raise more grass to ther square acre——"

"Vell, how apout hayseeds? You raise dose ub there py der quandity, I pelief me?"

"What makes ye think so?"

"Because your hair vos full of id."

"What's that? what's that?" cried Ephraim, in astonishment, quickly removing his cap and clawing through his hair with his fingers. "Hayseed in my hair? Darned if I believe it!"

The boys roared, and the face of the country lad grew crimson.

"You're havin' a gol derned pile of fun with me," he said, sheepishly. "Wal, sail right in an' have it. I kin stand it."

"Begobs! it's nivver a bit roight at all, at all," said a boy with a rich Irish brogue, and Barney Mulloy pushed his Dutch friend aside. "Av it's a soldier yure goin' to be, me b'y, it's instructions in military tictacks you nade. Now, sur, in case ye wur on guarrud at noight, an' should foind yure post invaded by the simultaneous appearance av the commandant an' corporal av th' guarrud on th' roight, the gineral-in-chafe an' staff on th' left, an' a rigimint av red-headed girrulls behindt yez, all wearin' bloomers an' arrumed to th' tathe wid corrun-brooms an' feather-dusthers, which would yez advance firrust wid th' countysoign?"

This sort of a question, put to a plebe with all sorts of twists and variations, was time-honored at Fardale, whither it had come from West Point, where plebes are puzzled with some variation of it year after year.

The country boy grinned a bit, and, still with his little fingers touching the seams of his trousers and the palms of his hands turned to the front, lifted his left foot and scratched his right shin with his heel, till a sharp rap on the ankle brought the foot down to the ground again, and caused him to brace up stiffly, drawling:

"Gol darned if I wouldn't be so scat I'd surrender on ther spot ter ther red-headed gals in bloomers."

These words do not look very humorous in print, but they sounded comical as they came from the mouth of that raw countryman, and the crowd roared with laughter again.

"Be me soul!" exclaimed Barney. "It's yersilf thot knows a hape more thin Oi thought yez did. Ye show yer good judgmint in surrunderin' to th' girruls, fer wan av thim alone wud capture yez av she set out to, an' ould Nick take th' countysoign—she wudn't nade it!"

Next the country lad was invited to sing, "to develop his vocal organs."

"Oh, say!" he awkwardly grinned. "I can't sing—I really can't, by gum!"

"Oh, you vos too modest alretty yet," declared Hans. "You peen goin' to ged ofer dot britty soon pime-by."

"But I hain't got no voice, an' I can't sing a tune no more than a mule kin."

"Me b'y," said Barney, "Oi admire yer modesty, but ye'll foind it necessary to sing fer th' intertainmint av Ould Gunn an' under professors av ye stay in th' academy, so ye moight as well begin now."

"You'll laff."

"Nivver moind that."

"It will sp'ile me so I can't sing. If I couldn't see ye laff I might do——"

"Dot vos all righdt," declared Hans. "You bet my life we been aple to feex dot britty soon right avay queek. Shust gif me your bocket handerkerchief."

"Whut you want of it?"

"Nefer you mindt dot. Shust gif me to id."

The country boy produced the handkerchief, and Hans quickly folded it in a thick strip about three inches wide.

"Now I feex id britty shlick so you don'd see us laugh oudt loudt," he said, as he quickly tied the handkerchief over the boy's eyes, while several of the others made Ephraim submit and stand with his little fingers still glued to the seams of his trousers.

In a few seconds the boy from Vermont was securely blindfold-ed.

"Now you sing dot song," commanded Hans.

"Whut shell I sing?"

"'Yankee Doodle,' begobs!" cried Barney. "It's patriotic songs Ould Gunn admoires."

"I can't git the tune," said Ephraim, "an' I don't know the words of only jest one varse."

"Well, sing pwhat yez know, an' kape repeating it over an' over till yez are told to stop."

"Dot vos der stuff. Let her go, Gallup!"

So the country lad opened his mouth and began to sing in a droning, drawling way:

"Yankee Dewdle came ter taown
'Long with Cap'n Goodwill,
An' there he saw the boys an' gals
As thick ez hasty poodin'."

"Louder!" commanded several voices.

So Ephraim repeated the stanza, singing still louder.

"Dot vos petter," complimented Hans; "bud id don'd peen loudt enough to blease Lieudenant Cordan."

"Louder! louder!" ordered the yearlings. "Open your mouth and let the sound out. You can never expect to sing if you pen the words up in such a cavern as that."

This time Ephraim shouted the words at the tops of his lungs, and he was complimented on all sides, while Barney Mulloy hastily said:

"Kape roight at it, an' kape on singing till ye're towld t' stop by me. Ye know my voice, an' don't ye moind another thot spakes to yez. Av he kapes bothering av ye, tell him to let ye alone, ur you'll kick th' back-strap av his trousers clane out through th' top av his head. Oi'll shtand by yez. Now, let her go again, an' kape at it."

The country boy began once more, and this time he bellowed the words so they could be heard for a mile.

The grinning yearlings lost no time in slipping quietly away from that locality, and taking positions at a distance, where they could watch what followed.

All alone in the street in front of his tent stood the blindfolded plebe, bellowing the words at the full capacity of his voice, and repeating them over and over.

In a very few seconds Lieutenant Gordan, the regular army officer at the academy, came marching briskly down the street in the dusk, his face so red that it almost seemed to glow like a light. Stopping short in front of the lone plebe, he called:

"Sir!"

Ephraim kept on with

"An' there he saw the boys an' gals
Ez thick ez hasty poodin'."

"Sir!" came sharply from the lieutenant.

Ephraim began the stanza over again, roaring it louder than before, if possible:

"Yankee Dewdle came to taown
'Long with Cap'n Goodwin——"

"Sir!" cried Lieutenant Gordan.

"Git aout!" snorted the boy from Vermont. "I'm here ter sing, an' I'm goin' ter fill ther bill, by gum!"

Then he began at the first of the stanza, and howled straight through it, for all that the lieutenant spoke to him twice.

In the dusky shadows not far away the cadets were convulsed with laughter they could not suppress.

"Sir!" thundered Lieutenant Gordan, "you are making a fool of yourself!"

"Ef you don't shut up an' stop interruptin' me, I'll be gol darned ef I don't kick you clean inter the middle uv next week! You ain't ther feller that sot me ter singin', fer your voice is of a diffrunt color than his. Naow you keep mum, ur I'll take this handkerchief off my eyes, spit on my hands, an' sail right into you, by thunder!"

Then Ephraim began once more:

"Yankee Dewdle came to taown
'Long with——"

The exasperated lieutenant snatched the handkerchief from Ephraim's eyes, almost bursting with rage.

"If you don't quit this howling, I'll lodge you in the guardhouse!" he declared.

The boy came near smashing the lieutenant with his fist, and then, seeing who it was, he gave a gasp and nearly fainted on the spot.

"Where's them fellers?" he murmured, looking around for his tormentors. "By gum! they've slipped! I've bin fooled!"

After giving him some sharp advice, the lieutenant sent him into his tent, and departed.

CHAPTER XXXIX.

AN OPEN INSULT.

The spirit of mischief seemed to break loose in the camp that night. A dozen times were some of the plebes hauled out of bed and slid around the streets enveloped in their own blankets, ridden on a tentpole, or an old wheelbarrow, tossed in tent flies, or nearly smothered with smoke that filled their tents from the burning of some vile-smelling stuff.

Time after time was the guard turned out to capture the perpetrators of these tricks, but still alarm followed alarm, and not one of the jokers was captured.

Every inspection seemed to show the older cadets all in their beds and sleeping with amazing soundness, considering the racket that was going on.

Lieutenant Gordan was at his wits' end, for never had there been such an outbreak in camp since his coming to Fardale, and he began to believe there was something radically wrong about the system as enforced at the academy.

The professors were driven from their tents and compelled to take refuge in the academy in order to get any sleep, and they all felt like resigning their positions and seeking occupations in other walks of life.

At West Point such things were once possible, but the introduction of long rows of gas lamps put an end to it by illuminating the camp so that the pranks could not be performed without the greatest danger of detection.

At Fardale the gas lamps were missing, and a dark night during the first weeks of each yearly encampment was certain to be a wild night.

It happened that Fred Davis had been assigned to guard duty on this particular night, and, for a long time, none of the disturbances took place on his post.

At length, however, when things had been quiet for an ominous length of time, Fred saw three figures coming swiftly toward him through the darkness.

"Halt!" he commanded, promptly. "Who comes there?"

"The corporal of the guard," was the reply, given in a muffled tone of voice.

"Advance, corporal of the guard, and give the countersign."

Then followed a suspicious hesitation. Fred fancied he heard a faint sound in his rear, but, before he could make a move, a blanket was thrown over his head, and he was hurled to the ground.

He struggled with surprising strength, but he was helpless in the hands of his assailants. His musket had been torn from his hands, and he seemed to feel something slitting and tearing his clothing. Once he was struck or kicked with great violence.

After a few moments of this treatment, Davis managed to get his head clear of the enfolding blanket and shout for help. His cries produced another alarm in camp, and his assailants quickly took to flight, leaving him in a badly battered condition.

Fred got upon his feet, and was standing dazed and bewildered when the corporal of the guard actually appeared, with the guard at his back.

Lieutenant Gordan, who had been on the alert for another outbreak, showed up at the same time; but Davis was so bewildered that it was several moments before he could answer their questions.

It was finally found that he had been robbed of his gun, his belt slashed, and his uniform cut in half a dozen different places, so it was quite ruined.

By this time Lieutenant Gordan was thoroughly angry, and he declared he would give his time and attention during the next week to the discovery and punishment of the perpetrators of the outrage.

"There is going to be an end to this hazing of sentries," he asserted. "Somebody shall be made an example of, and we'll see if that will do any good."

Fred was told to go to his tent and get to bed, and he was only too glad to do so.

Somehow, in the morning, the report got around that Davis had been stabbed or cut in the attack upon him. Frank lost no time in investigating, finding his fag attending to duties about his own tent.

In answer to Merriwell's questions, Fred said he had not been cut in any way, but his clothing had been mutilated, and he had been robbed of his gun, cartridge-box and bayonet-scabbard. He showed Frank his clothing, and the latter was scarcely less indignant than Lieutenant Gordan had been.

"This is not fun," Merriwell declared. "It is malicious and wanton brutality, and I fancy I can lay my hands on the fellow who was at the bottom of it."

The search for Fred's rifle had proved unsuccessful, and so he was given another from the armory, while a new uniform was ordered for him.

Lieutenant Gordan came around, and questioned the unlucky plebe again concerning the assault upon him; but it had been too dark for him to recognize any of his assailants, and the voice of the fellow who had announced himself as corporal of the guard had been muffled and disguised.

It now began to appear that the unusual activity during the night had been for the purpose of drawing the attention to the side of the camp opposite Davis' post, so that the attack upon him might be carried out successfully.

The boys found enough to think of and talk about during such opportunities as were given them.

At dinner the conversation was almost entirely about the tumultuous events of the night, and, by keeping eyes and ears open, Frank sought to discover who knew the most concerning those things which had taken place.

Bascomb seemed in high spirits. Over and over, in a sarcastic way, he repeated Lieutenant Gordan's assertion that such actions were outrageous, and must be stopped, appearing very grave as he did so, but winking slyly to some particular friend.

And Frank noted every fellow to whom Bascomb winked.

The big fellow could not keep his bullying propensities suppressed, and the sight of Fred Davis seemed to arouse him. Singling out the little plebe, he took a station at the opposite side of the table, observing:

"It is really too bad anybody should haze a pretty boy like him. Look at the tender blue in his eyes, and the delicate pink in his cheeks. Isn't he just too sweet to live! Oh, the fellows won't do a thing to him here—not a thing!"

Fred paid no attention to Bascomb, although the hot blood rushed to his face.

The bully continued:

"Before you, gentlemen, masticating his rations, sits a section edition of the late lamented George Washington. Those who are conversant with history are aware that little George found it impossible to tell a lie. Evidently Baby has heard of George, and seeks to emulate the Father of his Country, for he also finds it extremely difficult to tell a lie. Gentlemen, you may, at this very moment, be regarding a future president of the United States. The thought should overcome you with awe."

Bascomb's friends snickered, and the big yearling proceeded to address himself directly to Davis.

"Look here, Baby," he said, "I want you to tell us just what happened to you last night. We want to know the exact facts of the case."

With a trace of spirit, Davis looked up, and asked:

"Don't you, sir?"

"Don't I what?" demanded Bascomb, harshly.

"Don't you know?"

"What do you mean by that? How should I know?"

"I thought you might remember," said Fred, in a low tone.

That was enough to give the bully his opportunity to rave and bluster.

"That is an insult!" he fiercely declared, glaring at the little plebe as if he longed to devour him. "Such an insinuation is an insult! Do you mean to say that I had anything to do with the assault upon you?"

"I don't mean to say anything more about it."

"Oh, you don't? That is actually an open defiance. But I am going to put a question to you, and see if you will refuse to answer me. What do you know about it?"

"I know enough to mind my own business."

Frank laughed softly, and it was Bascomb's turn to flush angrily.

"You are very cool about it," grated the bully, reaching out and picking up a glass of water. "Perhaps this will make you still cooler."

He flung the water full and fair into Fred Davis' face.

CHAPTER XL.

FOR THE UNDER DOG.

In an instant every lad save Davis was on his feet, for all knew what naturally followed an act of this sort.

But the natural order of events did not take place. Davis slowly and carefully wiped the water from his face with the napkin. His hand trembled a little, and his cheeks were pale, the color having fled from them in a moment.

Frank had taken a quick step forward, ready to see fair play.

Although it was generally known that Davis was a peaceful sort of a fellow, who would not get into trouble if he could avoid it, still all expected he would show resentment at this open insult.

Bascomb stood with an insolent sneer on his face, waiting. As Davis made no move, he broke into a short laugh.

"There's courage for you, gentlemen!" he said, scornfully. "Why, the fellow hasn't as much spirit as a dead mouse!"

Frank was about to speak, when Davis slowly rose to his feet.

"I suppose I am expected to fight in a case like this," he said, his voice shaking.

Some of the cadets who were always eager to see a fight of any sort, no matter how unevenly the antagonists might be matched, quickly said:

"That's right. You must fight."

"I have never done such a thing in my life," declared Davis; "but I do feel like it now. You have laughed at me because I promised my mother that I would not lie, and I will give you a chance to laugh again. I promised her I would not fight, and I shall keep my word."

"Baby boy!"

"Mamma's petsie!"

"Softie!"

These terms of derision came from several sources, and Frank was swift to note every one.

Bascomb laughed again.

"You are altogether too good to live, Baby!" he said. "You make me sick!"

Frank had kept quiet as long as was possible. He saw that Davis did not mean to fight, and he made a resolve to save the plebe if possible by taking up his quarrel.

With two swift steps Merriwell confronted Bascomb.

"Sir," he said, speaking rapidly, and in a low tone, "I have been a witness to this entire affair."

"Well?" sneered the big yearling.

"I want to say that I think Davis perfectly right in refusing to fight you. You are larger and older than he is, you have nearly, if not quite, twice as much strength as he has, and your reputation is that of a slugger. He would not stand a show with you, and you know it, for which reason you have seemed to select him as an object of your bullying attentions."

Frank looked Bascomb straight in the eye, and the big fellow's face grew black with anger.

"What do you want?" he muttered.

"I want to tell you what I think of you, and I am going to do so. Davis has been reared like a gentleman, and it is but natural that he should recoil from contact with such as you."

"Do you mean to say I am no gentleman?"

"That is exactly what I mean to say, sir. No gentleman ever plays the bully, as you have done."

Bascomb made a move, as if he would do something desperate, and, on the instant, two of his particular friends caught hold of him, saying hastily:

"Not now, old man—not here! It would spoil everything."

Now Bascomb was not longing for a fight with Merriwell, and he would gladly have done something to cause the officers to interfere; but, to his regret, he saw that he had been too slow about it. So he sullenly muttered:

"All right, fellows; I won't smash him here."

"But you'll meet him later—you'll have to," eagerly said Rupert Reynolds, a fellow who made a pretension of being "sporty," and who was a great admirer of gamecocks and prize-fighters, for which reason he had grown very friendly with the slugger of the academy. "This affair must be settled in the regular manner."

"I didn't suppose I'd have to fight the whole academy," came sulkily from the bully. "If every sneak in school had somebody to step in and fight his battles, things would soon undergo a change."

As he said this, he cast a contemptuous glance at Davis, who was looking on, in a helpless way.

"You may fight or not, as you like," said Frank, serenely. "But you know what I think of a bully who is too cowardly to tackle a fellow he fears may be his match."

And then, unmindful that Bascomb made another move and was held back by his friends, Frank turned his back and walked round the table to Davis.

"Come," he said, "we will go."

There was a murmur of applause when he turned away, with Davis at his side.

Still Frank knew very well that he had taken an unpopular stand by espousing the cause of a plebe who did not seem to have nerve enough to stand up for his own rights, and he was breaking all precedent and traditions by a show of friendliness for his own fag.

However, Frank was a lad who firmly believed in standing by the right, no matter whether the cause were popular or not, and his sympathy was invariably with "the under dog in the fight." He could not bear to see the weak oppressed by the strong.

His generous heart had gone out to the lad who had been so tenderly and delicately reared, and who declined to lie or fight because he had promised his mother he would not do such things. Somehow Davis did not seem at all like a "sissy-boy" to Merriwell, who believed the plebe had a great deal of moral courage, if he were not physically brave. And Frank had come to believe that moral courage is a higher qualification than physical courage.

In this world there are two classes of heroes, and one class is likely to be grievously misunderstood. First comes the physical hero, the fellow who defiantly faces dangers that are sufficient to turn to ice the blood of another, and yet may succumb to some simple temptation that he knows will lead him into wrongdoing.

Then comes the moral hero, who resists the strongest temptations to do wrong, who fights and conquers in many a silent battle with his passions and desires, who bravely faces ridicule and scorn because he is confident that he is doing right, yet who quails, cowers, trembles, and flees in the face of physical danger.

Who will say which is the greater hero?

As soon as they were in the open air, Davis turned to Merriwell, his voice shaking, as he said:

"You must not fight with that fellow on my account."

"Why not?" asked Frank.

"Because you must not. It would not be right. He is big and

strong——"

"But I am not afraid of him."

"That may be true, and still it is not right for you to fight in my place. That will not help me any. I can see that I will not be thought any better of if you fight in my place. You must not fight him!"

Fred was very agitated and excited.

"The matter rests entirely with Bascomb now," said Frank, calmly. "I have expressed my opinion of him in public, and I shall be forced to back up my words if he challenges me."

CHAPTER XLI.

BIRDS OF A FEATHER.

Reynolds and Bascomb came from dinner arm in arm.

"Your time has come to knock out this fellow Merriwell, Hugh," declared the big fellow's sporty companion. "You'll have to do it."

"It looks that way," admitted Bascomb, but there was something ludicrously dubious in both his face and voice.

"Looks that way!" exclaimed Rupert, in a fiery manner. "Of course it looks that way. There's nothing else to be done, and I should think you'd be well satisfied with the opportunity."

"But I am not sure I can do it," confessed the bully, hesitatingly.

"Do it! Why, you ought to do it with one hand tied behind your back."

But Bascomb was not so easily reassured.

"I have boxed with him," said the big fellow, "and I know he is not easy fruit for anybody."

"You boxed in the gym?"

"Yes."

"And there it was necessary to conform to certain rules."

"Of course."

"That wasn't much like a genuine fight."

"I know it; but I found it impossible to hit him a soaker with my left. He is up to all the tricks."

"That's all right. Fight him in the evening, where you are not liable to be interrupted till you have finished him. The darkness will be an advantage to you, for he cannot see to guard or avoid all your heavy blows, and you will soon do him up. If you work it right, you can get him into a straight fight from start to finish, so it will not be a matter of rounds, which would accrue to his advantage. Once you get at him, you can follow him up till he is done for."

Reynolds' words gave Bascomb new courage.

"I don't know but you are right," he said. "The darkness would be to my advantage, and I ought to be able to get in a knockout blow sooner or later. By Jupiter! I believe I can polish him off!"

"Of course you can!" exclaimed his delighted companion. "Merriwell has put on a big front, and succeeded in making everybody believe he is a terror, but the time has come to cook his goose. Give him a good licking, and he will not be so high and mighty. His popularity will mighty soon begin to wane."

"You do not seem to love him."

"Not much! The cad has called me down on parade several times."

"Me, too."

"I'd like to get a grip on him that would disgrace him and cause his dismissal."

"You are not the first fellow who has thought that way, but, somehow, the cad has the luck to get out of every trap set for him, and he turns the tables on anybody who tries to trap him."

"He can't be that lucky always."

"I should hope not."

"Shall I act for you?"

Bascomb hesitated. Something told him that Frank could fight quite as well with his bare fists as he could box with gloves. But how could he retreat? If he did not meet Merriwell he would be regarded with scorn by every one, and, like Wat Snell, who had refused to meet Bart Hodge, be ostracised in the school.

"Davis ought to fight me first," he muttered.

"Oh, hang that plebe!" cried Reynolds, contemptuously. "He doesn't count with Merriwell. You can attend to him when you have disposed of Merriwell. If you go into this business determined to finish the fellow, you'll be sure to do it. Knock him out some way, fair or foul."

"I suppose a fellow might get at him foul in the dark, and not be detected."

"Sure. Only he wants to be slick about it. Say, I can tell you a trick."

"'Sh! Don't speak too loud; Dunnerwust and Mulloy are a little distance behind, and they're both particular friends to Merriwell."

So Reynolds lowered his voice, and talked rapidly to Bascomb in a low tone. The bully listened eagerly, finally slapping his thigh and crying:

"That's the scheme! That will do it!"

"Shall I see him, and make arrangements for tonight?"

"Yes; but wait till the last minute—take him after supper."

"All right. It's settled then?"

"All settled; and Merriwell will have a dandy pair of eyes on him to-morrow!"

Dunnerwust and Mulloy had been watching Bascomb and Reynolds.

"Vot you pelief dose shneaks vos down to, ain'd id?" asked the Dutch boy.

"Well, Handy, me b'y," replied Barney, "it's me proivate opinion, which Oi don't moind publicly ixprissing, thot they're plannin' mischief."

"Yaw, I pets me your boots you vos righd. Dey don'd haf their headts togeder near vor nottings, py shimminy!"

"Oi'd loike to take th' spalpanes by th' ears an' rap their hids togither wance," declared the Irish lad. "Oi'd make thim see stars."

At this moment Bascomb clapped his thigh and cried:

"That's the scheme! That will do it!"

"Uf dot don'd mean somedings, Parney, you vos a liar!" exclaimed Hans.

"Av course it do."

"I pelief me dot means drouble vor Frankie."

"Oi wouldn't wonder, Handy."

"You und me hat pesser dell him to keep his vedder eye vide open tight, ain'd id?"

"Thot's pwhat we will, me b'y. An' Oi propose to watch thim spalpanes a bit mesilf. Oi moight catch 'em at something crooked, Oi belave."

So it came about that Frank was warned that Bascomb and Reynolds had apparently been plotting.

Frank acted as first sergeant, and that very afternoon both Bascomb and Reynolds appeared in ranks with their belts disarranged. This was an open defiance, and, of course, was something Merriwell could not overlook.

"Fall out, Bascomb, and arrange your belt," he commanded, sharply. "You, too, Reynolds. You know very well that you have no right in ranks in that shape. Fall out!"

Bascomb and Reynolds obeyed in a sullen way, the big fellow beginning to mutter.

Merriwell had started back to his post, but he whirled sharply, saying:

"Silence, sir! This is the third time I have been compelled to warn you against muttering in ranks. You will be severely dealt with in case you repeat the offense."

Once more he turned, but he had not taken five steps before he heard some one say:

"Who's playing the bully now!"

Frank turned again, but Bascomb did not appear to have spoken, and Reynolds looked innocent. Having fixed their belts, they were again in ranks, standing at ease.

Not a word did Frank say, but his face expressed a great deal. No further murmurs were heard, and the drill was soon in progress; but Frank knew his enemies had tried to place him in a false light before the corps.

CHAPTER XLII.

THE CHALLENGE.

hat night, immediately after supper, Rupert Reynolds appeared at the door of Frank's tent.

"Mr. Merriwell," said Reynolds, stiffly, "I am here in the interest of my friend, Mr. Bascomb."

"I presumed as much," came quietly from Frank's lips.

"You have openly insulted Mr. Bascomb, and he demands an immediate apology."

Frank whistled.

"Is that all?" he exclaimed, with a queer twist of his face and a twinkle in his eyes.

"You will find this a very serious matter, sir," said Reynolds, with an assumption of great dignity.

"Mr. Bascomb may also find it serious."

"Will you apologize?"

"You may tell Mr. Bascomb that I will apologize to him when he is man enough to apologize to Fred Davis, and publicly acknowledge that he treated the little plebe in an unmanly and bullying manner."

Reynolds made a scornful gesture.

"Mr. Bascomb will not do anything of the kind!"

"Very well; I shall not apologize to him."

"Then you must fight him."

"I will do so with the greatest of pleasure."

"Oh, you won't find much fun in it," sneered Reynolds. "It isn't going to be that kind of a fight. Bascomb is thirsting for your life. It was with the greatest difficulty I persuaded him not to challenge you to fight a duel with deadly weapons. He said he would take satisfaction in meeting you in an affair of honor where he could run a blade through your body or perforate you with a bullet."

Frank whistled again.

"Why, he has become very courageous since he took to bullying boys! He is really bloodthirsty."

"He is determined to square accounts with you, sir. He says you have been boning military at his expense for some time, just to show your authority."

"Which he knows is absolutely false," Frank flashed back. "I have reprimanded him when compelled to do so by his utter disregard of what is right."

"That may be your opinion; Mr. Bascomb thinks differently. He demands that this fight take place without delay."

"The sooner the better."

"What do you say to making the time immediately after dark?"

"I am agreeable."

"As Lieutenant Gordan has been watching the old boathouse of late, it will be necessary to have the fight take place elsewhere."

"All right."

"It may be stopped if it is anywhere in this vicinity."

"Yes."

"Black Bluff is but a mile away."

"That's all."

"Why not go there?"

"The place is satisfactory to me."

"Then it is settled. Be on hand with your second as soon as possible after dark."

"I will."

Reynolds walked away with his head held very high and his neck very stiff.

Of course, the boys had been expecting Frank would receive a challenge, and no small number had been watching the two lads. Immediately on Rupert's departure, Frank's friends came swarming around him, asking scores of questions.

"Pwhat did th' b'y want wid yez, Frankie?" asked Barney Mulloy, eagerly.

"Oh, not much," smiled Frank, who did not believe in letting the entire gathering know exactly what had happened and what was going to take place. "He informed me that Bascomb demands an apology. Of course, I did not apologize, which may lead Bascomb to challenge me."

"An' he didn't challenge yez alridy? Wurra! wurra! Oi thought there moight be a foight on hand, so Oi did."

"Dot's vot's der madder mit me," sighed Hans Dunnerwust, in disappointment. "It vos peen so long alretty yet since I haf seen a scrap dot I don'd know vot it vos."

"G'wan wid yez, Dutch!" cried Barney, who was in ill-humor on account of the failure—as he supposed—of Bascomb to challenge Merriwell. "Thot Yankee from Vermont called yez a balloony sausage t'-day, an' ye nivver did a thing. Av ye wur dying fer a foight, ye'd challenge him. Ye're th' biggest coward on th' face av th' earth. Ye give me distriss!"

"Vos dot so!" retorted Hans. "Don'd you pelieve me! Vos id my blace to fight mit a blebe?"

"Of course it is yer place, ye ignoramus."

"Vell, I didn't know dot. Maype I fight him some dime pime-py right avay soon alretty yet."

"Oh, no ye won't."

"Von't I?"

"No, ye won't dare, ye Dutch coward. Av ye had a bit av spunk in yer body, ye'd challenge him to wance."

"Vell, you pet me my boots I don'd vos a coward," declared Hans, emphatically. "I'll vight dot feller!"

"Thot's th' shtuff, me b'y!" cried the delighted Barney. "Let me take th' challenge."

"Nod py a plamed sight! I don'd vant a pog-drotter to done some uf dot peesness for me, ain'd id? Uf I shoose mein second, I dakes Vrankie Merrivell alretty!"

For all that he had serious work on hand, Frank was ready for a frolic, and he instantly said:

"I will carry your challenge, Hans. You may depend on me."

"All righd, Vrankie, my poy; led her go."

"You wish me to hunt up Ephraim Gallup, and demand an apology or a fight?"

"Yaw."

"And you really mean it?"

"Yaw."

"Will you fight if he agrees to meet you?"

"Yaw."

"All right. There can't be any backing out now, understand that. You are in for a fight, if Gallup doesn't apologize."

"Yaw; but you mighd influence him to abologize uf you couldt, ain'd id?"

"It would not be proper to bring any undue influence to bear on him. I shall carry your challenge to him immediately."

As Frank started to find Ephraim Gallup, Barney Mulloy slipped from the crowd and joined him. The Irish lad's eyes were full of mischief.

"I say, Frankie, me b'y," he said, quickly, "can't we put up a job on thot Dutchman, an' hiv som' fun av this, Oi dunno?"

"Leave that to me," smiled Frank. "I fancy I will find a way to get plenty of sport out of this business. You know those two old horse-pistols that are hung up for relics in the armory?"

"Yis."

"Go for them yourself, or send somebody who can get them immediately."

"Pwhat do yez want wid thim?"

"I will show you, if I can make my scheme work."

"Oi belave Oi know," chuckled the fun-loving Irish lad. "Mursha! Won't thot be fun, Oi dunno! Oi'll hiv thim roight away," and off he darted.

As Frank expected, he found Ephraim once more surrounded by a mob who were having sport at his expense. Fortunately for Merriwell's scheme, the country boy was rather angry, and felt more like fighting than doing anything else.

"Mr. Gallup," said Frank, as he forced his way through the throng and confronted the Vermonter, "I am here in behalf of a friend whom you have sorely insulted."

"Git aout with yer nonsense!" retorted Ephraim. "I wish you'd quit yer foolin' an' let a feller alone."

"You will discover this is not fooling, sir," said Frank, sternly. "My friend demands that you fight him immediately. Will you do it?"

"Wal, I be twisted if I don't!" snorted Ephraim, as he spat on his hands and prepared to remove his coat. "Where is ther consarned critter? I'll bark his nose quicker'n a brindle caow kin kick over a pail of milk, by gum!"

CHAPTER XLIII.

DOUGHTY DUELIST.

Ephraim was in earnest.

"Hold on," said Frank, quickly, "what are you going to do?"

"Fight, by gum!"

"But you can't fight here."

"Why not?"

"You would be arrested and placed in the guard tent."

"Wal, ef a feller can't fight, whut ye makin' all this taowse abaout?"

"You can fight, but not within the limits of the camp. The duel must take place outside."

"Who is this consarned critter that says I've insulted him?"

"Mr. Dunnerwust."

"Wal, ef he wants to fight me, he'll find he never dun er wust thing."

Frank staggered and clutched at his heart.

"Don't!" he gasped. "I'm not particularly weak, but I'm not strong enough to stand many of those."

Ephraim grinned all over his long face.

"Oh, them things come natteral like with me," he said. "I kin reel 'em off by ther yard when I git started. Folks up aour away say I'm ther funniest critter that ever growed in them parts."

"Well, you have agreed to meet Mr. Dunnerwust?"

"Yep."

"The meeting must take place without delay, so there may be daylight enough for its consummation."

"Is that anything good to eat?"

"What?"

"Consummation."

"Not exactly."

"Didn't know but 'twas. Sally Golander up aour way she went

to Boston, an' when she kern home she told abaout havin' consummation soup, ur something of that sort. Say, you'd oughter seen that air gal arter she got back from Boston! She put on more style than a prize pig at a caounty fair, by gum! Why, you couldn't touch her with a ten-foot pole! She walked as ef she'd fell daown an' stepped on the small of her back, and she ripped open ther sleeves on ev'ry one of her dresses, an' bought caliker an' stiffenin' an' stuff ter put inter 'em to make 'em swell aout like a blowed-up bladder. I tell you she did cut an amazin' fast pace in aour taown."

"You are wandering from the issue," said Frank. "I presume you will be ready to proceed to the scene of the duel in a few moments?"

"Ready any time."

"All right. Choose your second."

"Whut do you mean by that?"

"You have to have somebody to look out for you and see that you have fair play."

"By chaowder! Ephraim Gallup kin look aout for hisself, an' don't you fergit it!"

"But it is absolutely necessary that you have a second."

"I'll act for Mr. Gallup," said Sammy Smiles. "He may depend on me to stand behind him as long as he stands in front of me."

"You'll do well ez anyboddy."

"All right, Mr. Smiles," said Frank, with a wink at Sammy. "Come aside, and we will make all arrangements."

It did not take long to make arrangements; but, as every one who knew about it was anxious to see the fun, it was not a little difficult for them all to get out of camp without attracting too much attention. There was a strip of woods close by, however, and the boys succeeded in vanishing into this cover one by one, after which they soon hastened to the spot where the encounter between Dunnerwust and Gallup was to take place.

The seconds took good care to have the two principals on hand, and Barney Mulloy was there with the old horse-pistols, which he kept carefully concealed.

Frank took Hans aside and said:

"This affair has assumed a much more serious aspect than seemed possible at first."

"Vos dot Yankee abologized alretty yet?" asked Hans, anxiously.

"Far from it."

The Dutch boy gave a groan of dismay, but stiffened up to say:

"Dot seddles his coose! I knocks uf him der sduffins oudt."

"But he refused to fight that way, and, as he is the challenged party, I was forced to allow him to select the weapons. He chose pistols."

"Bistols?" gasped Hans, turning pale.

"Yes."

"Dot vos murter in der virst degree! I don't meed dot veller mit bistols!"

"But you will have to meet him now. If you refuse, you will be drummed out of school—you will be tarred and feathered."

"Bud I don'd like dot peesness uf sdanding oop to be shod ad mit a pullet oudt uf a bistol. Somepody mighd ged hurt, ain'd id?"

"Oh, there's no danger that you'll get hurt any more than to have a bullet through your head."

"Vot vos dot?" gurgled Hans. "A pullet drough mein headt. Shimminy Gristmas! Uf dot don'd vas pad enough, vot you vant? Oxcuse me!"

"Now, don't show the white feather," urged Frank. "That Yankee has done this to scare you. I don't believe he really thinks you will dare meet him with pistols, and so he is going to make a laughing stock of you."

"Vos dot his game? Vell, I pets you your life he makes der piggest misdake vot he nefer seen."

"That's the stuff! If you brace right up and pretend you are eager to fight with pistols, the chances are ten to one he'll back down before the word is given to fire."

"Vell, uf dot veller don'd dink I vos apout grazy for dot tuel, you can kick me mit der neck in."

Frank saw that he had fixed it all right with Hans, and he wondered what success Sammy Smiles was having with his second.

Sammy was not finding it very easy to convince Ephraim it was his duty to fight a genuine duel with pistols, and he was talking swiftly, for it was past sunset, and would become dark in a very short time.

"I be hanged ef this air ain't ther biggest scrape I was ever in!" gasped the lank country boy, wiping the cold sweat from his forehead. "I wish I'd stayed away frum this thunderin' skewl, an' bin contented ter keep right on hoein' 'taturs an' cuttin' grass daown on dad's old farm. Say, ain't ther no way this air matter kin be settled up 'thout shewtin'?"

"It's too late for that now. You have accepted Dutchy's challenge, and you'll have to fight this duel."

"I never was so thunderin' scat in all my life, by gum! My knees don't feel strong enough to hold me up. Haow duz a feller feel when he's goin' ter faint away?"

"Oh, you're not going to faint. That's what the Dutchman's counting on. He wants to scare you out of it. He's even made his boasts that you Yankees haven't any courage, and that you'll run."

"Oh, he has, has he?" grated Ephraim. "Bust his skin!"

"He doesn't believe you'll dare fight him," continued. Sammy, concealing a grin with his hand. "That's what he's counting on. If you put on a bold front, you'll scare him out of his shoes. I'll bet he'll run away before the word is given to fire."

"Think so?" asked the Vermonter, eagerly. "Do ye really?"

"Of course. Look how much more of him there is than there is of you. Why, you'd be sure to hit him the first shot, while he has not one chance in a hundred of hitting you. He has been chuckling over the way your long legs will look when you run away."

"That settles it, by the jumping blizzards! Give me holt of that air hoss-pistil! I'll show him whuther a Yankee'll run ur not, by chaowder!"

"That's the stuff!" complimented the delighted Sammy, reaching up to pat the tall plebe on the back. "Stick to that, and you will scare him into convulsions. You must look as fierce and desperate as you can, so he'll think you are thirsting for his gore."

The preliminaries were soon over, and the valiant duelists were placed facing each other at a distance of fifteen paces. The old pistols, loaded with heavy charges of powder, but minus bullets, were thrust into their hands.

CHAPTER XLIV.

A COMEDY DUEL.

Both Hans and Ephraim were ghastly pale. The Dutch lad's teeth were chattering, and the Yankee boy's knees shook beneath him. But both tried to put on a bold front.

"Are ye ready, jintlemin?" demanded Barney Mulloy, who had been chosen to give the word.

"Vait a moment," commanded Hans, waving his hand frantically at Barney. "I vos goin' to gif dot feller a shance to safe his life. Uf he vants to abologize now I vont shood him drough der heart mit a pullet."

"Hurry up this business!" blustered Ephraim, waving the big pistol. "If ye fool around here all night it will git so thunderin' dark I can't see ter hit ther middle button on the Dutchman's coat."

"Vos you goin' to abologize?" shouted Hans.

"Be you goin' to run away?" demanded Ephraim.

"Uf you don'd abologize, I voss a dead man," cried the Dutch lad, threateningly.

"Ef you don't run away, you're a dead man," declared the Vermonter.

Now it happened that Sammy Smiles had brought along some stale eggs which he had been keeping for some festive occasion, and he had given one of them to Frank, while they had come to a perfect understanding as to the proper manner and the right moment to use them. With the eggs concealed in their hands, they were waiting for Barney to give the word.

"Come, come, jintlemin," called the Irish lad, sharply. "Take yer positions, fer Oi'm goin' t' give th' worrud."

"This is your last chance to run away, Dutchy," faltered Ephraim, who seemed to be losing confidence.

"Dis vos your lasd obbortunity to abologize, Yankee," said Hans, rather weakly.

"Ready to foire at th' worrud," called Barney.

Hans' teeth were plainly heard to rattle together like dice.

"One!" counted Barney.

"Uf he don'd run avay, I vas reaty to hear him abologize," murmured the Dutch lad.

"Say!" Ephraim hoarsely whispered to Sammy. "Git a rope an' tie me, quick! Hang me ef I don't believe my legs is goin' to run the best I kin do."

"Two!" counted Barney.

"Shimminy Gristmas! vere vas someding I can hide pehind?"

"Great thutteration! I'm a goner!"

"Three—fire!"

Both of the bold duelists turned their heads away, pointed the pistols at something, and fired.

Bang! bang!

Frank and Sammy Smiles let the eggs fly, and the aim of both was accurate.

Sammy's egg struck Hans behind the right ear, and spattered all over the side of the Dutch lad's head, while Frank's egg landed on Ephraim's neck.

"I vos a deadt man!" squawked the Dutch lad, as he went over in a heap.

"I'm shot, by gum!" squealed the Yankee, as his knees collapsed and he measured his long length upon the ground.

"Smoke!" cried Barney Mulloy, grasping his nose with both hands. "It smells loike ye'd both been corpuses fer a long toime!"

"By Jove!" gasped Frank. "That odor is strong enough to lift a safe!"

The other witnesses of the duel roared with laughter, but Hans was bellowing and Ephraim was groaning so loudly that neither of them heard the sounds of mirth.

"I can feel mein prains runnin' all ofer der side uf mein headt!" howled Hans.

"Send for a doctor!" shrieked Ephraim. "I'm covered with blood! My jubilee vein is cut clean in two, an' ther blood is runnin' down my neck!"

"I vos dyin'!"

"I'll be dead in a minute!"

Sammy Smiles held fast to his nose, and made haste to bend over his principal, whom he pretended to examine.

"Bring bandages!" he shouted. "Help me to stop him from bleeding to death."

"It's nary a bit of use," groaned the Vermonter. "No feller ever lived with his jubilee vein cut in two!"

"Merciful goodness!" cried Frank, in pretended horror, as he hovered over Hans, also taking care to cling to his nose. "The whole top of his head is shot away!"

The Dutch boy gave a wild, despairing wail.

"Und you said dot feller vos goin' to run avay! Dunder und blitsens! I vos a fool dot I don'd run avay meinseluf pefore mein prains he shot oudt!"

"Never mind," said Frank. "You will die like a hero, and we'll bury you with all the honors of war."

"Yah!" snorted Hans. "Dot vos nice—I don'd pelieve! I don'd care apout dot honors uf var! Oh, Shimminy Gristmas! vot a fool a blamed fool vos!"

"I am surprised at you," said Frank, sternly. "You should be proud to perish in such a heroic manner."

"Oh, yaw! I peen tickled to death—mit a pullet. Id vos fun!"

"I am afraid you are not a success as a hero."

"Vell, I dudder peen a success as a coward und kept avay from dot pullet."

In the meantime Ephraim had recovered from the shock sufficiently to detect the powerful odor of the stale egg that had struck him.

"Great gum!" he gurgled. "What was that Dutchman's pistol loaded with? Something must have crawled inter ther pesky thing an' died there!"

"Do you really smell anything?" chuckled Sammy Smiles.

"Do I?" howled the Yankee boy, sitting up and gasping for breath. "I ruther think I do, by gum!"

"You must be mistaken. Being seriously wounded, you imagine it. It is the result of your injury."

"Is that so? Wal," he wildly panted, "if that's ther case, I hope I'll die soon an' git aout of my misery!"

The spectators were convulsed with merriment, and Ephraim began to smell a rat—if, indeed, it were possible to smell anything but the ancient eggs.

"Say!" he snorted, "you fellers don't act like there was anybody dyin' around here. An' by chaowder! this smell is jest ther same ez I struck when I crawled under dad's old barn to find where the speckled hen was layin', an' crunched up some aigs that hed bin there two or three months. Ef that Dutchman loaded his pistol with a ripe aig an' shot me in the neck, I'll paound the stuffin' aout of him, by gum!"

"Vot vos dot?" roared Hans, also sitting up, and glaring at the

Vermonter. "You don'd peen pig enough to bound der sduffin oudt uf nottings!"

"Wal, dern my skin ef I don't show you! Ef I'm mortally shot, it'll be some satisfaction to die thumpin' you, by gum!"

"Keeb avay off!" squawked Hans, as Ephraim began to crawl toward him. "Keeb avay off, ur I vos goin' to bulverize you britty queek right avay soon!"

"You pulverize, an' be hanged! All I want is to git holt of ye."

Hans began to scramble out of the way.

"Holt on! holt on!" he cried. "Dot don'd peen no fair to sdrike a man mit haluf uf his heat plown off!"

"Your head's all right, only one side of it is plastered over with some yaller stuff. You shot me in the neck, and I'm all kivered with blood, but I kin do ye, jest ther same!"

"Dot vos der gweerest colored plood vot I nefer saw! You don'd peen shot ad all."

"Then, by gum! I'm goin' ter lick ye anyhaow!" and Ephraim scrambled to his feet.

"Vell, you don'd done dot till you catch me, py Shimminy!"

Hans also scrambled up, and immediately took to his heels, with the tall Yankee in hot pursuit, leaving the spectators of this ridiculous duel to exhaust themselves with merriment.

CHAPTER XLV.

ANOTHER KIND OF A FIGHT.

It had already grown quite dark.

The fun for the time being was over, but there was an engagement of quite a different nature to take place.

Barely had the Dutch boy disappeared, with the Vermonter at his heels, when Frank and several others of the party slipped away into the shadows and made for Black Bluff.

Bascomb and a large number of his friends were waiting when Frank arrived, and Merriwell heard the big fellow sneeringly observe:

"He has really come at last! I didn't know but he was going to take water. I was afraid I'd lose the satisfaction of giving him the licking he needs."

Frank bit his lip, and remained silent.

Bart Hodge was on hand, and he was quickly at Frank's side.

"Where have you been?" he asked. "I was beginning to fear Bascomb had put up some kind of a job to keep you away, so he could claim you were afraid to meet him."

"I have been acting as second in another affair," said Frank. "I want you to represent me in this. Will you?"

"You have no need to ask that, for you must know that it will give me pleasure. I want to see you give that big brute the drubbing he merits, so he will keep still for a while. He has been trying to injure you ever since you entered the academy, and he has said here to-night that he proposed doing me up to square an old score after he had finished you. I tried to get him to take me first, for I told him there wouldn't be anything left for me to fight when you were through with him. He said he was going to polish you off easily, and he has been whispering and laughing with that sneaking Reynolds. Somehow, I feel as if they have put up some kind of a job to get the best of you, and that is why they feel so well. You want to be on your guard for tricks, old man."

"I will," assured Frank, as he began to "peel" for the fight. "Go over and make arrangements with Reynolds. If you can get him to agree to make it a go-as-you-please till the best man whips you will suit me."

"All right; I'll stand for that."

Away went Hodge to consult with Reynolds, and Frank did not dream that he had proposed just the kind of a fight that Bascomb and his second most desired.

The wind was coming in across the bay, and the sea was moaning at the ragged base of Black Bluff, on the heights of which the fight was to take place. There were scudding clouds in the sky, but the night did not promise to be very dark.

It did not take Hodge long to complete arrangements with Reynolds, and he soon returned to inform Frank that it was to be one straight fight from start to finish, with no rests till one or the other whipped.

Frank had not supposed there would be near so many spectators present, and he well knew that the most of those assembled were fellows who were secretly envious of him because of his popularity, although nearly all had made protestations of friendship in the past.

Frank did not care for the friendship of such fellows, as there was nothing in the world he despised more than a hypocrite. He could respect a foe who was open and frank; but he had no use for anybody who wore two faces.

Fred Davis had not been told where the fight was to take place; but he had scented it in some way, and he came panting to the spot, just as Merriwell and Bascomb were about to meet. He rushed straight to Frank, exclaiming:

"You must not fight on my account! You shall not! You haven't any right to do it! This must stop!"

"Here, Bart," said Merriwell to Hodge, speaking quietly and firmly, "turn this boy over to Mulloy, and tell him to keep Davis from making any fuss."

"But you must listen to me!" cried the little plebe, on the verge of tears. "People sometimes get killed in fights. If you are badly hurt, I'll never forgive myself. Can't I do something to stop it? Why, I will apologize to Bascomb, and——"

"That would simply place you more in contempt, and would not let me out in the least, boy. Take him away, Mulloy," Frank spoke to the Irish lad, who was now at hand. "See that he doesn't get into trouble."

Seeing it was impossible to put an end to the contest, Fred gave up in despair.

Merriwell and Bascomb now faced each other. There was no demand that they should shake hands, and neither offered to do so. The boys formed a circle around them, and, at the word, they leaped at each other and the fray had begun.

Bascomb made an effort to clinch immediately, but Frank landed two blows that sent him staggering. This was an advantage which Merriwell followed up, and Bascomb was forced to keep falling back for some moments, shifting the battle-ground considerably from the point where the struggle began.

Spat! spat! spat! sounded the blows; but it was not always an easy thing to tell who was getting the worst of it.

To and fro, forward and back, moved the fighting lads, their movements being breathlessly followed by the spectators. Sometimes it would seem that one of the lads had the advantage, and then it would appear to be the other.

With his hands clasped together and his heart beating wildly, Fred Davis strained his eyes to see it all. To him every moment seemed an hour of acute agony and suspense.

Bart Hodge and Barney Mulloy were both intensely interested and excited, but neither of them entertained a doubt but what, barring accident, Frank would come forth the victor.

The breathing of the fighting boys became short and loud, and Bascomb occasionally muttered fierce words. Merriwell fought silently and fiercely.

At length the tigerish determination of Bascomb's foe began to drive the big fellow back again. Several times he clinched Frank, but his hold was quickly broken on each occasion. Three times both went down; but the strength of neither seemed sufficient to get the advantage and hold the other.

At length, as they were apparently on the point of grappling again, Bascomb was seen to make a quick move of one hand, and Frank immediately cried:

"My eyes! Oh, I am blinded! They are burning!"

Instantly there was the greatest excitement.

"Foul play, by the eternal skies!" shouted Bart Hodge, leaping forward. Instantly someone gave him a blow that sent him reeling.

"Howld on, ye imps!" roared Barney. "Ye can't play your dirty thricks here!"

"Keep them away!" grated Bascomb. "Keep them away, and I'll fix this fellow now!"

Frank heard the bully's voice, but he could not see Bascomb.

With a cry of unutterable fury, Merriwell leaped for his foe, caught him, grappled with him.

Then was seen such a mad struggle as not one of the boys present had ever before witnessed. Merriwell seemed like a tiger that had been stung to ungovernable rage, and Bascomb exerted every bit of skill and strength he possessed.

Round and round they whirled, away they reeled, and then a cry of surprise and horror suddenly broke from the crowd.

The beginning of the fight had been at a long distance from the brink of the bluff, but, all at once, it was discovered that, in the darkness, they had shifted about till they were close to the verge. And, unconsciously, they were staggering swiftly to the edge.

"Stop them!" shouted Hodge. "Quick, or they will go over!"

Fred Davis leaped forward, clutched at the struggling lads, but could not hold them. In a twinkling they tore away, and reeled on.

Others would have interfered, but it was too late. Both Hodge and Mulloy did their best, but Bascomb and Merriwell escaped their outstretched hands.

Then another cry of horror went up.

The fighting lads were tottering on the brink. They realized their peril at last; but, before they could make a move to save themselves, they went over.

"Merciful Heaven!" gasped Hodge. "That is the end of them both!"

CHAPTER XLVI.

RESULT OF THE CONTEST.

or a moment the horror-stricken witnesses stood and stared through the darkness at the place where the foes had disappeared over the brink of the bluff, and no one seemed capable of making a move or saying a thing immediately after those blood-chilling words came from the lips of Bartley Hodge.

Fred Davis was the first to recover. Down upon the ground he flung himself, peering over the verge of the bluff, and calling:

"Frank—Frank Merriwell!"

Immediately there was a faint, muffled answer from near at hand.

"Thank Heaven!" Fred almost wept. "He has not fallen into the sea! He is near at hand! I can hear him! Frank, where are you?"

"Here—clinging to this vine," was the faint reply. "The thing is giving—it will tear away! Quick—grasp my wrists!"

Fred saw that the dark form was dangling immediately below, and, without delay, he reached down and found a pair of hands which were clinging madly to a stout vine.

The vine was really giving way, and Davis instantly grasped both wrists of the imperiled lad.

"I've got him, boys!" he shouted, joyously. "Pull us up—pull us up! I can hold fast if you pull us up at once! He has hold of one of my hands now; he will not let go. Pull us up, and he will be saved!"

"Lay hold here!" shouted Hodge, grasping Davis by the shoulder. "Down on your faces, two of you, and clutch Merriwell the moment he is lifted far enough for you to grasp him. Work lively, now! Are you ready?"

"All ready," came the chorus.

"Then hoist away, lads, and up he comes!"

So, with a strong pull, the imperiled youth was dragged up over the brink to safety, falling prostrate and panting at the feet of his rescuers.

"Poor Bascomb!" exclaimed one of the boys. "I am afraid he is done for!"

"Not much!" panted the boy they had just saved. "But that was a mighty close call."

"What's this?" shrieked Fred Davis, dropping to his knees and staring into the face of the fellow he had helped to rescue. "This isn't Merriwell! It's Bascomb!"

Exclamations of astonishment came from every lip, for all had thought they were rescuing Frank.

"Great Jupiter!" gasped Bart Hodge. "It must be that Merriwell went clean down the face of the bluff!"

"An' thot manes he is a dead b'y!" declared Barney Mulloy. Fred Davis quickly leaped to the brink, and wildly shouted:

"Frank Merriwell! Frank Merriwell! Where are you? Frank! Frank!"

No answer save the moaning of the wind and the gurgle of the sea which came up from the base of the bluff, like the last strangling sound from the throat of a drowning person.

"He is gone!"

A feeling of unutterable horror came over the little party on the bluff, for they all seemed to realize what a terrible thing had happened.

Fred Davis fell to sobbing and moaning. Again and again he sent his voice down the face of the bluff, shouting into the darkness that hovered over the surging sea:

"Frank Merriwell! Oh, Frank, where are you? Frank! Frank!"

A night-bird swept past, and answered his shouts with an eerie cry; but the voice of Frank Merriwell did not come up out of the darkness below.

"It's no use!" came hoarsely and hopelessly from the lips of Bart Hodge. "Merriwell is a goner! It was most remarkable that Bascomb caught hold of that vine and so escaped."

Fred Davis sprang to his feet, and rushed at Bascomb, who was cowering and shivering in the midst of the boys.

"You killed him!" screamed the little plebe. "You're responsible for his death! It was murder!"

"Thot's roight!" came from Barney Mulloy.

Bascomb cowered and retreated before Davis. All his bullying spirit was gone, and he shivered when the little fellow declared it was murder.

"You shall be hanged!" wildly cried Fred, shaking his clinched hands in Bascomb's face. "I will testify against you! You shall be arrested and hanged!"

"Take him away, somebody!" muttered Bascomb, hoarsely.

"Touch me if you dare!" defied Davis, who seemed quite beside himself. "I have been a coward long enough, and I am not afraid of you all now! If I hadn't been a coward, I should have fought here to-night, instead of Merriwell, and he would be alive now! Oh, I'll never forgive myself for letting him fight in my place! But I'll do my best to avenge—I'll swear he was murdered!"

"That's rot," said Rupert Reynolds, rather weakly. "It was a clean case of accident."

"I am not sure about that," came significantly from the lips of Bart Hodge. "We all heard Merriwell cry out that he had been blinded. That meant something. There was foul play here, and the parties who were in the dirty game must suffer for it."

"Faith, an' thot's roight, Bart, me b'y!" exclaimed Barney Mulloy. "It's as clane a lad as iver brathed thot wint over Black Bluff to his death th' noight, an' somebody will pay dear fer this pace av worruk."

Bascomb still remained silent, seeming incapable of offering any defense.

"It is useless to waste any more time here," said Hodge, sharply. "This awful business must be reported in camp. We must get boats from the boathouse, and search for Merriwell's body."

He started away, and the boys began to follow him. Bascomb stood quite still, and saw his late supporters, with the exception of Reynolds, draw away and leave him, as if he were some creature to be avoided.

"Oh, that's the way!" he grated, bitterly. "They're afraid they will be mixed in it some way, and so they sneak! I am left to face the music alone!"

"Brace up, old man," urged Reynolds. "You may not be in such a very bad box. I don't see how they can do anything but expel you from the academy, and it is likely I will have to take the same medicine, as I was your second."

"Oh, you're trying to show a bright side; but I tell you, Reynolds, there is something worse than expulsion to follow this!"

"What do you mean?"

"You heard that plebe Davis declare he would charge me with murder?"

"Sure; but he's deranged for the moment."

"He will make the charge, just the same; and I'll have to face it."

"But it cannot be proved against you."

"I am not so sure. If I hadn't flung red pepper in Merriwell's eyes I'd have a better show. Now it will look as if I did that to blind him, so I might force him over the bluff."

"I don't believe anybody can think you as bad as that. You certainly had no desire to do anything more than whip Merriwell by some means, fair or foul."

"It is easy enough to say that, but I'm afraid it will not be easy to make people believe it. I swear, Reynolds, it's a terrible thing to have anything like this hanging over a fellow! Why, it has taken all the nerve out of me! I'd give my right hand to see Frank Merriwell alive and well at this moment!"

"Don't go to pieces that way, Bascomb!" entreated Rupert. "You've got to keep a stiff backbone. Come, let's hurry after the others."

Reynolds got hold of Bascomb's arm, and fairly dragged him after the other lads, who were making their way toward camp.

Each step that brought the big fellow nearer camp made him more desperate. Finally, he declared:

"I'm going to know what Hodge and Mulloy mean to do."

Then he hastened forward till he came upon Bart and Barney, who were accompanied by Fred Davis.

"Look here, fellows," said Bascomb, "I've got some questions to ask you."

"Well, ask them," directed Hodge, shortly, as the boys halted and clustered again.

"I want to know if you actually think I am wicked enough to wish to kill a fellow cadet and classmate?"

"As fer mesilif, Oi dunno," admitted Barney. "Yure a big scoundrel, but Oi don't loike ter think any felly's villain enough to do murther."

"But it looks mighty black for you, Bascomb," said Bart. "We all heard Merriwell cry out that he was blinded, and then you seemed to drag him straight for the brink of the bluff."

"It was an accident!" declared Bascomb, hoarsely. "I did not dream we were anywhere near the edge of the bluff."

"It was not accident!" cried Fred Davis. "It was murder, and I will swear to it!"

"You hear that," came huskily from the lips of the accused. "If you fellows stand by him, I am done for."

"We'll have to be given time to think it over."

"No, that is wrong, for you'll be forced to make some explanation as soon as you get into camp."

"We'll simply tell the truth."

"That will ruin me!"

"Which cannot be helped. The truth is the only thing that will stand in a case like this."

"All right. There's no show for me."

Bascomb turned about in a blind way, and Reynolds caught him by the arm, asking:

"Where are you going? What are you going to do?"

"I don't know," was the hopeless reply. "It doesn't make any difference where I go or what I do now!"

The most of the boys moved toward camp again, leaving Reynolds talking earnestly with Bascomb. Before the camp was reached, Reynolds came running and panting after them.

"Bascomb has gone crazy!" he cried. "He said he was going to kill himself, and he broke away from me and ran into the woods! It is terrible!"

CHAPTER XLVII.

ALIVE!

"I don't know but suicide is his easiest way out of this scrape," said Hodge.

"It is the only way he can escape hanging!" came from Fred Davis, who seemed to be aroused to a point of relentless hatred for Bascomb.

"Merciful goodness!" came faintly from Reynolds, who seemed to be weakening. "What a dreadful affair this is! I'd give anything in my power to give if I were well out of it!"

"An' ye'd be gittin' out chape at thot, me hearty," declared Barney Mulloy.

"If I'd ever dreamed what would come of it, horses couldn't have dragged me into the affair!" almost whimpered Reynolds.

"An' now ye're in it, it won't do yez nivver a bit av good to who-ine, me b'y."

"All you can do is brace up and face it out," said Hodge. "That's what the rest of us will have to do. It's likely we'll all be fired from the academy for our shares in the business."

"I wouldn't mind that if it would bring Merriwell back all right," asserted Reynolds, and there was a sincere sound in his voice.

"We'd all take our medicine without a murmur if it would restore him to life. He was the whitest boy that ever breathed!"

"I think you're right," admitted Rupert. "I don't like him, but I presume that was my fault. Perhaps I was jealous because he was so popular. He never did me a mean turn."

"Och! an' he nivver did anybody thot!" quickly put in Barney. "It wur ivver a good turn, av it wur anything at all, at all."

And so, talking of Frank's virtues, the boys approached the camp. It was decided among them that Hodge should report the affair to Lieutenant Gordan, and they should all get into camp without being challenged, if possible. For this purpose they separated, and slipped in one by one, by various ways.

Hodge himself found a little difficulty in getting past the sentinel, by whom he did not wish to be challenged and taken in custody, as there would be a certain amount of red tape business that would delay him from seeking the lieutenant immediately and making his report.

He finally succeeded in getting into camp, and hurried directly to his own tent. As he entered, he was surprised to see a lamp had been lighted, and somebody was wringing out a towel in the water-bucket, at the same time having his head and face well swathed with another towel, that was dripping wet.

"Well, who in thunder are you? and what are you up to here?" demanded Bart, indignantly.

The fellow with the towel about his head pulled enough of it away from his mouth to reply:

"Hello, Bart! I am soaking the red pepper out of my eyes, and incidentally bathing my bruises at the same time. I couldn't see to guard for all of Bascomb's blows."

Hodge reeled backward, and came near collapsing. He caught hold of the tent pole at the front, and clung to it for support.

"Frank!" he cried, faintly.

"That's my name," affirmed the other, as he unwound the towel from about his head, and looked at Bart with a pair of very red eyes. "You look as if you saw a ghost."

"Well, I couldn't be more surprised if I saw a whole regiment of ghosts. Is it really you—alive?"

"To be sure."

"But—but—didn't you go over Black Bluff?"

"Yes."

"Then how do you happen to be here? It can't be you fell all the way down into the water, and then swam out?"

"No."

"Then what did happen? For mercy sake, tell me, and relieve me of this suspense."

"Why, I didn't fall far—not more than ten feet. I struck on a shelf, and lay there stunned."

"And Bascomb clung to some vines till we pulled him back to the top of the bluff."

"Those vines fell all around the shelf I was on, and I was half-covered with them when I recovered enough to thoroughly realize my position. It is likely that, while he was clinging to them, Bascomb partly covered me with them by winding his legs about them, thus changing their position after I fell."

"And he covered you so that the vines and the darkness prevented us from seeing you."

"I suppose so."

"But why didn't you answer? Davis called to you more than twenty times."

"I was stunned, and I did not hear him at first. When I did hear, it was impossible for me to answer, although I tried to do so."

"And we went away and left you there."

"Yes."

"How did you get off the ledge?"

"My strength came to me swiftly when I realized my position. As soon as possible, realizing I was alone, I sought a way to get to the top of the bluff. I was successful, for I found some clefts in the rock for my feet, and, aided by the vines, I climbed up. Then I lost little time in getting into camp, for I didn't know what sort of a report you fellows would bring. I did not expect to reach camp ahead of you, but it seems that I did, although I had not been in the tent two minutes when you showed up."

Up to this moment Hodge had held off, as if not quite able to believe it possible Frank had escaped. Now, with a cry of joy, he sprang forward and embraced his comrade.

"This is the happiest moment of my life, Frank!" he declared, with tears of joy in his eyes. "Why, I was about to report you as dead, and start out an expedition to search for your body! I couldn't have felt so bad had you been my own brother. Davis is distracted. He has charged Bascomb with murder, and swears he will stick to it in court. Mulloy was also inclined to look on it as a case of murder, and Bascomb became so scared that he ran away while we were returning to camp. Reynolds said Bascomb swore he was going to commit suicide."

Frank straightened up quickly.

"Look here, Hodge," he said, "you must act, and you must act swiftly. I do not want to go to Lieutenant Gordan in this condition; but you must go to him, and tell him that Bascomb seems to be out of his head and has run away, threatening to kill himself. The lieutenant will be sure to send out a detachment to search for the poor fellow. If you see Mulloy, tell him I am all right, and get him to keep Davis still. The plebe mustn't blow the story all over camp. Let everybody know I am all right. As soon as I can soak this red pepper out of my eyes, I'll be ready to help in the search for Bascomb, if I am needed. Go quickly!"

"All right; I'm off."

Hodge darted out of the tent, and Frank wrapped another wet towel about his head and eyes.

CHAPTER XLVIII.

BABY'S HEROISM—CONCLUSION.

All night the search for Bascomb continued, the cadets carrying on the work in relays.

Hodge had convinced Lieutenant Gordan that Bascomb had suddenly become deranged, and had succeeded in having the search instituted without telling the real cause of the disappearance.

The joy of the boys when they knew Merriwell was safe in his own tent had been boundless, but they were forced to keep it suppressed, fearing that too much of a demonstration would arouse suspicion, and create an investigation.

Davis wept for joy. At first he could not believe such good news could be true, and he had rushed straight to the tent, where Frank was already receiving congratulations.

"You don't know what a terrible load this lifts from my shoulders!" cried the little plebe, in ecstasy. "Nobody shall ever fight for me again! I can't lick anybody, but I will stand up and take my thumping when it is necessary. I am going to write to mother tomorrow that it is absolutely impossible for a fellow to get along here without fighting, and I am going to ask her to release me from my promise. I won't lie for anybody, but I am going to fight when I have to!"

"I do not believe you will be forced into many fights when the boys understand you," said Frank.

Frank reduced the inflammation in his eyes so he was able to take part in the search, and he declined to be relieved, continuing in his efforts through the entire night.

Near sunrise, with a company of plebes under his command, he was beating a piece of woods along the bank of a river about four miles from the academy. Davis was one of the company. The little fellow had grown intensely anxious for the quick discovery of Bascomb, hoping the big bully had done no harm to himself.

"If he should commit suicide, I'd feel that I must be responsible for that," said Fred.

"You are altogether too conscientious," declared Frank. "There are none of us but hope to find Bascomb all right, but no one save himself will be to blame if he has taken his life."

Birds were singing their morning songs, and there was a rosy tinge spreading upward in the eastern sky. The breath of the morning was sweet with the perfume of June; but the boys heeded none of the beauties of nature around them, for they were fearing that at any moment they might come upon some ghastly thing there in the heart of the green woods.

All at once, they did come upon a haggard, pale-faced lad, who was sitting on a fallen tree, and seemed to be waiting for them to approach.

It was Bascomb.

"I have dodged searching parties all night, and I am not going to run any——"

Thus far did Bascomb get, and then he saw Merriwell. He stopped, and his jaw fell, while he shuddered, showing the strongest symptoms of terror. His eyes bulged from their sockets, and the expression on his face was one of unutterable horror.

"Bascomb!" cried Frank. "I am glad I have found you!"

He stepped toward the big fellow, but Bascomb leaped to his feet, shrieking:

"Don't touch me! You are dead—dead! Go away!"

And then, before another word could be said, before anybody could do a thing to prevent it, Bascomb turned and fled through the woods—fled as if pursued by fiends, shrieking forth his terror.

"After him!" cried Frank. "Don't let him get away! He is so scared that he will surely do himself injury if he escapes."

The pursuit began, and Merriwell soon found that Fred Davis was rather fleet of foot. In fact, Fred was able to keep near to Frank's side.

It was a wild chase through the strip of woods. Impelled by terror, Bascomb ran as he had never run before. Under ordinary circumstances, Frank could have overtaken him easily, but this was far from an ordinary case.

At length, however, Frank and Fred began to gain on the fugitive.

Casting wild glances over his shoulder, Bascomb discovered this, and his terror knew no bounds. He had been running parallel with the river, but he suddenly changed his course and made straight for it.

"He is going to try to drown himself!" cried Frank.

Then an accident happened to Merriwell. He tripped in some underbrush, and fell heavily to the ground. When he got upon his feet, he saw Bascomb leap from quite a high bank into a deep part of the river.

Fred Davis was not far from Bascomb's heels, and he was stripping off his coat when the big fellow plunged into the water. The coat was flung aside in an instant, and then Frank saw Fred boldly plunge into the water after Bascomb.

"By Jove!" exclaimed Merriwell; "the little fellow has courage, after all!"

He hurried forward, and when he reached the bank, he saw a struggle taking place in the river.

Bascomb did not want to be rescued. Made crazy by the horrors he had experienced through the night, and by the sight of Merriwell, whom he believed a ghost, he was determined to drown himself in the river.

Three times Davis struck at Bascomb's temple with his clinched fist, and he finally landed with sufficient violence to stun the big fellow.

Then, with the skill of a veteran life-saver, the little plebe swung the heavy yearling over his back, and struck out for the bank, swept down stream by the current.

Frank ran along the bank till Davis came near enough to be pulled out with his burden, and Frank dragged both the water-dripping lads to solid ground.

"By gracious! Davis, you have proved your value this morning!" cried Frank, as he clung to the panting little plebe. "Bascomb will owe you his life, and no one can call you a coward from this time on."

The other boys came running to the spot, breathing heavily, and Frank soon explained exactly what had taken place. They looked at Davis with increased respect, and one of them proposed three cheers for "Baby," which were given with a will.

The sound of the cheering seemed to arouse Bascomb. He opened his eyes, and the first person he saw was Frank. With a moan and a shudder, he covered his eyes with his hands, gasping:

"Take him away! Don't let him touch me!"

"You have no reason to be afraid of me," assured Frank, quietly. "I am no ghost; I am alive and well."

"No, no; it cannot be!"

"It is the truth. I did not go to my death over Black Bluff, as you thought. I did fall, but I was saved by a rocky shelf."

Then Frank slowly and distinctly explained everything, finally convincing Bascomb that it was really true.

The horrors of the night he had spent alone in the woods overcame Bascomb so that he was quite prostrated, having to remain in hospital several days, and barely escaping a fever.

But he was very happy to know that Frank still lived, and this happiness led to his quick recovery.

As for Frank, although Bascomb had played a most contemptible trick on him in flinging the red pepper in his eyes, he knew the bully had been punished quite enough, and he decided to let the matter drop. As it was, there were many other matters to claim his attention, some of which will be related in the next volume of this series, entitled: "Frank Merriwell's Foes."

The report of Davis' exploit in rescuing Bascomb became generally known, and, instead of being called a coward, Fred was regarded as something of a hero. The boys thought him peculiar, but there were not a few who came to uphold him in refusing to fight when he had given his mother his word that he would do nothing of the kind.

From the time that he dragged Bascomb out of the river he had very little trouble in the school, and there were ever dozens of champions ready to fight his battles when he did find it necessary to fight.

But Frank had been first to defend the little fellow, and there never came a time when Fred did not think Frank the noblest and bravest lad in all the world.